ADVANCE PRAISE FOR *THE WHITE DEER*

"Regina McBride's new book evokes a loving nostalgia for a place we've never known—Chekhov's Russia. Set in the summer of young Anton's twentieth year, the novel centers on a young woman whose family is losing financial control of their estate—an estate famous for its orchards. Anton is the guest of a neighboring doctor, and the two young people become entwined in a romantic friendship—*une amitiée amoureuse*. McBride's story comes at Chekhov's from the side, presenting us not only with the family's eccentric and complicated history, but the vision of the author himself, as a character in the work. A beautiful and eloquent rendering of a place and time we somehow feel is ours."

—Roxana Robinson, author of *Leaving*, NYT Editors' Choice

"McBride has always been a gifted and lyrical storyteller, but never more so than in this gorgeously written novel of nineteenth century Ukraine and Russia, in which she brings a young Anton Chekhov to life. The story will remain with you long after you've turned the final page. Superb."

—Gabriel Byrne, author of *Walking with Ghosts*

"This gentle but profound novel takes you on a quietly magical journey through nineteenth century Ukraine, mixing the Chekhovian sensibility with contemporary spirit to create the effect of delightful immersion."

—Lara Vapnyar, author of *Divide Me by Zero*

"This restrained and beautiful book utterly transported me to summer in Russia in the late nineteenth century: to a lovely old estate with a neglected peach orchard. McBride beautifully suggests how shards of the daily material of life can be picked up by an extraordinary writer and transformed into art. I never wanted to leave the enchanted, doomed world she conjured."

—Rachel Pastan, author of *We're So Lucky to Live Here*

"This transportive novel sweeps the reader up into a vivid, melancholic dream set on a nineteenth century Russian estate. Regina McBride creates her own Chekhovian tragi-comedy that delights as it captures a lost world frozen in time. *The White Deer* is a gripping must-read for anyone who loves literature and a love story gone awry."

—Virginia Pye, author of *Marriage and Other Monuments*

"In this stirring tale, McBride evokes a sense of place with lush depictions of birch stands and daisy fields along with a soundtrack of Tchaikovsky and folk tunes, creating a backdrop for Vera's tender and chaste friendship with Anton. It's an evocative portrait of a vanishing way of life."

—Publishers Weekly

"Through his friendship with an introspective woman, Anton Chekhov's story is revealed in Regina McBride's thoughtful historical novel . . . With deep empathy and a light spiritual touch, *The White Deer* explores the complexity of human relations to others, power, and the past."

—Foreword Reviews

The White Deer

The White Deer

GREEN CITY BOOKS
BOOKS

GREEN CITY BOOKS
Bend, OR

ISBN: 9781963101232

First Edition
designed by Isaac Peterson
Cover uses a photo by Евгений Карепанов
licsensed through Pexels
Author Portrait by Neil Scott Johnson

Library of Congress Cataloging-in-Publication
Data has been applied for.

23 24 25 LSC 10 9 8 7 6 5 4 3 2 1

Also by Regina McBride:

Stranger from Across the Sea

Ghost Songs (memoir)

The Fire Opal

The Marriage Bed

Land of Women

The Nature of Water and Air

Yarrow Field (poetry)

The White Deer

A NOVEL
OF ANTON CHEKHOV

REGINA MCBRIDE

For Phil Chapman,
acting teacher and dear friend,
who first introduced me to
Chekhov's plays.

1879

Volkhov Estate

Polkova Oblast, Ukraine

Prelude

". . . something always seemed to remain that was hidden and unattainable, beyond the power of human penetration."
—Turgenev

I awakened early to sleigh bells and looked out my second-floor window. It was mid-April, but snow had fallen at night. I saw Petya in his faded sheepskin coat near the stable tending to a chestnut mare, preparing her to pull a sled. I'd seen him preparing horses like this numerous times in the past, fitting the padded section around the horse's neck and shoulders, adjusting the traces, straps, and chains, connecting the collar to the sled. He patted the horse on the neck or the rump as he checked the tension or the tightness of the apparatus, all the while speaking to her, clouds of condensation carrying his words.

The bells on her harness rang each time she nodded or shook her head. She shifted her haunches as he kissed her on the nose.

Since the time we were small, Petya had been good with horses. I had been afraid of them as a child, so it had been something to see, a small boy my own age leading the giant black stallion named Count Orloff, beautiful but nervous and mistrusting of everyone, but so gentle and obedient with Petya and so willing to follow him.

"Animals can read character, often better than people can," a summer guest, an ornithologist from Moscow, had said once, observing Petya, ten years old at the time, with the stallion.

This chestnut mare belonged to the blacksmith from the nearby village of Korablin. I'd heard from Nickander, one of the servants, that the blacksmith had come the day before by carriage, not expecting snow. He'd brought an iron-work gate, custom-made for the old summerhouse, which had been, for as long as I could remember, permanently under repair, parts of the roof collapsing almost every winter under heavy snows no matter the fortifications built into it each summer.

Petya had been gone for six months but had been back, working on the estate now for three days, but only temporarily. This I had also learned from Nickander. My uncle and aunt were in Kharkiv, so there'd been nothing preventing Petya from asking for me. But he hadn't. I waited expectantly for him to look over at my window and see me there.

When I was little there had been no children my age on the neighboring estates. My sister was seven years older and had always been of a serious disposition. Even as a child, she hadn't been like a child.

But Petya, the son of two servants, was born in a small annex house on our property three days before me. While my birth had been celebrated with toasts of champagne, his had happened quietly.

When I was small I used to see him sometimes through this window or other windows on the second or third floor, running errands, carrying handkerchiefs or cigars out to guests on the lawn.

I was seven years old when my aunt first called upon him to play with me. We were allowed to play in one area around the mulberry tree that could be seen from the downstairs kitchen. Old Aniuta, the servant, was charged with keeping her eye on us. One of the servants put up a swing on that tree. At first Petya was cautious. I had to persuade him to use the swing. He gradually became more comfortable and we ran around the tree and we played with small toys in the grass. He had long, sandy-colored hair that was always neatly combed. I had once seen his mother kneeling before him, combing it. He didn't speak much but I was always asking him questions because the sound of his voice gave me pleasure. Even as a child, it was at a low register and sounded a little hoarse. Having no other friend, I was careful not to forfeit what was between us. I had tried to make him feel that my advantage as a child of landowners meant nothing between us.

My Uncle Pavel, my father's older brother, had objected to me spending time with Petya.

"This is one way we make use of him, Pavel," his sister, my aunt Marya told him. "Vera is a child. She needs to play." My uncle rarely won in disagreements with his sister. Aunt Marya had the hard task of running the entire estate while he did nothing much but walk around muttering, casting a disapproving eye. Only in the presence of guests did Uncle Pavel transform into someone benevolent and welcoming. But it was a mask. This was a theatrical family and that was the role he had learned to perform. When guests departed, the true taciturn man who had been waiting behind the smile returned.

At first, in his labors with the horse and sled, Petya had seemed unself-conscious, but I noticed a new tension in his posture. He may have glimpsed me in his peripheral vision. He seemed to be deliberately avoiding looking up at my window.

Many times over the years Petya had waved to me as he led one of the horses in or out of the stable. Sometimes he'd done a little dance or performed an exaggerated bow. We were nineteen now and for several years he'd been more formal with me, even distant. I was sure it was on the advice of his father who he'd told me had always felt uneasy about him spending time with me. Like almost everyone else, Petya's father believed that there were boundaries that should have been marked between the landed and the serving classes.

When we were still children and it was raining, Petya and I stayed in the kitchen. Aniuta would clear spots for us at a rough wood table, place a lamp between us, and we would draw pictures.

It was apparent right away that Petya had a talent for drawing. I would often put my pencil down and watch him, awestruck, as he drew. Sometimes I lay my head on my arms on the table, watched the movements of his pencil and listened to its soft breathing as it grazed the dry paper. From that angle I could see the circle of concentration around him. It reminded me of a halo on an icon. Slowly, whatever he was envisioning began to appear on the blank sheet of paper, becoming more and more dimensional.

Even when we were small Petya had a strange, sourceless maturity. Of course I couldn't articulate that back then. He knew himself in some way that I didn't know myself. His drawings somehow showed that, too. They were textured with so much dimension. He could see whatever he was drawing in his own memory; he needed no models.

He defied everything I'd been taught about servants. How could a lesser being, as I was always being told servants were, draw and focus the way he did? How could someone less human than me observe the world with such intensity?

When we were seven or eight, he told me a story about a tiny girl who married a grasshopper. One day the girl was seen making her way through tall blades of grass, her face streaming with tears. She climbed on the back of a blackbird who flew away with her. Petya did not know why the girl had escaped. He had fallen asleep when his aunt was telling the story. She had left Volkhov the next day so we never found out what happened. The two of us tried to imagine why the tiny girl ran away.

I had watched, mesmerized, as with an astonishing precision, Petya drew a large grasshopper. When it was finished he held it up for me to look at. I recoiled at the eyes, two bald globes covered all over with minute, barely visible squares, a smeared dot in the center of each eye.

He looked at his own drawing in horror, as if it had come from somewhere else and not through him. Always reticent, he asked me, "Why would she have married him?"

I could still hear the sound of his quiet, low-pitched voice as he asked the question.

It was terrifying how alive the grasshopper was, so alive it was threatening. Petya and I looked at one another and a chill seized my back and shoulders. I was afraid the enormous insect would hop off the page, so I asked him to put the drawing outside in the grass. We both knew that day, watching from the kitchen door as the rain blurred the image and darkened the paper, that Petya had a gift. It was not my gift. It was his, but he included me in it somehow. In some way, we shared it, or he shared it with me. Maybe because he was afraid, as I was afraid, and it was better that there were two of us.

Aniuta kept icons in a small dark alcove room near the stove, the faces of saints quivering and shifting in candlelight. The first time we came into the kitchen together, Petya expressed awe of the little room and stood at the doorway staring in. That day after he'd drawn the grasshopper and put it out in the rain, he went in that little room for the first time and I followed. The room was so small I had to stand behind him. Being very near him in the trembling candlelight I'd felt breathless. I was so close I could smell him, a soft diffused scent of hay or dried grass and something else, which I decided was the wind, which his clean muslin shirt had likely hung out in to dry. I breathed Petya in, filled with elation. I thought I might float upwards.

After we stepped out of the room, Petya drew Theotokis, the holy mother with her sacred little boy. He didn't draw her in the stiff manner of the old icon itself, but lovely and soft in her veil and garments, she and her little boy of human proportions. And Petya's Theotokis had compassionate eyes, not the cold vacant ones you saw in the stiff figure of the usual icon. After that day he drew Theotokis repeatedly. And I used to think his Theotokis looked like his own mother, a quiet woman who worked as a seamstress, embroidering dinner napkins or the collars of shirts. His saints all had the faces of real people from his life. They were not stiff unfeeling figures. Not flat and without dimension. Sometimes he drew St. Nicholas of Winter, who, in his eyes, looked like our servant, Nickander, who'd been a teenager when we were children, a very large man even in his adolescence, with a wide, kind face. Sometimes he drew St. Ambrose with his gray double-pointed beard, always with the face of his father, Fyodor. But mostly, besides drawing horses and a certain linden tree, he drew Theotokis with his mother's face.

I now pressed my forehead to the cool glass. Petya stood before the mare with a hand on either side of her neck. She nodded, then pushed the length of her face against his chest and stomach.

When we were fourteen, Petya was in constant demand, helping his father on the estate. With childhood over, everything was different. It came to be understood that Petya and I were not allowed to spend time alone in the company of the other. My Uncle Pavel first decreed this, and my aunt finally agreed with him. But Petya used to leave his sketchbook hidden in the downstairs kitchen in a place where he knew I would find it and look at his drawings. He knew the effect they would have on me and I believed it was important to him that I look at them. I would go down there when I missed him, which was often.

The wind animated everything Petya drew, the mane and tail of a horse, the branches and leaves of a tree. That had started when he was little, but it became more prominent as he got older. It was almost a little strange. While Petya had a quiet stillness about him, his drawings were full of duress, everything listing to the right as if with the force of the wind. Even with a figure from an icon, the veil or the garment or sometimes the hair blew dramatically. And the figures had expressive hands and reached with their arms or twisted from their waists. Some lifted their faces or turned their heads in profile while their bodies faced front. It was as if there was so much forceful emotion in him as he drew that the figures could not help but communicate it. And if he drew the flame of a candle, it was always leaning far to the side. And looking at it, I could feel the movement and force of the air that blew it. It was as if he had drawn the wind itself.

One day when we were fifteen, we ran into each other on the avenue of birch trees, the carriage road on the estate. For almost a year we had only seen each other from a distance. He was much taller than the last time I'd stood beside him. His physical being in transition, a beautiful, amorphous state between childhood and manhood, caused a sensation of wonder in me. He looked at me, too, with a new awareness. We escaped together into the trees, and walking where we were unlikely to be seen, came across a dead bird. Petya was very solemn as we gave it a service. He scraped the ground with his hands and dug a tiny grave. We buried the bird, pressing earth into a mound over it, our hands or fingers occasionally, inadvertently touching. Still kneeling, Petya picked up small stones from the ground around us and slowly placed them one by one on the grave.

As children, he and I had been like one being with our secret life built around his drawings, and the games we had created and played together, but adolescence had taken that from us. As we knelt there in silence and Petya kept placing small stones carefully on the mound, I sensed that his life had become in some way larger without me. His parents had always been attentive and protective and I wondered if there was some kind of plan in his future because I could feel something there to the side of him, another life. Whenever I'd seen him walking past, through a window or from the veranda, there'd been a feeling of purpose to his walk. I had no other life, no other preoccupation to the side of me. Though I had a tutor and studied and read books, Petya was still the center of everything for me. I had taken for granted that because he was a servant, he would not have any kind of plan for his future, but as we knelt there in silence together, I could feel that he did and it did not include me. A devastating idea struck me: a wife might have been found for him. But the thought brought so much pain I had to reject it.

When I said we should find a way to spend time together, maybe even to just sit in Aniuta's kitchen and draw, he stiffened. Keeping his eyes fixed to the burial mound, holding one small stone between his finger and thumb, he told me that his father had gotten very angry with him recently when he mentioned that he would like to see me. To stress to Petya how dangerous his feelings for me were, his father told him about something that happened decades back.

My family had kept more horses then and employed a farrier, a handsome young man named Afanasy. My grandmother took him as a lover. This was done discreetly at first though the maids knew everything. According to one of the maids, after a few months of trysts whenever my grandfather was away from the house, Afanasy disappointed my grandmother by trying to put an end to the affair. My grandmother did not take it well. She accused Afanasy of trying to steal her jewels. He was arrested and sent to the Krasnoyarsk Saltworks in Siberia. After three years of hard labor he escaped. Petya's father saw him in a neighboring town where he was hardly recognizable and described what he'd been through. He had contracted typhus in the camp, was sickly, and lived only a year after returning.

I had heard something once about my grandmother having sent a servant to Siberia, but these details appalled me and I apologized to Petya as if, by virtue of having my grandmother's blood in my veins, I'd had some hand in this terrible crime.

"You know me, Petya. I would never do anything that would cause you harm."

He remained silent.

"I don't see why we can't draw together or even just sit and drink a glass of tea."

His father reminded Petya that my Uncle Pavel had a particular dislike for him, but that anyone in my household might take umbrage to seeing me socializing with Petya. Any of them might make Petya's life a misery.

We heard footsteps crunching on the earth nearby. Petya rose up quickly from his knees. Still holding the one small stone between his thumb and forefinger he took a few steps backwards, shot me an earnest look, then disappeared between two poplars.

There were moments in his faded sheepskin coat, as he adjusted the belly strap on the mare, that he was almost unrecognizable. In this last year Petya had shot up in height. We had, as children, been present for so many incarnations of each other, so many selves in the constant state of evolution. Even the face of fifteen-year-old Petya had been softer, less structured-looking than this adult stranger's face. At certain angles, I could see a familiar shadow on his forehead or his cheek bone, or he'd move an arm or turn quickly to look at something, the way he always had, and those flashes of recognition made my heart quicken.

He may have now been a tall young man, I told myself, but he was the same Petya I'd spent so much time with as a child. We had chased and tackled each other, wrestled laughing in the snow. I had once pressed a dry kiss to his cold cheek. In the years since we had buried the dead bird, we had smiled at each other forlornly across distances.

And during that time I'd struggled to think of ways to bridge the intolerable distance between us.

One morning a year ago, I heard a woman from Petersburg, who was visiting, tell my Aunt Marya and Father Ivan, a beloved local priest, that the only way out of poverty in this country was if someone had a talent of some kind! It was like a flash of lightning. I retrieved the notebook of Petya's drawings from the place he kept it hidden in the downstairs kitchen, then met privately with Father Ivan and showed it to him.

The priest looked through the pages, his mouth open in a circle of awe.

He said he would speak to the drawing master in Korablin and show him the drawings.

It took a little time but the drawing master finally came. All of Petya's drawings impressed him, particularly his drawings of Count Orloff the stallion. The drawing master appeared both amazed and distressed by the icons; they strayed so far from the traditional images. Even still, he kept coming back to them, focusing on them in silence.

Uncle Pavel objected to the idea of an apprenticeship, but Father Ivan said that it would be a sin against God if Petya Fyodorovich was not given the chance to use such a gift to make the world better. My aunt had always been more liberal and she cared about Father Ivan, so things went forward. She signed papers in support of Petya and an arrangement was made.

I thought the apprenticeship would be in Kiev and I would be able to see him and spend time with him while he was there. My father lived part of the time in Kiev and was often asking me to go and stay with him there. I'd imagined what it would be like: Petya studying during the day; my father, a kind man who would in all likelihood be moved by my intervention and Petya's sudden change in fortune, taking us for carriage rides and to dinner in the evenings. But to my disappointment, the apprenticeship offered was in Sevastopol. We had no family connections there and it was far away to the south, and according to my aunt an uninteresting place.

Early on when Petya was gone, I dared to entertain a notion that we could marry when he finished the six months away. He would find work in Kiev where we would live. I knew there would have been vehement objections and I would have had to be careful about how such a marriage was undertaken. I knew that even my father, despite his disdain for the class system, despite himself, would still not approve. And yet I believed that I would be able to somehow manage it.

During the six months he was gone, I often envisioned Petya wearing a finely tailored dark green serge coat.

I wanted to have such a coat made for him, and barely restrained myself from organizing that.

Petya stepped beyond my view, outside the frame of my window, and a short time later reappeared with the blacksmith from Korablin. I surmised that the girl with them, a girl with long brown braids and a pink and green floral kerchief, must have been the blacksmith's daughter, whose name I had heard was Yulia. Just as she was about to board the sled, she turned and exchanged words with Petya, then moved close to him. Smiling up at him, she pushed a strand of his hair back on his forehead. My ears rang. Blood rushed so hard to my head, I couldn't see.

Petya stood watching and saying goodbye as the blacksmith took the reins and the sled cleaved a pathway through the snow.

Half an hour or so later, with my heart skipping, I started off toward the summerhouse to find Petya. I was not sure what I would say. I had no plan and struggled to constrain my out-of-control breathing. It was clear and cold, the snow beginning to harden on the ground. I saw Petya with Nickander and Osip, another servant, striding off toward the end of the road in the distance. They didn't see me. I thought of calling out. Instead I went into the summerhouse. Substantial work had been done to the staircase, which had been one of the jobs in progress. It looked almost complete. Other work was also being done on one of the ceilings where there looked to be water damage.

Lumber, stones, and sacks of mortar filled a large area cleared of furniture.

Curtains were closed on many of the windows, but daylight came from one room at the end of the hall where I saw a pallet on the floor. Petya had likely slept here the night before, working late and trying to finish.

Petya's father, Fyodor, who had always been in charge of the construction on the summerhouse, had hurt his back a few weeks before and had gone to Korablin where he and Petya's mother had family. Having just returned from the apprenticeship, Petya had come to Volkhov to help Osip and Nickander, and make up for his father's absence. But he was only here temporarily, and from what Nickander had told me, planned to go to Kiev to look for work as a draughtsman.

I was about to leave when I spotted a pencil on the floor near the pallet. It was Petya's pencil, pale-grained wood with thick graphite in the middle, the kind he had always used. Some intuition told me to look in the cabinet near the stove. Inside I found a sketchbook, another pencil and a piece of charcoal. I sat on a stool near the stove and swooned as I looked at the drawings: houses under dark skies complex with thunderheads, drawings of trees in a storm seen through a rainy window. There were drawings of the blacksmith working at a forge, one of a man nailing a shoe to a horse's hoof. And my heart expanded when I turned a page and found a new drawing of a particular linden tree, its branches straining, its leaves dappled in light. When he drew this, had he thought of the time we had taken shelter under it from a rainstorm? The tree was imbued with his rich, internal life, a heightened world, full of deep shadows and wind. A rush of emotion shot up through me from some depth. His skills had sharpened, his shading with more dimension, an intense contrast between light and dark. Could a tree ever be drawn more beautifully by anyone? Looking at it was like being near him, but he was nowhere to be seen.

Then I turned the page and found a drawing of Yulia, looking very forthright and intelligent, wearing the wool babushka she had been wearing that morning before getting on the sled. This was the most recent drawing, and only blank pages came after it. I looked at Yulia with her intelligent eyes, Yulia, who, as a poor blacksmith's daughter would be the natural wife for Petya. I closed the notebook, placed it where I'd found it, and went home, lost, not sure where I was in the world.

I paced my room in tears.

In need of a distraction, I put on a dark green velvet opera dress that my cousin Nadia had sent me from Kiev, hoping to lure me into visiting her. For years I had been refusing her invitations, and invitations from my father to go to Kiev because I could not bear to forgo the chance of seeing Petya, however slight. Even when he'd been gone these past six months I stayed, on the odd chance that he might return.

I stood before the mirror in my room, my face blotchy from crying. I felt exposed in the dress with its low-cut, bosom-enhancing neckline and could not imagine being at ease in public in such a garment. I slipped on the small jacket that had come with it. As I stood before the mirror buttoning it up to my neck, I heard footsteps crunching in the snow below and hurried to the window where I saw Petya crossing the yard. I knew he was on his way to the back door that led to the kitchen.

Uncle Pavel and Aunt Marya were expected back from Kharkiv anytime. It was possible that they were already in a nearby village, and that the snow had delayed them from returning to Volkhov. Once they were back there'd be little chance of Petya and I meeting and talking. I went halfway down the stairs and waited awhile, wondering if I would hear my name mentioned as Petya and Aniuta talked, but I didn't. I descended farther and loitered near the door that led down to the kitchen. Aniuta had been baking, a savory fragrance wafting up the stairs. I waited long enough for Petya to have eaten a meal, and then crept down quietly. Aniuta was cleaning the dishes while Petya sat near the stove drinking tea. His coat hung on a hook near the door. He was wearing a rumpled work shirt, his pants marked with the dust of mortar.

I said his name, and they both started at the sound of my voice. Aniuta looked at me through the soapy steam from her dishwater.

"Please come and help me with something."

I ran back up the stairs and soon heard his slow footsteps behind me. I asked him to carry the gramophone from the drawing room downstairs to the ballroom on the other side of the house. Without answering he went to the drawing room and picked up the heavy contraption, then carried it through the hallways, following me another flight down to the empty ballroom.

After he set it up, I asked him to start a fire. Again, without looking at me or answering, he crossed to the fireplace on the far side of the room. Once he'd gotten the wood to crackle, he stood, his eyes on the flames.

Outside the many windows of the vast, empty room, flakes drifted in circles and fell over the white embankments of the buried garden. His eyes flashed for less than a second in my direction. With his head lowered, he began to walk toward the door.

"Petya Fyodorovich, I need you for something else."

My words, though spoken softly, sounded like a plea, piercing the resonant silence in the empty room. His eyes set themselves squarely on my face, and I read in them both caution and curiosity.

"I think I might move to Kiev."

He averted his eyes from mine.

"I have to practice dancing the waltz. Everyone there dances it."

When he made no response, I said, "So I need you to help me."

"Vera Sergeyevna . . ." Petya quietly saying my name exerted a peculiar power, like an undertow of water, pulling me somewhere I could not breathe. "You know I don't know how to dance the waltz."

"I'll teach you, and then I can practice with you. You will need to know how. When you find work in Kiev, you might be invited places and have occasion to dance the waltz."

As he considered, he seemed for a moment not to move. Then with a nod of the head, signaled assent.

My blood quickened. "Wait here," I said, making sure it sounded like a command, lest he decide to leave. I had never commanded him before and I felt for a moment like some darker extension of myself. I ran across the hall to one of the storage closets where several of my grandfather's military tunics hung, picked a dark green one covered in crests and medals, and brought it back. Attached to the tunic was a belt with a long, curved sabre in a metal sheath, the kind of sabre Petya used to say the hero, Ilya Muromets, had brandished against his enemies. Again, I was afraid to ask, lest he say no, so I issued it as a command. "Wear this."

He looked at me sidelong, at first with a slight, suspicious smile as if I might be toying with him.

"It will be fun," I said. "I am dressed up, too."

I saw, in his face and in his posture, that he understood I wanted to play as if we were still children.

He took the tunic from me and put it on, and as he buckled it around his waist, smiling slightly, he gave me a penetrating look that sent a thrill through my body.

My love of his drawings had given him oxygen since childhood and now, with freedom from servitude, he carried himself with a new confidence, which caused my heart, skipping hard, to raise itself in my chest, a confidence that worried me. I thought of the blacksmith's daughter.

I put on the record and began teaching him the steps of the waltz.

Every time he made a mistake I gave him a disapproving face. I disliked myself for this little mask of reproachful impatience, but somehow it guarded the softness and intense confusion of my feelings.

I fixed my gaze over his shoulder, watching the window through which I could see the snow-covered garden, new flakes falling lightly over it.

When he made two mistakes in close succession, and I squawked at him, he let go of me and took a step back. I put my hand on his shoulder in an effort to begin again, but he took another step back. I burned with indignation, which gave way to a deeper feeling of pain and surrender. We stood without moving, my eyes filling with tears that would not fall. He had offered no excuse for not having sought me out. I thought of reminding him that he had promised to come tell me about his experience as soon as he was back from Sevostopol, but it seemed useless to mention it. Expecting him to go, I waited for it, but he didn't and as the moments passed, a single tear streamed slowly down my right cheek. His arm faltered as he reached for my hand and put it on his shoulder then put his other hand on my waist. He led me in a dance, sweeping freely across the room. More instruments joined the orchestra and the music quickened its pace. He spun me suddenly, a thrill rushing through me. I laughed, ease and old familiar feelings reawakened. He shifted the sword so it hung behind. We were as we had been as children, engaged in an equal and playful give and take.

"You look like a dragon with that stiff tail," I said, casting a glance at the mirror on the north wall of the room to see myself in his arms.

When the music stopped, I went to the gramophone. I realized I was sweating in spite of the coldness of the room. I turned the record over, but before placing the needle onto it, found myself listening to my breaths, staring at the rotating disc. Petya had followed me and was standing a few feet back. I could feel his expectation, his excitement to continue dancing. I listened to the soft exertions of his breathing at a slightly different rhythm from my own, and felt something open in my body. I remembered Yulia's face. I left the arm with the needle on it to the side, though the record continued to turn. I undid the buttons of my jacket, took it off, and let it slip to the floor. His attention went immediately to my figure in the dress, and it lingered there a moment before his eyes again met mine.

"I want you to draw me," I said, my heart accelerating.

He began to study me with what looked at first like detached concentration. He turned abruptly and opened the window we were closest to. A gust of wind rushed in and the fire came to life with sparks escaping from the flames. Sweet whiffs of burning pine filled the room. He stepped a few feet back from me, and I felt him transfiguring me with his eyes, imbuing me with penumbra and wind, placing me in that vivid inner territory of his vision.

Yulia touching his hair. Yulia looking up into his face.

I put a hand to each of my shoulders and lowered the straps of my dress, pushing it down to my waist. The soft shadow at his forehead appeared then disappeared. He was not unnerved, but seemed even more present in his body. A flake of snow blew in and stung one of my bare breasts. Petya watched it melt, then run in a tiny rivulet on my skin. He went still and looked at the floor and an awful moment came when I thought he would leave. But he raised his eyes again slowly, all his focus given over to studying me. I experienced an unbearable intensification of the senses, more powerful than if he had been touching me. Maybe it was the stillness, the absolute stillness that allowed me to hear something like a faint chorus, barely audible, through the open window. I was not sure I even heard it, so attenuated, so vague was it, perhaps made only of other sounds like snowfall, rushes of wind, the fire crackling. Still I heard exalted voices coming from very far away in the sky, resounding as if there were thousands of them, yet so quiet, blurred by great distance.

All at once, as Petya turned away, the sound was gone.

He walked across the room where he took off the military tunic and belt, then set them carefully on a chair. Without another word, he left the ballroom.

I ran up to the third floor, looked out the window, and saw him walking with purpose on the snowy pathway that led to the summerhouse.

Around two hours later, I saw Petya below, entering the stable.

A flurry of snow blew against my face and hung on my eyelashes. The wet door made no sound as I pushed it open. Inside, the acrid smell of horse urine presided on the cold air. By the yellow light of a kerosene lamp, Petya was covering one of the mares with a rug.

"I want to see the drawing you did of me," I said.

He stiffened, then turned and faced me.

"Where is the drawing, Petya?"

"In here." He pointed to his temple. "You are in here, Vera."

I could see silvery gray dust on the tips of his two middle fingers, the ones he used to smudge pencil or charcoal when he drew. My pulses threatened to deafen me.

I moved close to him and reaching up with one shaking hand, touched his hair the way I had seen Yulia do.

He squeezed his eyes closed.

"Petya," I whispered, my voice shaking. "Petya."

I placed a hand on each of his shoulders for leverage, went up on my toes, and touched my lips gingerly to his. He kissed me back, at first softly, then with more pressure, the world unraveling, falling away around us. With his arms around me he pulled me close, breaking the kiss and burying his face in my neck, breathing at my ear. I felt his hardness, tight as whipcord against my belly.

A noise of bells caused us both to jump. Petya stepped back.

"It's only the horse, Petya."

Flustered, he struggled to catch his breath. I approached him again but he took another step away.

"No, Vera," he said, his voice quiet, almost sad. "We are not thinking."

He grabbed his lamp but stopped before reaching the door. He stood facing away from me, his head lowered.

I said his name and heard him exhale, as if in defeat.

"Come," I pleaded. He turned cautiously to look at me, and I opened my arms, taking a step back toward a shadowy corner of the stable.

He set the lamp down and followed. He embraced me, kissing my hair, my face. He took off my coat and his own, then went to his knees, kissing my dress at the waist and the belly, kissing my dress over my thighs. He reached for my hands and brought me down to lie with him in the hay.

A heavier snow fell that night, the whiteness of the sky through my window illuminating my room. I lay in bed, sleepless, moving from unease to euphoria and then to dread. My body felt slightly crushed all over, my pulses ticking like clocks.

Petya's intensity had taken me off guard, even shocked me at moments. I wasn't sure exactly what I'd been expecting to happen, something softer and slower. I had only known that I wanted to be near him, as near as I could, to secure him to me.

Lying in my bed now with the snow falling outside, I relived certain heightened moments between us, each one delivering a renewed shock, followed by a starburst of desire.

Afterward, we'd both been shaken. He had lain heavily next to me, breathing harshly, his forearm over his eyes. When he moved his arm, he took a deep breath and released it. He stared up into the shadows of the wooden rafters.

"Are you all right, Vera?" he whispered.

Lying here in my room now, I tried to understand if it was the question, or the way he'd asked it, that had made my heart sink.

As we'd stood brushing hay from our clothes, he told me he had been given several addresses and was going to Kiev in a few days to look for work as a draughtsman. When I told him I was sure he would find a position, his eyes glazed over. He felt impossibly far away from me. I hesitated, but then spilled out my dream of us marrying.

He was buttoning his coat when I said this. His fingers slowed around one button. He kept looking down.

"Petya? How would you . . ." I began in a shaky voice. "How would you feel about that?"

When he didn't move or speak I made an involuntary sound, a soft, upset exhalation, which caused him to look at me in earnest. Suddenly he took my hands and covered them with kisses. Squeezing his eyes closed he pressed my hands to his forehead.

I would play and replay this moment in the coming months. When it was happening, I took it as his way of saying that he wanted to marry me. But he had never said it out loud.

It was almost dark when we left the stable. Before we separated I told him I would come and see him the next day at the summerhouse.

In the middle of the night I heard sleigh bells outside and got up. I watched a sled glide away below in the near darkness, propelled forward like a boat sluicing through quiet water. I wondered who could have been leaving the property. There were four or five people it could have been, though it was odd to leave late, in the dark.

When light finally returned to the sky, everything looked odd, and I felt disoriented. The candles were still burning in the sconces in the hallway, each wearing a bright, fizzing halo.

The laden branches leaned in from either side, forming a white canopy over the long avenue. I made my way through foot-high snow, my breath smoking on the air around me, the summer house finally materializing through the whiteness.

Massive icicles hung like a jagged curtain from the awning all around the veranda. A new area of the roof had collapsed under branches and snow.

"The eternal project," my aunt had once called the summerhouse. No sooner was one thing fixed than another would break.

"It is cursed," Uncle Pavel used to chide her. "Why do you keep trying?"

Petya could not possibly have slept in there, but maybe he had, or maybe he'd slept in one of the annex houses with Nickander and Osip.

I dug under the snow-covered mat on the porch and found the key that Aunt Marya always left there. The hasp of the door was frozen and I had to shake and pull at it for a while before it gave. Everything was iced over inside the glassed-in veranda. Water had frozen in the watering can and ice crystals had formed over the gardening tools. Some of the windows had cracked under the heaviness of the ice.

The main door resisted and eventually groaned open, a concentrated gust of cold rushing to meet me. I called out Petya's name. I could see where the roof had buckled and a high bank of impassable snow blocked the stairs to the upper floor. The rails of the banister that had so recently been repaired had snapped and fallen away. Cold drafts circulated through the house.

I called out again, but there was no answer and in the silence I could feel that the house was empty.

Amazed by the glittering destruction, I moved through the corridor, looking into the rooms. In places the snow had not reached, furniture had fallen and crockery lay shattered.

I came to the room Petya had slept in. The pallet was rolled up and placed on a shelf. A short, much-used wooden pencil lay on the floor near the cabinet. The sketchpad wasn't inside, only a piece of fabric pushed far to the back. I closed it. I thought of the sled leaving in the middle of the night and felt sure now that it had been Petya.

Holding back tears, I stood at the window that had been closest to where Petya slept and breathed on one pane until a fog of condensation formed. With my index finger, I wrote *Petya* in ornate script. As the word wavered there, beginning to drip, I thought of the cloth in the back of the cabinet and went to open it again. I could see the tiniest edge of paper behind the cloth. Reaching far back, I managed to dislodge a page of drawing paper, which was rolled into a scroll.

Part 1

". . . desires and dreams and griefs were breeding."
—Pushkin

Two and a half months later

Chapter 1

Carrying a heavy book, I took a shortcut through a field of weeds and wildflowers then crossed the road and reached a stand of poplars and a path, which led to Dr. Mitrofan's large wooden house with its old world window sashes, painted blue and white. It was a warm, bright day near the end of June, breezes rushing through the birch trees.

The front door was open, creaking back and forth. Stepping inside, I called out, but it was quiet. Curtains in the front room blew in and billowed, then clung to the screens. Old Lika, who worked in the kitchen, a small half-blind creature in a starched ill-fitting apron, materialized, looking dazed, as if I'd awakened her, and told me that the doctor had gone to town with his wife who was taking the train to Odesa to see her sister.

I explained that I was just returning a book my aunt had borrowed and told her I'd put it back on the shelf where it belonged.

I walked slowly up the hall but before reaching the library, stopped at the doctor's consulting room, the door wide open, held in place with an iron doorstop.

Embracing the heavy book against my chest and stomach with both arms, I stepped inside. He usually came to us when anyone in our household was ill, but we had on occasion come to him here.

The bare walls were painted white. Everything was white except a brown wooden frame around the window and a brown leather chair near an oak desk in the corner. I felt light-headed. The hem of the bleached, heavily starched sheet on the examination table quivered on gusts of air from the hallway.

Since Petya departed, I had not had my monthly flow. Most of the time the idea of having a child did not seem real and it was only in moments when I felt the sting of an unfamiliar ache in my belly or my breasts that the reality would paralyze me. But there were moments when I missed Petya so much, and felt so lost, the idea of carrying him within me gave me a kind of comfort.

I sat down in the brown leather chair, grasping the heavy book tightly against me. The room was so quiet I could hear myself breathing, the walls so white they hurt my eyes.

Since Petya left that snowy night, I'd been telling myself that he would come back when he found work in Kiev or he would send word to me. But so much time had passed and it kept passing. Sometimes I could not help but think he was gone from my life.

I began to cry and bent forward over the book, clutching it close. My weeping became more intense and spasmodic.

With a gasp I sensed a presence and opened my eyes. A figure stood in the doorway, difficult to see through my tears.

"I'm sorry," the figure said in a quiet voice of such familiar timbre, I thought it was Petya.

I blinked quickly and wiped my eyes with my sleeve.

My heart sank. I guessed he was my age, nineteen, or maybe twenty, dressed in an off-white muslin shirt and dark blue sail cloth trousers.

"I didn't mean to surprise you," he said in a voice I could now distinguish from Petya's. "I was in the library reading and I heard footsteps." It was a voice of a similar texture, but belonging to someone less reticent.

I took a shaking breath. "I came to return this book," I said, but did not stand up.

"Is there something I can do?" he asked.

"No," I replied.

For a few moments neither of us spoke.

"I'll leave you, then," he said and seemed to wait for me to respond. When I didn't, he bowed and vanished from the door frame.

The windows of the library were thrown open, the sun shining directly in. The young man stood near a desk at the window. He was tall, taller even than Petya, inches over six feet, I was sure. His hair was darker than Petya's, but there was something similar about his face. He introduced himself formally as Anton Pavlovich Chekhov, a friend of the Mitrofans'.

"I'm Vera Denisova. Vera *Sergeyevna* Denisova," I added, mirroring his use of the patronymic.

A large book had been left open on a side table near an armchair. I guessed it was the book he'd been reading when he'd heard my footsteps.

"You live down the road past all the linden trees," he said.

"Yes, at Volkhov."

A sudden strong breeze caused the white curtains to stir brightly, tousling his brown hair, a reddish halo where the sun touched his head.

"You have an outdoor stage at Volkhov."

"We do," I said, still embracing the book.

"I hear the great violinist, Anatoly Slezkine, will perform an adagio one night soon! Doctor Mitrofan has invited me to accompany him there to hear it."

There was an underlying tranquility about Anton. I could see it whenever he moved, even slightly, something relaxed in his physicality. He stood very still and focused on me. His eyes, thoughtful and alert, drew and reflected all the daylight in the room.

"I have no talent for music myself, but it is probably the only force that can bring me to tears."

I smiled. "The maestro should arrive anytime. But if you come, I'm afraid that after listening to a genius perform, you will have to suffer through amateur theatricals."

"I am a great fan of amateur theatricals," he said, a frisson of excitement in his voice. "My brothers and I participated in them ourselves. And spent as much time as we could at the local music hall."

He took a few steps toward me, cocked his head and tried to read the title from the spine of the volume I held.

"*The History of* . . . I can't see the rest."

"The History of the Chinese Empire," I said.

"You're interested in history?"

I shook my head. "My aunt borrowed it. I'm returning it for her. Not a book I would choose for myself. I find reading history too . . ."

"Dry?" he asked.

"If that's the polite way to say that it bores me, then yes," I replied.

I did not want to let go of the book but it seemed strange to keep clinging to it. I walked to the bookcase and slid the heavy volume onto the shelf.

We stood looking at each other, the silence extended and slightly awkward. He exuded a quiet magnetism that interested me.

The wind came in and stirred the pages on the thick volume he'd left open.

"Is that the book you were reading?" I asked.

"Yes."

We both laughed as the wind kept turning the pages.

"Now you'll never find your place again!" I said.

He held his arms wide and shrugged.

"What is it about?"

"The respiratory system."

"That's another subject I would never choose to read about," I said.

"It requires a certain kind of . . ." He looked up and to the side as if searching for a word. "Intention." His eyes met mine again.

"You don't like it either."

"It's demanding," he said, nodding, "but I am learning to like it. I have to!" He smiled. "I am about to begin medical school."

"Where will you go to study?"

He told me he'd dreamed of studying in Zurich, where Dr. Mitrofan had studied. Though it would have been difficult to arrange he might have been able to do it, but his oldest brother persuaded him to stay in Russia. He paused, then tensed his mouth and added in what struck me as a sardonic tone, "For the sake of the family." He looked down and shook his head slightly. "I'm going to Moscow University."

"I've heard it's a good place to study medicine."

"It is, I'm sure. I am just anxious to travel, to see Europe. But I'm spending a month here at the doctor's invitation. I'm making use of his library. Getting a head start."

He suddenly pulled a handkerchief out of the breast pocket of his white muslin shirt, pressed it to his nose and mouth, and coughed convulsively into it, muffling the sound. He coughed a second time, squeezing his eyes closed.

"I'm sorry," he said as he put the handkerchief back in his pocket. He struggled a little to catch his breath. "I'm recovering from a mild case of bronchitis."

"I'm glad it was mild and you're recovering."

"It's *not* contagious," he added.

I nodded and we stood there, each offering the other the hint of a smile. The two of us might have been observing formalities, but the room felt animated around us, a new reckless breeze rushing in, the curtain billowing wildly, papers flying off the desk and onto the floor.

Anton went over and retrieved them. Rather than closing the window, he gathered the rest of the papers and put them in a drawer.

"Dr. Mitrofan told me that your grandmother was Dashkova, the actress," he said.

"Yes."

"And he told me that your father also used to be an actor."

My heart began beating hard. "My father, Sergei Denisov, is *still* an actor," I said quickly.

I heard the defensive tone in my voice and tried to arrest it. "Well, it is true that he has taken time off from acting, but my father is *still* an actor. He still performs."

The reality was that, devastated by a bad review, my father hadn't set foot on a stage in almost fifteen years. It was general knowledge but he pretended otherwise. He told people that he was in demand, constantly being offered roles. People sometimes questioned him and it became awkward. Some of those people were in the theatre and asked for details, trying to put my father on the spot. I never liked it when my father told people this, but he was not here to say it himself, so I repeated the lie for him.

"He is constantly offered roles and I'm sure that when the right one comes he will accept." I avoided Anton's eyes.

My beloved father, who lived much of the year in Kiev, was several days late in arriving for the summer and had sent no word. I was anxious to see him. He had always been so tenderly indulgent of my moods and emotions. The past few days I had been sitting on the veranda listening for the clopping of horses and the wheels of a carriage, but any conveyances that arrived had delivered neither Petya nor my father.

My face felt hot. Anton had inadvertently touched a nerve, however I hoped nothing in my demeanor gave that away. But he looked pained. He told me in a hushed, sincere voice that my father was an actor of great notoriety. I smiled inwardly at his sweet attempt to soothe or appease me. I wondered if he'd ever even heard of my father.

"Well it was nice to make your acquaintance, Anton Pavlovich Chekhov," I said, and looked at the giant book he'd left on the side table, pages still stirring, his place irreparably lost. "I will let you get back to the respiratory system."

As I started toward the door, he stopped me.

"Dr. Mitrofan told me that you sometimes help out at the Zemstvo school in Ilyakin."

"Yes, I try to be useful in some way."

"The weather is particularly beautiful today." He smiled. "Breezy as it is."

"Yes," I nodded, my heart still beating like a muted drum in my ears.

"If you are going to the school now, might I walk you there?"

"I'm not going to the school today. My father could arrive anytime so I don't want to be far."

"I was hoping to take a break from all the studying."

"If you'd like, you can walk with me to Volkhov."

Chapter 2

The sun brought forth the reddish glint in Anton's thick, brown hair. I led him through the same shortcut I had taken to get there, the air buzzing with insects.

"Dr. Mitrofan told me about the summer parties on your estate."

"Yes, started by my grandmother." I described to him how the parties sometimes lasted the entire month of July, guests constantly arriving or departing, some staying indefinitely. "Celebrations go until dawn sometimes and spread out over the park and around the duck pond. Many of the guests are luminaries of the theatre or writers. Artists and intellectuals with conflicting views of the world."

"I imagine there are sometimes quarrels," he said.

"Oh yes," I laughed. "Western culture versus Slavic. Feudalism or capitalism. At least one terrible fight each summer."

Anton laughed, then began to cough, bending forward and holding both hands to his mouth. A first bout of coughing turned into a second. When he recovered, he apologized, his eyes damp and red. I asked him if he was all right and he dismissed my concern, asking me to go on with what I was saying.

"Most of the time guests talk about unremarkable things." I described drifting from tobacco-fueled arguments about the Latin names of mushrooms to gossip about infidelities.

I told him there were a few guests on the property now and that more would arrive in the coming days and make themselves at home. "I pray that this summer we won't be overrun with people."

Navigating the high weeds, we laughed at the exuberance of the grasshoppers hurling themselves at Anton's legs or getting caught in my hems.

Since we'd come outside into the daylight, my mood had lifted, the bright air washing away my sadness, making my predicament less immediate.

"I'd like to avoid running into my sister, Sasha," I said, once we reached the avenue of birch trees. "She might come looking for me to rehearse our scene from *Twelfth Night*."

I explained that we were going to perform it after Slezkine's adagio and that we had been rehearsing for hours the night before. I felt frustrated with my part in the scene and could not quite find my way with it. "My father should have been here days ago. I need his help. I'm dreading the performance."

For her part, Sasha was obsessing about doing well. She had invited Prince Miranov, a thin, cold man with blue eyes as cloudy as moonstones, someone she was interested in, but whom I did not like at all. When she'd asked me to do the scene, though I hadn't wanted to, I'd agreed. All my life I'd been looking for ways to endear myself to Sasha. And I thought it might be a chance to get closer to her so I could take her into my confidence. But even if I told her the condition I believed I was in, I could never have told her that Petya was the father. I knew that Sasha accepted the conventional "wisdom" that almost everyone else accepted, that servants were inferior beings. In moments of desperation I fantasized about opening her eyes, teaching her how small-minded that position was. I imagined getting through to her and being able to confide in her. But I also imagined her telling me that my love for Petya was shameful and that the condition I found myself in was unforgivable, a disaster that would cause only suffering.

Another reason I had agreed to do the scene was because I thought it might be a distraction. But it was proving to be the opposite.

"I used to love performing snippets and monologues from Shakespeare in the past. But now I'm uncomfortable."

"Why?"

"Everything I do or say feels false. I'm only there to give Sasha her cues, so it shouldn't matter so much. But it does and I don't know why."

"It's good that it matters so much," Anton said.

"I'll tell you what it feels like. Imagine that the scene is a room. I keep coming in clumsily through the wrong door. I need to somehow find the right door."

"Ah," he said. "You feel there is a way in. You just haven't found it yet."

I steered him onto a side path where the chances of running into Sasha were smaller, and pointed out the empty summerhouse when it came into view. Anton drifted in its direction and I followed, telling him that the roof was damaged, that a small crew had spent every spring and summer since I could remember, trying to repair it.

"They would succeed almost every year, but always too late in the summer to house the guests, which is what my aunt wants to use it for."

No plans were currently in place to repair the parts of the roof that had buckled under the April snowfall.

"It could still serve as a shelter for vagrants, but my uncle insists it be kept locked." Periodically over the years, especially in the cold weather, I'd unlocked the door and when my uncle found out he yelled. "You will meet my Uncle Pavel at the performance, Anton," I said and shook my head. "I am always butting heads with him. Why shouldn't people use it for shelter if they need it?" I took the key from a pocket in my skirt and showed it to him. "I went to check yesterday to make sure it was unlocked but there were so many spiders on the screen. I don't mind insects, Anton, but I hate spiders."

"I'll check," he said.

I gave him the key and he walked over, found the door locked, unlocked it, and pushed it open. He stepped inside for a few seconds and I could hear him coughing. When he came back out, he closed the door and gave me the key. "Yes," he said. "Lots of spiders inside, too, but I'm used to them. In the small room where I was living until recently they crawled all over me in my sleep and built their webs around me."

Taking a back pathway, we could see people in the distance, dressed in white and swiping at the air with butterfly nets.

"They go after the blue butterflies but only catch the hawkmoths," I said.

Anton pointed in the direction of the orchard and asked what kind of fruit grew there.

"Peaches," I answered.

"And will anyone be pruning those trees?"

"I'm not sure."

"Did they flower in the spring?"

"Not as much as usual. Last year there were pink blossoms for as far as you could see."

I had heard summer guests talking under their breath about the orchard being unmanaged as if it were a bad omen. Even the ground under the trees, someone said, was overgrown with chickweed and dandelions. And the fruit that was growing was being eaten by Japanese beetles. It bothered me to hear these things, but I could not keep my focus on any of it. I told myself that it would somehow be addressed. There had been other problems in the past and my aunt had fixed them.

A couple emerged through the birches ahead of us walking on an adjacent pathway. A stout man in an immaculate white suit and a woman in pale blue, wearing a tall hat embellished with sprigs of lily-of-the-valley.

"Vera Sergeyevna," the woman called over to me. "Did you hear about the sighting this morning? A white deer on the back acreage. A doe, it is believed, or it might be a young buck. There are plans for an excursion later to look for it."

They kept walking past us but we could hear the rest of their conversation. The man, whose boots creaked as he walked, said that a white deer would make a great prize.

The woman, a commanding sort of person, a regular grand duchess, linked her arm firmly with his, and said, "You do not hunt a white deer! A white deer, buck or doe, is a miraculous occurrence in nature."

"Why then go look for it?" the stout man asked.

"You are crude, Victor Victorovich!" she said in a chastising voice, though she did not let go of his arm. "Crude and insensitive. It is in order to glimpse the miracle of it."

"I am crude, I admit," Victor Victorovich confessed mournfully. As his voice trailed off we could hear him say, "I rely on you, dear Anya Leonideyvna, to show me a different way."

We watched them retreat.

"This woman, Anya Leonideyvna," I said, "has taken it upon herself to civilize Victor Victorovich."

Anton raised his eyebrows. "Why does he need civilizing?"

"He overindulges in everything. A confessed voluptuary."

"That does not strike me as such a terrible crime," Anton said. He smiled as he reached into a deep pocket in his sailcloth trousers and brought out a small oval charm formed of soft metal, flat on one side. On the other side, sealed in some kind of clear resin, the tiny, slender figure of a white deer stood surrounded by green, the suggestion of trees or a forest.

"I am not a superstitious person, but they say it is providential to glimpse a white deer, especially at a time of change in one's life," Anton said.

"Really?"

"A white deer, it is said, invites the person lucky enough to see it to exchange an old life for a new one."

At these words, a charge of emotion rose from deep within me. I peered at Anton. "Then I would very much like to see it."

The quality of his attention as he gazed at me caused a shiver to run up my arms. The moments of our first encounter in the doctor's office hung in the air between us.

Right away in my mind the white deer became inseparable from Petya. An encounter with it, I told myself, would herald Petya's imminent return. A fugitive part of me knew it wasn't realistic, but the longing, hopeful side attached itself to the idea.

"When I know more about a search party, Anton, I will come tell you."

We kept walking. I imagined seeing the white deer at every turn ahead. I imagined it leading me far into the property, a place deep and dark green where I would find Petya waiting for me.

"So many old trees," Anton said, "and so many different kinds."

"These trees are my family members. I have known them all my life."

Anton wore a rapt expression.

"Our forests are similar, I've been told, to the beautiful Carpathian forests in southwestern Ukraine."

"There is a feeling here," he said, "something very old." He took a deep breath as if he might breathe the atmosphere into his lungs. He did not seem inclined to go back to his studying.

"You must have beautiful gardens here at Volkhov," he said. "You know, Vera, deer are sometimes drawn to gardens because they love to eat flowers."

I told him that a rare wild orchid was growing in one of the gardens and he said that perhaps a rare deer would be drawn to a rare flower. Taking a circuitous way to the garden, we had to pass an extension at the back of the main house where many of the guests usually stayed. I stopped when I heard a gentle high-pitched female voice through an open window. She seemed to be asking someone a question.

"Listen," I whispered to Anton. "It's Vova, a young chambermaid, a summer hire. She talks to herself."

A fleeting shadow crossed his face as if it made him uncomfortable to listen, but if he was, he seemed unable to help himself and stood perfectly still, his head raised.

I could not quite hear what Vova was saying, but her words had a musical urgency to them.

There was a pause as if she was waiting for an answer to her question, then she spoke as if surprised by something.

"Are you sure there isn't someone in there with her?" Anton whispered almost soundlessly near my ear.

"She's alone."

The window was too high off the ground for us to glimpse what lay inside, but we stepped closer to listen. She must have been making a bed, because there was a sound like a sheet snapping on the air.

"The carriage never comes. You said the carriage would come."

Anton looked serious, barely breathing as he listened.

"But the carriage *doesn't* come," she said in an argumentative tone of voice. Again there was the sense that she was listening to someone and that she heard another response.

"I wait and it *does not* come!" she cried with feeling.

Her words and the emotion in her voice shook me. Like me, Vova was waiting. I felt suddenly protective of her and guilty for having instigated the eavesdropping.

I beckoned Anton and we walked away.

"She seems to be trying to understand why someone left her behind," Anton said. He gazed at the ground as we walked, his brow fraught.

"I've heard her talking but this is the first time I've heard clearly what she's saying. I hope you don't think badly of me for telling you to listen."

"No," he said thoughtfully.

"I grew up in a house where people keep things from me, so it's a habit. Not something to be proud of, but I listen at doorways sometimes."

"We are human beings. We are curious. She is probably a person with a sad story. There was nothing unkind in you suggesting that I listen. I was interested so I listened."

"You are absolving me?" I asked with a smile.

He raised his hand, showing me the flat of his palm in a priestly gesture. "I am absolving you."

We walked quietly for a little while.

"She is the second sad young woman I've encountered today," Anton said, feigning wistfulness and looking off to the side.

I felt color rising to my cheeks.

We arrived at the garden and I pointed out the bearded slipper orchid, growing in a patch of delphiniums. "This orchid travels."

He raised his brows and looked at me expectantly, but I detected amusement.

"You think it's funny?"

"I am a practical-minded person. That sounds . . . fanciful."

"There really are traveling orchids, Anton."

He pressed his lips together, resisting a laugh.

"The vine that the orchid is attached to has sudden growth spurts, so it looks from day to day like the orchid has traveled."

"Well, I have learned something new."

"So don't be so condescending," I said, smiling at him and feeling satisfied.

"I didn't say a word."

"Your eyes did. For a few minutes you were asking yourself who this silly girl is who believes that flowers can walk."

"I should never put it past nature to be strange and unpredictable." He bowed his head, pressing a hand to his heart. "I beg your absolution, Vera."

Now I raised my hand and showed him the flat of my palm. "I grant it to you."

I'd begun worrying that Anton would say he had to go back.

In his company I felt suspended in a light joy I had not felt for a long time. I had only just met this tall young man in the white muslin shirt and blue sailcloth trousers, but a feeling had formed itself quickly that he was someone I might trust. It could not be explained any better than to say that it was something felt in the tissues and the nerves.

As Anton admired the speckled orchid with its long, asymmetrical petals, I stood before a Russian olive tree, just one of many that grew at Volkhov, the silvery backs of the long slender leaves catching the sunlight, and thought that because Anton had met me while I was in the throes of emotion, he knew me more deeply right away, than if we had met in more conventional circumstances. When I'd seen him in the doorway I had felt intruded upon, but only briefly. Thinking about it now it filled me with wonder how quickly any shame or unease had dispersed. I had been instantly curious about him and wanted to be again in his company. Did I have a more intimate sense of him, too, because of what he'd witnessed? I decided as I looked at the leaves of the Russian olive tree that yes, I did. I looked over at him and he looked at me, a smile less on his lips and more in his eyes, the air between us awash with an almost strange, premature affection.

He suggested that an excursion of too many people would likely be noisy and the white deer would hide, that we'd have more luck just the two of us walking quietly and that it was probably a good idea for us to look for it right away.

"Dr. Mitrofan told me that the grounds of Volkhov span far in each direction."

"It's true. In some directions, the property spans as far as two versts. A person could feel quite isolated in some places on this estate. People who venture into the back acreages sometimes get lost."

"Do you have any idea where a rare deer might be on your property?"

I led him to a less trodden pathway, hoping for a sighting. He paced his walk to match mine and kept his hands interlaced behind his back, an expectant smile on his face.

When the path we were on became overgrown and less defined, we heard movement and stopped walking, hoping it was the white deer, but through the branches, the figure of a large man came into view, his silvery blond hair catching the sunlight. He did not, at first, see us.

"Who is that?" Anton whispered.

"My Uncle Boris, my mother's brother," I said.

Uncle Boris moved slowly across a grassy clearing, wearing a blue Napoleonic-looking jacket, elaborate frogging on the chest. And then I saw the rifle.

"Oh no." I took a step closer to move a branch and he turned, aiming in my direction. "Uncle!" I cried out.

He lowered the rifle.

"You cannot hunt rabbits at this hour. There are guests on the property!" I yelled impatiently.

He looked sternly down at the ground a moment before disappearing into the branches.

"He would never shoot the white deer, would he?" Anton asked.

"He is only allowed to hunt rabbits and only very early in the morning. It is too late for him to be out here with his gun. I've seen him point his gun at rabbits but he never shoots. I don't know why. I don't think he's ever actually fired the gun."

"Curious," Anton said. "Dr. Mitrofan mentioned to me that you have an uncle who got back last year from a Siberian prison camp. Is that him?"

"Yes. He labored for years mining gold."

We walked away from the area toward an embankment of the river, dense with willows, the air bright with the songs of chaffinches, darting from one tree to the other.

Speaking quietly, still on the lookout for the white deer, Anton said, "Dr. Mitrofan told me your uncle suffers from consumption."

"Yes, the White Plague. He contracted it in the Kara Gold Mines."

Chapter 3

Anton and I found our way to a remote area of the estate, and stood on the edge of a hill overlooking a valley covered in wild grass and weeds. He whistled at two borzois we saw below, and they came loping up to us, excitedly wagging their tails. They circled as we talked to them, both of us petting them vigorously. They belonged to a woman named Proskovia, who soon appeared, quite winded, climbing the ascending hill. Her red hair, tousled by the breezes, looked like dry bursts of flame around her head.

Proskovia was my favorite of all the guests. She was the only person I had confided in about my feelings for Petya, but I had stopped short of telling her what we'd done together and my near certainty that I was carrying a child.

"Proskovia read my tarot cards!" I told Anton.

She was getting nearer to us but still struggling up the hill. She tended to isolate herself from others and never appeared at meals or gatherings. I described how, after feeding her dogs in the morning, she would arrive early to the buffet and fill her cloth bag with food to last her the day, then wander the grounds, often quietly humming, the two dogs always following or running ahead at a distance, then circling back around to her.

I asked him if he had ever heard of Maxima Gabinskaya, a famous eccentric who used to play the piano for the Petersburg Philharmonia, a woman who wore a long black skirt, but otherwise dressed as a man in a collared shirt and suit jacket. He said he hadn't. "Maxima is my mother's only friend. She plays the piano more beautifully than I've heard anyone play. This lady, Proskovia, came to Volkhov as Maxima's guest."

When she reached us she was breathless, one hand on her heaving chest. "This area," she asked, sweeping her other arm back toward the valley from which she'd just ascended, "was it once marshland?"

"I believe it was," I replied.

"What a shame that it dried up!" she said.

I introduced her to Anton and she told us she was looking for the greenhouse.

I said that we would escort her there.

"I am breathless," she said, "but it is not because of the hike or the rough roads." She stopped a moment and lifted a foot to show us one of her sturdy climbing boots, that clashed with her silk organza dress patterned in orange and yellow fleur de lys. She was a tall woman with prominent cheekbones and an ample bosom.

"My dear children, I am tired because I am up at all hours. I never sleep well."

She focused on Anton as if she recognized him, but was not sure from where. She spoke to us in a personal, confiding way, as if we were intimates. "Many nights I don't sleep at all, and then, after the passage of days I will sink into a state of catatonia for a little while. And I do this in the most inopportune places. In a busy hallway, or once in a kitchen during meal preparation. I sleep on the floor and sometimes don't even close my eyes. I can see people who come up and address me and try to make me get up, but it is as if I am behind a thick wall of glass. I want you both to know in case you see me in a slump on the floor or in the grass, not to be alarmed."

There was about her such an air of sincerity. When she looked away a moment, Anton shot me a smile. I could see by his eyes that he liked her.

"By the way, dear Vera. Your sister was looking for you earlier."

"Oh, yes," I said. "I will see her a bit later."

"She seemed as if it were important."

"My sister always behaves that way. It's fine," I reassured her.

Proskovia looked at Anton with curiosity. "Tell me more about who you are and where you came from."

He told her he was a poor medical student on his way to Moscow, but had been spending lazy days visiting Dr. Mitrofan.

"You could pass as aristocracy."

He shook his head. "My papa sold herrings."

She was tall, but Anton was taller so it was funny when she addressed him as Little Antosha. "Enjoy a bit of leisure, Little Antosha," she said. "How nice for you. There is something about you. I might have easily thought you were aristocracy. I would say that you and I are alike in that way. We both live more in a gray area."

She turned to me. "Your aunt and your uncle don't quite know how to treat me, dear girl. I came with Maxima so they are confused and think that perhaps I am an important person as she is, but they are not sure. Let me tell the two of you the answer to that mystery." She looked at each of us with wide mischievous eyes and whispered, "*I am not!*"

She smiled sweetly, a green jewel gleaming between two of her teeth.

"Some of us do not fall into easily identified categories."

"I don't fit easily either," I said.

Proskovia touched my wrist and leaned toward me. "And you, too, dear, if you want to occupy such a limbo with Little Antosha and me!"

As we strolled slowly along, she told us that she had grown up backstage, that her mother had been a seamstress for the ballet. Some of the ballerinas had been educated types and there was one who was a gypsy. The educated ballerinas taught her reading and writing, while the gypsy taught her about the influences of the planets, and how to read cards. The ballerinas did not have children because of what it would do to their bodies. They all pampered her and called her their little girl. "I was fortunate enough to have many mothers."

We entered the greenhouse where Proskovia took a microscope out of her large tapestry bag and examined the flowers closely. She knew most of their Latin names, but could not remember the Latin name for the Queen of Prussia roses. She said that someone was not pruning them correctly, that they were too fat. She bent to smell one then quickly recoiled. "They should not have such a strong fragrance," she said with tears in her eyes. "They should not intoxicate quite so powerfully."

We tagged along with Proskovia and the dogs. Anton showed no signs of leaving to get back to his studies. I resigned myself to the fact that Sasha would be angry later.

"You are an old soul," Proskovia said to Anton. "Anyone with any intuition can see that if they look. People will love you for that, Little Antosha, but some will hate you for it."

"I hope more love me than hate me," he said.

Anton had already told Proskovia that he was recovering from a mild case of bronchitis, but each time he coughed softly into his handkerchief or his sleeve, something that I was getting used to, she gave him a sidelong look of concern.

"I think you will defy all odds. Perhaps you will become a redemptive political figure in one of the southern oblasts."

"Perhaps!" Anton laughed, throwing his hands out with an odd jubilation. "Perhaps all the medical studying will come to nothing."

Proskovia pressed a palm to her chest. "Can he be real?" she asked me in a whisper that Anton could easily hear.

Taking my arm, she led me a few steps away from Anton and with our backs to him, she said, "You see what I told you days ago, Little Veroushka? Someone new would arrive to replace Petya Fyodorovich." She had said these words in a low voice, but one loud enough, I was sure, for Anton to hear, and I wondered if she'd done that on purpose. She smiled, the green jewel in her teeth winking at me.

A wave of sadness went through me. If she had not been so in earnest over my happiness, I might have told her that Petya could never be replaced by anyone.

When we faced him again, Anton looked curiously at me, one eyebrow raised.

We walked awhile until we came across an upholstered chair set out on a hill where a guest may have been enjoying the view earlier. She brushed a few leaves off the cushion, then sighed as she sat down, crossed her legs, and lit a small brown cigarette.

"It must have been interesting growing up backstage with the ballerinas," Anton said as the two of us sat down on the ground, facing out over the same view.

"I have good memories and I have bad ones, too. I loved all my mothers and if any of them suffered, I suffered, too.

"I could consult the cards for the two of you, but I do not want them to break your hearts. The cards, as we know now, dear Little Veroushka," she said shooting a glance at Anton, "can be fortuitous. But they can be wrong. In every reading I've ever had done since I was a child, the cards told me that I would have a daughter. I have always wanted a daughter, or even a son. I love young people. And I am thirty-eight years old and to be quite honest with you, I can't be bothered with men. Maybe it's the awful men who used to visit the ballerinas that made me mistrust the male of the species. I am sorry, Anton. Not you. You are still young and your eyes are clear and there is hope yet for you. Cards are not foolproof. Years keep going by and there has been no sign of this daughter. Yet the cards keep telling me she will come.

"I do not know if it was with my own mother or if it was with the ballerinas but I know I experienced euphoria at an earlier time in my life because a part of me remembers that feeling. I walk around aching to find that euphoria again, that closeness between mother and child."

"Could it be with someone else, not a child, that you could find that closeness?" Anton asked.

"No, no. It is very specific. It is a maternal instinct, a deep desire to give and to protect. You see, a wise ballerina once told me that a child anchors a mother to the earth. I am not anchored. I move like a shadow on the periphery."

A child anchors a mother to the earth. The words sent pleasurable chills over my arms and shoulders. For a fleeting moment, I pressed my palm to my belly.

"Like a shadow," she repeated wistfully. "Hmmmm," she uttered, blowing smoke skyward. "Hmmmm."

A cricket began a tentative song in the bracken.

"A fat man with a big cigar used to come backstage to see Viridiana, the prima ballerina. One night he brought her a pink velvet box of Belgian chocolates tied with a pale blue ribbon. That was the first time I ever had a chocolate. I felt changed by the taste. It was like entering a dark, sweet garden at nighttime. I felt elevated by the flavor, in awe over the fact that such a sweet dark explosion of sensation could exist in the world. But that same night, Viridiana came back in tears from her dinner with this man. She had marks around her neck, and would not go on for three nights. I refused ever to eat another chocolate and I didn't until last year when an acquaintance of Maxima's brought over a box of Viennese chocolates. I was offered one and took it. I had to go sit alone for an hour after tasting it, the pleasure was so intense. But that very night, my beloved little poodle, Dudinka, ate something sharp outside and choked to death."

The dogs grew anxious over Proskovia's tone of voice. The one she called Kingfisher trotted up to her and peered uneasily into her face, while Feokta, who had settled at her feet, seemed to plead with her with his dark eyes.

"I cannot eat chocolates with impunity." She looked at me and asked with grave curiosity, "Can you, dear?"

"I think so," I replied but worried that perhaps I'd been causing bad things to happen whenever I ate one.

"Chocolate!" she uttered wistfully. "Something demonic about it."

Feokta groaned and let out an anxious bark. Proskovia stared at the afternoon sky.

"There she is," she said, pointing with her cigarette to a pink star. "Venus, the goddess of love. It is fortuitous to see her impression there during the day." She paused and then said, "I do hope you and your beloved Antosha do not run into small-minded people with objections."

"Proskovia, we only just met each other."

"That doesn't matter. *The Lovers* came up as the last card in your reading. And you are too young to remain heartbroken over Petya Fyodorovich."

"Proskovia!" What I had told her about my love for Petya Fyodorovich was told in secret. I avoided Anton's eyes.

"I'm sorry, dear. I think it's fine to mention him in front of Little Antosha, don't you? But no one else."

A blue butterfly fluttered slowly past Proskovia. She drew at her cigarette and exhaled, the smoke drifting off to the side, following after the butterfly.

"A shame about all that marshland drying up," she said as if to the air.

Anton and I walked quietly awhile and stopped when we reached a hill looking down toward a grassy meadow. "This is where we will have fireworks one night soon. You should come and see them."

A man dressed in a belted, mustard-colored jacket appeared below. He seemed not to see us above on the hill. He stopped suddenly and consulted something shiny, probably a compass, held in his palm.

I made an irritated sound. "That's Oleg Radzitsky who used to be a cartographer and is now a businessman. He first came here months back with Sasha's Prince Miranov. Since then I've seen him wandering the property by himself. He takes the liberty of coming here without the prince and without an invitation. And he doesn't even go see my aunt or uncle. Just wanders around looking at the property."

"Is he interested in buying the estate?"

"No one can *buy* Volkhov, Anton. It isn't possible."

He gazed at me with a quizzical expression and after a silence asked, "Why not?"

"It's ours!"

He looked thoughtfully out over the view.

"He joined us uninvited for dinner months back and raved about how beautiful Volkhov is. He said a new railway would likely run nearby in the not-too-distant future and then he had the nerve to ask my aunt if she'd ever thought of clearing areas of land to build summer cottages, that there was money to be made."

"How did your aunt react?"

"She listened to him, which frustrated me. I think she was just being polite."

Oleg Radzitsky, still unaware of us on the hill above him, pocketed the compass. As he swatted at an insect on his neck, he reached into a different pocket with his free hand, took out a small notebook and pencil and, holding it close to his face, squinted and began scribbling something.

"How could a man sit at dinner with a family and talk about cutting down their trees to build cottages? I don't like Prince Miranov by himself, but having such a friend makes me dislike him even more."

"Maybe the prince thinks it's smart to cleave to a businessman."

"Why? He's an aristocrat."

"Things in the world seem to be changing."

Under siege by a sudden cloud of insects, Oleg Radzitsky swatted all around his face and head, backed into the trees, and disappeared.

"Dr. Mitrofan is probably back by now, and if he isn't, Lika will get cranky if no one is there to eat her cooking."

As we strolled along in the direction of the avenue of birch trees, Anton asked me who Petya Fyodorovich was.

At first I didn't answer and kept walking, but after a moment, stopped and faced him. "He was a servant," I said.

Anton raised his brows, his eyes bright with interest, but his expression, as he looked at me, became serious. I would wonder later what he saw in my face as we stood there looking at each other in silence. I was sure he knew now that Petya had been the cause of my tears earlier.

"I hope you'll come back tomorrow morning, Anton. We'll search more for the white deer."

He thanked me and said he would.

I turned and started toward the house, but looked back once. He was almost out of sight when he began coughing convulsively, muffling the sound with his handkerchief.

Chapter 4

Standing outside my mother's room I could hear Sasha talking about Prince Miranov. I heard only his first name, Timofei, and something about him having been recently in Paris.

I opened the door. The room was hot. My mother sometimes kept a fire burning even when the weather was warm, saying she felt cold. She was standing near her red velvet couch holding a slip, a few delicate garments folded on one of the cushions near her. My sister sat in a green wingback chair, a small basket on her thigh, sewing a button onto a lace glove. As she looked up at me, she stopped sewing, her needle poised in midair.

Sasha, like our mother, was blond and very fair, their complexions like milk tinged with rosewater. I was dark-haired and took after my father's side of the family.

"Where were you?" Sasha asked. Like our mother, she was perspiring from the fire's heat, wisps of hair clinging to her forehead and temples.

"I'm sorry," I said. "I met a house guest of Dr. Mitrofan's and was showing him around the estate."

"We'll go to my room in a few minutes and run our lines. Did you memorize the monologue?"

"I think . . . I think so."

She made a quiet noise of exasperation. "You're doing such a poor job with this, Vera, because you don't like Timofei."

"No, Sasha. That isn't why."

"Why then don't you at least memorize the monologue?"

"I've been distracted."

Sasha had come to my room months before, after the first time I met him. She lay next to me on my bed and told me that Prince Timofei Miranov wanted to take her to Paris. I listened in silence as she told me he wanted to introduce her to some of the Pre-Raphaelite poets and painters. "He thinks that Millais would want to paint me as Eurydice or as the drowned Ophelia."

When she asked me what I thought of the prince, I was honest with her, and told her that there was something about him that I didn't trust. She listened to what I said and wasn't angry, and it seemed almost as if she had come to hear me warn her against him. My opinion seemed to have confirmed something for her, but instead of making her wary of him, her interest had gradually intensified.

"When Timofei is here, Vera," Sasha said irritably, "I demand that you behave better to him!"

The prince liked to hear himself speak and his arrogance made me feel contrary and eager to correct him. The last time he had visited he said something I knew was wrong: that the Potemkin villages had actually been solid villages erected along the water and were still standing.

"They were only façades," I'd said, "and were taken down after Catherine the Great passed in the boat."

"No, no, no, little girl," he'd said coldly. He was a tall, looming, narrow-chested figure with a large jaw and a small, upturned nose.

"Yes, yes, yes!" I'd replied, and Sasha had looked horrified.

The prince had pretended to ignore me but his cheeks flushed purple.

As if Sasha too were remembering the moment now, she scowled at the glove, pulling her needle quickly through a few times. "So you'll behave?"

"I will be nice to him *for you*, Sashenka, but I had to correct him that time because he was wrong."

A crease deepened between her brows. "You only know what you've read in a book, Vera. I'm sure Timofei knows better. He's a man and he lives in the real world. Not in a book!"

"He was wrong," I muttered again quietly.

I had since found out that the entire story might have been a myth, but I still considered myself more correct because the story had been about façades, not actual buildings.

I sat down on the red velvet couch and watched her finish sewing the pearl button onto the glove.

"Even if you think he's wrong about something, don't correct him."

"For you I will hold my tongue, dear sister."

The sadness I'd felt earlier began again to overcome me. I reached over, touched Sasha's arm, and whispered her name. She paused her sewing a moment but then continued without looking at me. I watched her sew in silence but felt emotion surging inwardly. I softly squeezed her forearm.

"Stop!" she said and pulled her arm away.

When she'd tied the knot and cut the thread, she began stuffing a finger sleeve with cotton wool. Sasha had been born missing a finger on her left hand and always wore a pale pink or flesh-colored lace glove. She stuffed the empty finger sleeve so it was not apparent. Mostly, people did not ask why she wore only one glove, but it had happened a few times over the years that someone who had had too much to drink at a summer party did ask. She had a ready answer. She said it was embarrassing but she had a light rash on the palm of that hand and the doctor had told her it was best that it stay covered. She took great pains that no one know about the missing finger. In my opinion, Sasha's left hand overly preoccupied her. But I had begun to feel that her unease over it was a manifestation of something deeper that she felt missing, something wrong at the heart of her life.

My sister was a cipher. I often called her by the affectionate *Sashenka*, but she only ever called me Vera, and was rarely demonstrative. It must have seemed to other people that she had no time for me, but that was not right. We shared an intimacy of Sasha's design. She was often pensive and sometimes she'd come to my room, lie beside me on my bed, and talk freely, spilling things forth.

She felt a kind of yearning to understand herself and who she was meant to be in the world. She admitted once, at such a moment, that she thought that humor might be the function of a particular, mysterious organ that she had been born without, yet another curious anomaly. Entirely preoccupied with the mystery of her own incomplete being, she allowed me the great privilege of being her sounding board. She told me once that she should not exist. When I pressed her on why she would say such a thing, she went silent.

She put on the newly repaired glove and held her hand up. As she turned it at different angles, surveying the impression it made, she told me to come to her room in fifteen minutes to run lines. She got up, taking her little sewing basket with her, and closed the door.

My mother had three adjoining rooms. The front one with the fireplace opened onto a large communicating room with French doors that opened onto a balcony overlooking the front of the house. A door on the left wall of that room led to her bedroom, which was always dim, curtains kept permanently closed, a candle burning day and night in a green glass lamp.

When Sasha left, my mother went into the communicating room, where she opened a dresser drawer. I followed and watched her put away the little pile of delicate garments she'd been holding. She paused after closing the drawer, still touching the handle, and stared downward as if lost in thought.

I went close to her and leaned on the side of the dresser, touching the edge softly with three fingers, hoping she would focus on me.

But she didn't, and I froze there with the force of not being seen.

Some days my mother was more remote than other days. Burning a fire was always an indication that she was feeling introspective, agitated and harder to reach.

I recognized the expression on her face, a glazed inward look, as if she were absorbed by some urgent paradoxical question, something that both appalled her and seemed to fill her with wonder.

"What are you thinking about, Mama?"

She looked at me, bemused by the question.

"Tell me," I urged. "Are you remembering something?"

She shook her head. Her features were drawing together, something that happened when she was annoyed. I changed the subject.

"Mama, you should come to hear Slezkine when he performs."

She peered uncertainly at me. "I might come," she said. "Yes, I will come!"

She'd said other times that she'd come down to dinner or to hear a musician perform. But for the last year, she'd barely left these rooms. She had grown a little heavy and soft about the edges from lack of exercise.

"Yes, it would be a shame if you miss Slezkine's performance. Music is so important to you. He'll play an adagio, I heard, from a new violin concerto by Tchaikovsky."

She sighed and looked down again at the handle of the drawer, retreating again into her thoughts. She was more present for Sasha. I had to try harder to pull her from her reveries.

"You took singing lessons, didn't you, Mama? When you were a girl."

"I used to go to a lady, Madame Avilova. She played the piano and I sang. She had six cats and they walked on the piano when she played."

"On the piano, Mama?"

She laughed. "On top of the piano, Vera. Not on the keys!"

"That's why you have such a beautiful voice. You had training."

"It wasn't really training. She played the piano and I sang. And the cats meowed in the background."

"It's the cats really that taught you to sing, then."

"Yes, you're right, Vera!" she laughed.

"Did they have beautiful soprano voices?" I asked.

"Yes!" she smiled. "And one Siamese was a baritone!"

I picked up her round wooden hairbrush, which sat on top of the dresser. She brushed her own hair and Sasha's with this brush and the soft white bristles were enmeshed with long blond strands of hair. For a long time now my mother and Sasha shared a closeness that excluded me, though Sasha was often impatient, even angry with her. Our mother reacted very quietly to Sasha's irritability, collapsing a little into herself, and I think Sasha may have felt guilty sometimes about her anger, maybe even confused about where it came from, but seemed unable to curb it.

"Will you, Mama?" I asked, holding out the brush.

She looked vaguely startled. I knew she didn't want to be torn away from whatever she was thinking about, but she nodded and I walked back into the front room and sat on the red velvet couch unpinning my hair and spreading it over my shoulders. She followed, stood behind me, and brushed.

On the wall above the fireplace hung a framed map of Russia, which was practically all Siberia, all white uncharted territory barely marked. And then there was the crowded far western side where Ukraine was, Baltic Russia hinging itself to Eastern Europe and Finland and Lapland.

Until my mother was sixteen, she had lived with her family at a southernmost point of Ukraine on the edge of the Black Sea, which was clearly marked on the map at the bottom of the western side of the continent.

To engage my mother, I resorted to asking her questions about things I already knew the answers to, things I knew she would be happy to repeat.

"What is the name of the place south across the Black Sea, the nearest shore to where you lived when you were a girl?"

"Constantinople," she said, almost brightly.

My mother had spent the early years of her life breathing moist, salty air, gulls riding the spring and autumn winds.

"And you had a pet goat, didn't you, Mama? What was her name?"

"Her name was Dunya."

"She used to unlock the gate with her teeth," I said.

"Yes," she laughed softly. "I am convinced, Vera, that she understood everything I said to her. She was such a clever goat."

"And she had golden eyes," I said.

"Yes."

"And you had a red parasol."

"One summer, the sun faded it pink." She laughed softly again.

The brush slowed in my hair. "The paradise of childhood," she said, "didn't last."

Her family had been Old Believers, something they'd been, for generations, persecuted for. Sasha had explained to me what our mother had left unclear. Our mother's father, our grandfather, had been a writer, Alexander Belanovsky. He wrote a poem in which he claimed that the White Czar of the holy city in Russia's eastern lands was the only true czar of Russia. For this, everything our grandfather had written, all seven of his books, were banned and destroyed. He was arrested and sentenced to forced labor in the silver mines of Nerchinsk and his family accompanied him into Siberian exile. Once they reached the Vladimirka Road, our grandfather, who was an epileptic, was taken in chains by cart with a group of other convicts. Our grandmother, mother, and her older half-brothers, Boris and Dimitri, followed in a separate cart.

The weather had often been bad, but they were luckier than most. My grandfather at least was in a cart, while they often passed people who were chained to each other and wearing only rags, walking into exile. But even in the carts it took months to reach Lake Baikal, in a mountainous region of the Siberian forest, and it would have taken even longer to reach Nerchinsk. They still had weeks of traveling ahead but had stopped for the night. It was October and the winds were cold. Our grandfather underwent a seizure, and in his frenzy, choked himself with his chains.

The family remained grief stricken at the lake. A sect of Old Believers, the Children of the White Czar, had been camping nearby, celebrating the Festival of Kupala since the summer solstice. Thousands of pilgrims had been there but had all eventually left. This group of fifteen or twenty were about to travel north to try and reach Evankia, one of the most remote areas of Russia and the refuge for some sects of Old Believers. In his grief, Dimitri's religious fervor grew intense and he persuaded them to join the sect and follow the wanderers northward through taiga. This holy pilgrimage was rarely undertaken, except by the most devout.

They were stranded on flooded roads and tormented by furious winds, surviving mostly on powdered tea and dry bread. They tried to follow the river, where they were able to glut themselves on sterlets, which were easily caught. The cold began to get the better of them. Dimitri had repeated visions of a young woman in a pale blue dress leading a reindeer and pointing the way through the trees. There had been snow flurries all along, but one morning they awakened and the entire world was white, not a single branch visible on any tree. One of the horses had died before dawn and from then on they had to keep extra fires going all night to warm them. On the perilous journey, my grandmother's heart gave out. Very soon after, Dimitri, who followed his vision of the girl in pale blue up onto a mountain, fell into a crevasse in the snow.

Boris and our mother lost track of the caravan in the snowstorm. They were found starving and almost frozen to death, by a tribe of Nakut nomads, herding reindeer. One of the great ironies was that they were trying to find their way to the holy city, "true Russia preserved from the invasions of the Mongol hordes," as our mother had described it to Sasha, and they ended up living among the nomadic Nakut, who are of Mongol origin.

They lived with the Nakut for several years until a fur trader arrived and took them back to civilization, a village near Lake Baikal. And that is where our mother met Sasha's father.

Ilya Iunoshev, had been much older than my mother, and an important elder in the Orthodox Siberian sect of Old Believers known as *The Children of the White Czar*. In Eastern Siberia, this sect practiced their religion freely. Iunoshev had been a widower. His daughter, Yekaterina, still lived in the house with onion domes that my mother and Sasha had lived in, on a mountain overlooking Lake Baikal. When Iunoshev died, my mother traveled back to western Russia with my five-year-old sister, apparently a treacherous undertaking that took months and depleted any money he had left her. They were destitute and hungry when they at last arrived at the doorstep of Ilya Iunoshev's second cousin in Petersburg.

As my mother pulled the brush through my hair, I kept gazing at the map. Sasha had been born in Siberia, that infinite eastern territory of our mother's heart, exhausting in its scope, dwarfing Western Russia. All of that, steppe, taiga, and tundra, belonged to Sasha, that unimaginable territory some called the open-air prison.

On the map it was a vast, blank territory, white like a land covered in snow, a virgin purity to the image, ironic because there was only darkness attached to the idea of it. It was the place of loss and suffering my mother had fled after her husband died, yet in many ways, she still lived there.

She had taught us to believe in Siberian elementals: an old woman in the fire who, if you focused, you could see treading the flames. She told us that if we want to stir the fire, it must be done gently and respectfully. And there was the Vorsa, a monster that rushes through the forest, causing the trees to bend. Because of my mother, I believed in an undercurrent of magic driving everything in the world.

"They're only stories, Vera," Sasha had told me, but I never thought she was right. My mother believed in these things so, as a child, I had, too. Some part of me still did.

"Mama," I said.

She kept brushing my hair. "Yes, Vera?"

"I couldn't sleep last night, I've hardly been sleeping for weeks."

When she said nothing, I spoke again. "I'm so upset about something."

When she still said nothing, I said, "Please let me talk to you."

"There is no reason to be unhappy, Vera. You are safe here and you have everything you need."

"Please, Mama."

I felt her retreating from me, each stroke of the brush growing more half-hearted. More time passed between strokes and then she stopped altogether but was still standing behind me. I turned and looked up at her.

She was staring at the fire, her face damp and shining. I could see the bright lethargic movement of the flames, now gone low, on her eyes.

"You just told me but I can't remember. What was the name of the city across the Black Sea?"

"Constantinople," she said. "You can see it there on the map, at the very bottom."

To bring back her attention I talked about other things, about the young man I had just met who was on his way to Moscow to study medicine, and she listened quietly and began brushing again, gently tugging the brush through the thickness of my hair. I talked about Proskovia, how she'd grown up backstage at the ballet and how moved she was by the fragrance of the Queen of Prussia roses.

"Maybe I will meet her," she said.

"You have met her, Mama. She came with your friend, Gabinskaya."

"Oh yes," she muttered as she stopped brushing and came around to sit on the other side of the red velvet couch.

I felt a pleasant sensation when I looked at the hairbrush, still in her hands, a few of my long black hairs enmeshed in the bristles with Sasha's and my mother's blond ones. I thought of commenting on it, but refrained.

I watched with wary interest as she began pulling a comb in different places through the bristles until she released the mat of hair, the strands of mine like black errant threads interrupting a softer weave.

My heart plunged when she got up and threw the clump onto the embers, which hissed.

I didn't know if I was tearing up from the awful odor of burnt hair polluting the room, or the rejection I felt. Why couldn't my black hair remain in the bristles with hers and Sasha's?

I got up, went to the French doors in the communicating room, and opened them. The fresh air barely diluted the noxious smell.

I missed my mother, as if she wasn't in the next room. My yearning for her made her less tangible, made her lose her physicality. Her response to my needing her was to turn into air, polluted with the smell of burnt hair. The sky was growing overcast and the wind was blowing. I ached for my mother as I remembered her. For a protracted moment I was small again, back at a time when my father still lived with my mother in these rooms.

I remembered standing with my mother at this French door overlooking the park of windy trees. I could feel again, as if I was back in that moment, her soft hand touching my shoulder. She had knelt down close beside me, chills of pleasure on my neck as she whispered a secret Sasha was not meant to hear: "Look for the violet dress." It was her mother, my grandmother, who had died in Siberia, we were looking for. "I see her," I whispered so quietly there may have been no sound, that secret between us filling me with oxygen and light even in the dark of evening.

"Vera!" my mother called out from the other room, breaking my reverie.

I found her standing near the fire gently stirring the ashes and embers with the iron poker. She pleaded with me to go get one of the servant women, Varvara or Aniuta, to build the fire up again. She would not permit a male servant into the room to attend to the fire, or for any other reason, ever.

"I can build it for you," I said.

"No. I don't have the patience for that."

I agreed and was about to go when I noticed that an ash had settled on her damp cheek under one eye.

"There's an ash on your face, Mama. Let me get it off."

"Oh!" she said.

I stood close, facing her. When I touched it gingerly, it adhered to the tip of my fourth finger. I showed it to her and she smiled faintly.

"Mama," I said, leaned in and kissed her. A sad tenderness spread over her features.

"Constantinople," she said as if I had asked her again the name of the city across the water. She looked down at the embers and shook her head.

"Poor Mama," I said and put my arms around her.

My mother was broken, but something in me still ached for reassurance from her.

She wriggled out of the embrace with a gentle impatience, her attention returning to the ashes. "Please, Vera! Get Varvara or Aniuta."

Chapter 5

The morning was loud with birdsong. I saw Anton approaching me on the carriage road, the shade broken with smatters of sunlight. He was wearing the same dark blue sailcloth trousers but a different shirt, thin white cotton, breezes playing in its generous sleeves.

It struck me harder than it had the day before, how handsome he was, but the closer he got, the more I could see that he looked tired, a half-moon of shadow under each eye.

"Did your father arrive?" he asked as we got closer to each other.

I shook my head no.

"Do you remember your dreams, Vera?" he asked me.

"I do sometimes."

"I dream of cemeteries," he said. "In fact I dreamt about a cemetery last night."

"Did someone you love die recently?"

"My grandmother, Efrosnia, died of smallpox in February, and her husband, my grandfather, who my brothers and I called *the mobile bronze statue*, died in April. I've lost my other set of grandparents as well. Also an infant sister, three uncles, and two teachers. Besides cemeteries, I often dream about freezing to death. I was very cold as a child several times and I suppose it haunts me.

"Last night both recurring themes came together in one. I dreamt I was freezing to death in a cemetery." He laughed and then began to cough, fumbling for his handkerchief. "Anyhow, the dream is still with me."

"You must have felt relieved when you woke up," I said.

"Yes, but even this bright warm beautiful day does not quite eclipse the feeling of the dream. It's so much with me, I feel like I'm still asleep."

We strolled slowly, making little headway to the back acreage, the shade around us broken with patches of sunlight.

"I couldn't help myself, Vera. I asked Dr. Mitrofan about Petya Fyodorovich."

At the mention of Petya's name I stopped walking. Anton also stopped.

"He told me that Petya had an exceptional talent at drawing and that you helped him out of servitude."

"Yes," I half-whispered, my heart quickening. "He had a miraculous gift."

Anton looked at me with feeling.

We stood in a kind of spell, the day around us so clear, so temperate. A pleasurable breeze touched us, stirring his sleeve and the hem of my skirt.

There were things I wanted to say, to express to Anton about Petya, but the only words that came with any ease were about the priest, Father Ivan, and the steps he'd taken to make the apprenticeship happen.

As Anton listened expectantly, a dragonfly hovered near his shoulder, then darted away.

I explained how Petya and I had come to spend time together as children and how we drew pictures.

"Have you ever had the experience, Anton, of looking at a drawing and feeling that you are close to some unnamable depth in the person who drew it?"

"Yes, I understand what you are talking about. My brother, Kolya, is an artist. Sometimes I look at something he's drawn or painted and it astonishes me in some way I can't articulate."

"When I look at one of Petya's drawings I feel him present in ways that many people are not when they are in the same room with you. But he's not here. And yet, when I look at the drawing, some essential part of him is. There's a strange magic to that."

Anton turned from me and coughed. When he looked at me again, his eyes were damp and red.

"Is your cough getting worse?"

"No, no, it's getting better," he said and abruptly changed the subject back to Petya, telling me how impressed Dr. Mitrofan was with one of Petya's drawings of the stallion, Count Orloff.

On the pathway ahead of us, a grasshopper jumped to the left and lost itself in the tall grass. I told Anton the story Petya had told me as a child about the grasshopper and asked if he happened to know it because Petya and I never found out why the girl was running away. But he'd never heard the story. He mentioned another story, unrelated, about a cricket, and while he summarized it I only half-listened. A certain feeling in my chest and stomach had been intensifying as we talked about Petya, a desire to keep sharing my feelings and to possibly confide in Anton.

The day before, I had been vacillating between fear and euphoria over the pregnancy, but today, the euphoria was more consistent and the fear was becoming acceptance.

"I'll ask my sister, Masha, about that grasshopper story. She might know of it."

"Petya also told me a story about a boy whose spirit got stuck inside a samovar and escaped it by turning into steam. Do you know that one?"

"No!" he said, smiling. "I like that idea."

I told him that since Petya had been gone, I often thought about that story and sometimes imagined that he had turned himself into steam, and often thought that he was on the air in the house and could see me. I felt my face heat at this confession. "Maybe there is no such thing as distance when it comes to the spirit. Maybe that is what happens when a person longs too hard for another person but they are kept separate, that they find a way through the spirit to be near the other."

I had said nothing to Anton about being in love with Petya, but Proskovia's wording had suggested it and after this confession, I decided not to try and hide it from him. "I feel him here sometimes, Anton. If he is not actually here on the estate somewhere, then his spirit has traveled here. And I think he must feel my presence, too, wherever he is."

Anton looked at me evenly. "You are an altogether unusual young woman."

"What do you mean?"

"Born into an aristocratic family and . . . helping a servant who you are . . . attached to, leave servitude."

I was quiet.

He added, "And you feel that the spirits of the living travel freely great distances to see each other."

"I suppose I shouldn't have shared all these things."

"I'm not judging you, Vera."

"You told me the other day that you were a rational, practical-minded person. What I just said to you is very far from rational. I shouldn't give voice to everything I feel and imagine."

"I am honored that you feel you can share freely with me."

Encouraged, I shared with him more of my way of seeing the world.

"I think, Anton, that emotions are more complicated than we make them out to be. They are like forces, don't you think? We really can sometimes feel the presence of a person who is far away."

"Maybe," he asked gently, "the imagination supplies a remedy for agony?"

"So you think it is only imagined. And he isn't here at all," I said in a quiet, doleful voice.

"Don't you think it's imagined, Vera?"

"Common sense would tell me I imagined these things, but my senses tell me what I perceive is real. Sometimes I even smell him. But it's clear you are full of doubt, Anton."

He looked unhappy to disappoint me and shook his head. "I am a young man. There is much I don't know about the world."

The generosity of his words made me smile inwardly. I pressed my lips closed, holding back feeling. "It was Petya I was crying about in Dr. Mitrofan's consulting room the other day."

"Ah," he said quietly.

After a silence he asked, "Did you keep any of his drawings?"

"I have three of his drawings." My breathing quietly accelerated. "One of those drawings I looked at once but cannot bring myself to look at again."

"Why not?"

I turned my eyes to the sunlit water, blind spots of brightness flashing as it ran.

He repeated the question.

"It's a drawing of me."

"And you won't look at it?"

"No."

"Would you allow me to look at it?"

"Oh no," I said and let out a soft sudden laugh, which caused his eyes to widen.

I was relieved when he didn't ask me to tell him more. I wasn't certain I could have explained everything I felt about the drawing Petya had done of me.

We heard footsteps and two laughing voices, a man's and a woman's, as they walked at a swift pace along an adjacent pathway, hidden by bracken and trees.

"The dinner is always cold by the time it's served," the man said.

"Marya Mikailevna keeps a small staff," the woman replied. "Too many housekeepers or footmen would be an offense to anyone with strong democratic instincts."

Anton looked at me with raised eyebrows as the voices and footsteps of the invisible guests passed into the distance.

"I must be careful what I say on our walks."

"A bit further out there is privacy, but this close to the house in summer you never know who or what you'll overhear or who might overhear you."

Chapter 6

In a front parlor room, beneath a massive painting of a Napoleonic battle scene, all chaos and blood, a grand buffet presided for a few hours each summer afternoon, a colorful display over two long walnut sideboards. Guests came and dined at their leisure.

Anton and I arrived to the buffet at a quiet moment when no one else was there.

We each picked up a plate and were serving ourselves filets of hake in raisin sauce, when Father Ivan, the local priest I'd told Anton about, an enormous man with long black robes and a voluminous black beard, crouched in through the doorway, bringing with him into the room the cool and overweening odors of frankincense and something like kerosene. His tall hat interfered with the chandelier, causing it to chime. Before I had a chance to introduce him to Anton, my Aunt Marya issued through a back doorway, and on a sudden breathless gust removed her square wire frame spectacles, slipping them into the pocket of her skirt. Father Ivan apologized to her for having stepped on a champagne glass that someone left in the grass.

I introduced Anton to my aunt and Father Ivan, who each greeted him warmly.

Color was up in Aunt Marya's cheeks, as it always was when she was in the presence of Father Ivan, who appeared at Volkhov every summer to enjoy the festivities. They shared a warm regard for each other as well as the same liberal political views and always joined forces when impassioned arguments occurred at a gathering. When he was near her, the hundred things that were usually on her mind seemed to dissolve.

My aunt, having dispatched a young servant, Osip, to clean up the broken glass, rushed quickly into the next room and as we continued to serve ourselves, returned, having exchanged her practical black shirt for a lace blouse, the pins rearranged in her hair and a smear of badly blended rouge on her lips. She stood near Father Ivan at the buffet. I leaned near Anton and said in a low voice, "My two allies in helping Petya."

"This is very heavy fare for a midday meal, Marya Mikailevna," Father Ivan chided affectionately in his deep bass voice.

"Oh dear," she said vaguely.

He smiled at her look of concern, piling his plate with stuffed eel, grouse, mushrooms cooked in butter, and buckwheat kasha. It was the same fare always offered at a Volkhov summer buffet, and his remark to her was part of a little game I'd heard them play more than once in the past. She clearly knew he was teasing her, but she played along as if he were serious, and he seemed to get some pleasure from this. He looked at her fondly, chuckling under his breath, and mumbled something about the persistent vitality of old passions.

I had heard them once five or six years before, behind the closed door of my aunt's office, breathlessly uttering what sounded like urgent sentences, begun but left unfinished, interrupted by what must have been bouts of kissing. It had stunned me. I had always thought of my aunt as a sexless administrator, her only role the running of the estate. It had been remarkable, discovering this new dimension to her.

Another time I had seen her walking down the narrow hallway where her room was, the tall, corpulent priest in his wrinkled black frock following sheepishly after. I did not tell her that all that day one of the kinky hairs of his beard was clinging to her white blouse just below the left breast.

It intrigued me, the secret heated life she led. I imagined her many nights of the year alone in her room, desiring Father Ivan. How had she learned such patience? How had I?

Aunt Marya directed us all through the French doors into the conservatory, a vast, chilly, enclosed patio, occupied here and there by marble statues, armless and inward gazing. The priest took a place at the head of the biggest table, a chair wide enough for two people and covered with a red Moroccan carpet. Anton and I took places at the same table and Aunt Marya followed us in, a small hill of kasha on her otherwise empty plate and sat down. Only a prop, I knew the little pile of kasha would go mostly uneaten. Aunt Marya watched the priest taste a forkful of grouse and nod with appreciation. She smiled. I'd heard guests refer to my aunt as plain, but in Father Ivan's presence without her spectacles, with the color on her skin, she was softer and less efficient, and her eyes seemed to glisten.

Anton turned abruptly from the table and coughed into his handkerchief, then excused himself, explaining that he was recovering from bronchitis. "A mild case only," he added.

"I'm very glad that's all it is, and I hope you recover quickly," Father Ivan said and studied Anton with interest. "Dr. Mitrofan has talked about you, Anton Chekhov, the young man staying with him who is going to Moscow to study medicine. You have a brother who suffers from tuberculosis."

Anton, who had been enjoying his fish, put down his fork. "Yes, yes. My brother, Kolya, who is a painter."

"I hope things are not getting worse for him," Father Ivan said. "But, forgive me. Not the subject for a meal."

Anton began to tell the tale of how he had met Dr. Mitrofan. Five years before he had been traveling by oxcart with his oldest brother, Aleksander, on an errand. For days they had been caught repeatedly in the rain, and when the weather was clear, decided to take a swim in a cold river, which turned out to be a mistake.

"I became chilled and very sick. Someone in the area knew Dr. Mitrofan, who happened to be passing through. He diagnosed peritonitis, a bad case, then offered to treat me. He brought me back to his house, while my brother continued on with the errand. Dr. and Mrs. Mitrofan took excellent care of me.

"In the comfort of his house as I recovered, I began reading about medicine, and that is when I first became inspired to become a doctor myself."

Father Ivan nodded slowly as he chewed, leaning slightly forward and focusing in on Anton.

"I decided that in my life I would be on the other side of the equation," Anton continued.

"What do you mean?" I asked.

"I want to be the one who cares for the ill. Not the one who needs caring for."

"Being a doctor is not an assurance against illness," I said.

Anton seemed to only half hear me, keeping his focus on the priest.

Voices sounded in the next room at the buffet.

"The doctor tells me that you also write stories and plays," Aunt Marya said.

"Last year I wrote three terrible plays, all destined for the garbage bin. And I have tried my hand at a few stories. If they can be called stories."

"He said that they are humorous."

"Yes, crass little entertainments. I am trying to master the form enough that one day I might publish in a periodical like *The Clock* or *The Dragonfly*. Aleksander, my oldest brother, publishes in both those places, but nothing I've written so far seems publishable. I sent him a new story and a play, hoping for his approval. I'm waiting on a letter from him to hear his thoughts. I am hopeful he'll see merit in one or the other."

The priest nodded. "Maybe one day you will aspire to write something more meaningful than crass little entertainments. But I suppose people do need such diversions." He took a sip of water. "And how wonderful there is so much talent in your family."

"Both my brothers are brilliant. With me, it remains to be seen. But I love writing. It is a dream I aspire to, publishing stories or to see a play I've written performed by a talented company."

"You would be living a double life, Anton," I said. "A doctor and a writer!"

"My pen name will be Antosha Chekhonte, in honor of a former teacher who used to call me that as a joke."

"Antosha Chekhonte," the priest repeated.

"For some stories, though, I might use the name: The Man without a Spleen."

"You wouldn't do that, Anton!" I cried.

"I certainly would."

The priest laughed and clapped his hands. "It is so wonderful to be young, Anton, and still have everything before you. When I was your age I had dreams of traveling. I thought I would visit exotic places, be gone for years from the Russian continent, but then I experienced a vocation and became a priest. I have been to Moscow a few times but otherwise I rarely leave Ukraine."

"I have a dream of traveling, too, Father Ivan. My hero as a boy was Nikolay Przhevalsky, the explorer of Central Asia! I want to one day travel into Siberia."

"Why, Anton?" I asked.

"For many years I have been preoccupied with the fact that we send people there and we forget them. I hope to be a doctor by the time I make that journey and maybe I can help. But I would also like to write about whatever I see there so people know. The suffering that goes on there is our fault for looking away. For not wanting to know the truth."

"But you are not thinking of your own safety," I said.

The priest interjected here. "Vera, you are right that it would be a very dangerous undertaking, but Anton's intentions are deeply admirable."

"Father Ivan, forgive me but Anton could disappear there, as so many others have," I said.

Anton looked vaguely irritated with me. "I would plan it and undertake it carefully. It is something I aspire to do one day. Something I hope I will be able to do."

"You are a thoughtful young man, Anton Pavlovich," the priest said. "And you are right that it is unthinkable, hundreds of thousands of versts dedicated to exile and human suffering, away from the eyes of justice." He sighed and waited, respectfully pausing before spearing a fat mushroom with his fork.

"But it is suicide!"

"Vera Sergeyevna," Father Ivan admonished in a soft firm voice. "Anton Pavlovich is not going to Siberia any time soon."

"But . . ."

"Stop! You must stop, Vera!" the priest interrupted.

My aunt changed the subject, asking Anton about his family. Anton explained that he had grown up in Taganrog, a town in the south, on the Sea of Azov. He and his brothers worked in his father's store, which sold various practical things as well as groceries.

"And who will help your father in the store when his sons all leave?" the priest asked.

"The store is no more. My father went bankrupt. He and the rest of the family fled to Moscow."

"But you stayed in Taganrog?"

"Yes, to finish school and earn some money to send to them."

"And how did you earn the money?"

"Tutoring."

Father Ivan said he had been in Taganrog once and heard Mass in the very old Cathedral of St. Nicholas.

"That church was part of my childhood," Anton said and told us his father had made him and his brothers sing at dawn in the choir there while growing up. "They were very early services, and very late rehearsals. But in spite of the freezing conditions and the sleep deprivation, I will always love *akfisty*."

"There is no music as celestial as Orthodox church music," Father Ivan crooned as he wiped his mouth with his napkin.

The conversation continued, both my aunt and the priest directing questions to Anton.

Uncle Pavel and Lilia Petrovna, a woman from Petersburg who I had met before and guessed to be near forty, arrived to the table with plates of food, just as

Anton revealed that his father had been born a serf and that his grandfather had bought his family out of servitude, something that came as a surprise to me. Uncle Pavel raised his eyebrows and looked appalled.

When I introduced Anton and Lilia Petrovna, she greeted him politely, exuding a cloud of French perfume as she settled herself in a chair. The bodice of her silk dress was cut low, her bosom too much on display for this hour. She seemed dressed for an evening at the opera.

When introduced to Anton, Uncle Pavel nodded vaguely, avoiding Anton's eyes and pretending to be distracted by a missing spoon.

The priest was watching my uncle, having clearly registered the slight against Anton. It always impressed me how observant Father Ivan was of dynamics between people around him. He watched people's faces and paid attention to the subtleties of a voice or a gesture.

He shifted his eyes from my uncle to Anton. "You are very well educated, Anton, for a young man whose father was born a serf!"

"My father was adamant that all his children be well educated. And in this he has been successful. We are all readers!"

I watched my uncle closely as he settled into his chair and spread his napkin over his lap. I hoped to catch his eye and give him a disapproving glare for snubbing Anton, but he seemed to sense it and would not give me the satisfaction of returning my look.

Uncle Pavel must have felt Father Ivan's eyes on him, a pulsing vein becoming visible on his forehead. He was an unattractive man, but appeared particularly unpleasant looking in such moments. And he smelled strangely of caraway seeds, though he did not eat them and none were kept in the house.

While Father Ivan watched my uncle, Lilia Petrovna gazed intently at Father Ivan. I had seen it before. Father Ivan, a widower of seven years, and decidedly handsome in his gruff, bearlike way, had the power to enchant women though he seemed to make no outright effort to do so. Lilia Petrova's interest in him bothered me. Father Ivan, in my way of thinking, belonged to my aunt and I had my eye out for usurpers.

Lilia Petrovna also seemed to be watching Aunt Marya, as if trying to perceive what exactly was between her and Father Ivan.

"Did you hear, the poor Dolzhenkos had to sell their estate?" Lilia Petrovna asked. "Their family has been hundreds of years on that land."

"What a tragedy," Father Ivan said.

"Where is it?" Uncle Pavel asked.

"Twenty versts north of here. On the Dnieper. Bad investments by the patriarch, two decades or so ago. It has caught up to them."

Lilia Petrovna lifted her glass of Veuve Clicquot and addressed Aunt Marya. "It is wonderful that no one was reckless with the family money and you can still spend so lavishly."

My aunt colored at the words and looked away.

Lilia Petrovna then addressed the priest. "We were speaking earlier of servitude. I was just telling Pavel

Mikailovich about something in the *Petersburg Gazette* last week, a report about a man who had gotten angry with his servant and killed him. And of course," she said with a tone of disapproval, "the murderer faced no consequences."

If the priest had not been there I knew Uncle Pavel would have openly expressed indifference.

But Lilia Petrovna sold him out, perhaps in order to show herself in a more compassionate light to the priest. "Pavel Mikailovich does not think this landowner should be penalized. And of course I reminded him, Father Ivan, that there has been an emancipation, and serfs, as if it needed to be made official, are considered now to be human beings."

Father Ivan, who had listened with a shadow between his brows, emitted a low-throated growl then bellowed in *basso profundo*, "Servants are dehumanized at every turn! In the eyes of God they are much more human than their oppressors!"

Uncle Pavel smiled strenuously, and the vein came further forward, running from a spot on his bald hairline unevenly down and across to get lost in one of his eyebrows. Even through the cloud of Lilia Petrovna's perfume, I could smell caraway seeds.

"The landed classes indulge in games one after the other, cardplaying and croquet. And when do the poor get to indulge their pleasures?"

My aunt nodded thoughtfully. "We are, are we not," she asked the priest, "such self-indulgent creatures?"

She shook her head back and forth with an expression of remorse.

"And here we have a young man whose family paid their way out of servitude, who is becoming a doctor and wants to visit Siberia to shine a light on terrible oppression. This is an admirable young man. This is what we should all be doing, especially those of us with privilege, looking for ways to ease suffering." The priest looked directly at Uncle Pavel, who had become suddenly very interested in the soup in his dish.

When Lilia Petrovna casually remarked that Anton was a pious young man, very close to God, Anton shook his head.

Maybe to knock down the high pedestal the priest had just put him on, he said, "It is not a belief in God that drives me, Madame Petrovna, to want to visit Siberia. In fact I think of myself as an agnostic."

To have said this out of the company of Father Ivan would not have elicited much shock, but in his presence the air in the conservatory compressed into something unbreathable.

Even though Anton had not said it recklessly, but thoughtfully, openly and ready to be contradicted, my aunt and Lilia Petrovna sat frozen while Uncle Pavel's eyes lingered expectantly on the priest. My own heart had moved up close to my throat.

"I don't mean to offend," Anton said, observing everyone's shock.

When no one spoke, he smiled and went on. "It's ironic, really. It was always assumed that I would join the clergy because I got my best marks in religion."

Father Ivan raised his eyes slowly. "I cannot imagine God is not pleased with you, young Anton, even in your hours of doubt. You are an honest young man and it is clear you are not trying to offend but simply to speak the truth."

Uncle Pavel picked up the salt cellar and looked at it resentfully, and everyone else breathed again.

Anton smiled and said, "I did hope for a lively theological argument."

"No such debates during a meal," Father Ivan responded. "Very bad for digestion."

A brief conversation ensued, initiated by my aunt, about the impending arrival of the maestro, Anatoly Slezkine.

"He is a mushroom enthusiast, isn't he?" Father Ivan asked.

"Yes, I know it is early in the summer to pick mushrooms but we always have chanterelles growing in the northwest woods."

"I hear," Lilia Petrovna said, "that he is a shy man."

"Yes," my aunt replied, "he is easily flustered and overwhelmed by praise. Too much of it makes him uncomfortable, so we must be discreet with our adulation."

"We received a letter," Uncle Pavel began, "from one of the maestro's factotums, warning us that certain foods should not appear on the dinner table. No asparagus or artichokes. No crayfish or cheese. The sight of an uncut melon on a platter upsets him because it suggests the head of John the Baptist."

"So odd," Lilia Petrovna said softly.

"One must make allowances for genius!" my aunt said.

"I have heard that everyone weeps when he plays an adagio," Father Ivan said.

Aunt Marya murmured that it was true. "And after he plays Tchaikovsky, Vera and Sasha will perform the scene from Shakespeare."

"Remember," I said, "that Sasha is a polished actress. I am only there because she needs me. I only hope I don't embarrass her or myself."

Aunt Marya shook her head. "Why are you saying such a thing?"

"It was always a pleasure watching you in a summer play," Father Ivan said.

Lilia Petrovna spoke suddenly. "Father Ivan, I was told that you saw the production of *La Dame aux Camélias* in Kiev, starring the actress Sarah Bernhardt."

"Yes," the priest responded, "I have, in fact, seen Bernhardt perform that role, twice."

Father Ivan, a great advocate for the poor, liked to spend his leisure time with the moneyed classes, and whenever in Kiev or Moscow attended the theatre. He was a discerning critic, difficult to please, and could be coolly dismissive, so it delighted me to no end that he had seen my father as *Eugene Onegin* years back, before I was born, and still expressed admiration for that performance.

Lilia Petrovna praised Bernhardt lavishly for the range of her voice and her aptitude for tragedy. She paused, looking expectantly at the priest as if waiting for him to chime in in agreement. When he didn't, she continued with her praise. She should have taken his silences as cues to stop, but did not. Even as the blood rushed to her face and bosom, she went on speaking of Bernhardt's brilliance.

"Do you not agree, Father Ivan?" she finally pleaded, catching her breath.

"My dear lady, Bernhardt is all artifice. She fools people, that is all."

In a voice couched in breath she asked, "But you went twice to see her, Father Ivan?"

"I often accompany friends who provide me with tickets. I admit to you that she is a phenomenon. But it is her nerve that I find interesting. She leaves me cold."

My heart raced at the priest's words. "So you believe, Father Ivan, that an actress should feel the emotions she is performing?"

"All I know, dear Vera Sergeyevna, is that I do not like to be manipulated."

Lilia Petrovna's eyes glimmered. "So you are saying, Father Ivan, that I have been fooled?"

"I am sorry to tell you this, dear lady, but she has persuaded you into thinking she has a great soul while I believe the soul is missing or at least not present while she is on the stage."

Lilia Petrovna lowered her head and spoke in a quiet, grave voice. "I bow before your perception of the truth, Father Ivan."

Even as the conversation moved on to other subjects, Lilia Petrovna kept watching the priest with the same damp, humbled eyes. When he leaned in and whispered something to my aunt and she softly laughed, Lilia Petrovna reached for her glass and inadvertently knocked it over, soaking the tablecloth with Veuve Clicquot.

Before we left the house I led Anton to a parlor room to show him numerous portraits of my actress grandmother, mostly daguerreotypes, each in a different role. They went in chronological order. The earliest pictures as you entered the room were sepia images floating on archaic squares of whitened glass. As a young Titania, my grandmother's debut role, she looked up as if into a tree, her hands splayed, but softly, as a fairy might splay her hands. Of all the pictures it was my favorite, a grace and gentleness to her, a silky suggestion of foliage behind her and the occasional twinkling light, offering the impression of fireflies around her. And that gentleness still seemed present in her Juliet and in her Cassandra.

"Looking at these," Anton said, pointing at the first three images, "is like looking at you, Vera."

"Yes, I know that I look like her. Everyone has always remarked on it. I have the same black hair and the same eyes and forehead."

"And you have the same upper lip." He looked at my mouth, then at my eyes.

I averted my eyes from his, a wave of warmth rising from my chest to my face.

"She treated me special and wanted me to love her but she was unkind to almost everyone else. I looked like her so I think she saw herself in me! And I was the daughter of her favorite child. If I was the same girl but didn't look like her, she would have dismissed me, I'm sure."

In the middle of the gallery, a hardness came into my grandmother's expression: Clytemnestra, raising her arms, eyes wide, face given over to fury.

After Clytemnestra, her face was always the same: hard jaw and bold, staring eyes that seemed electrified by the universe in which she was the center, the burning sun itself. Every picture was a grandiose but empty indication of feeling. And every raised arm, tormented profile, bent spine, or fist to the sky, seemed only an attempt to compensate for feeling no emotion at all. But always, the staring, vacant eyes. I was frightened of those images as a child. When I was twelve or thirteen, years after she was dead, it occurred to me that my grandmother may have been mad, though it was not something I could have articulated. Her expression unsettled my stomach. But I had never commented on it. In spite of the fact that everyone but my father had been mistreated by her, saying anything remotely negative about my grandmother would have been heresy.

"I saw her act when I was six, when the Italian opera visited in the winter." I pointed to the final portrait, a picture of an old woman wearing what was clearly a long girlish wig, pinned crookedly and a bit too far forward on her face.

"She was seventy-six years old, and do you know what role she is playing here?" I asked him.

"I cannot begin to guess."

"Desdemona."

He raised his brows.

I described what I remembered of a scandalous evening. The parts I did not actually remember, my aunt had filled in for me: the tenor, Tomaglio, stealing everyone's heart with his thundering Othello, my grandmother hobbling, defiant against the infirmities of her age, upon the stage, prostrating herself before him and kissing the cuff of his pants. He and one of the servants had quite a struggle helping her back to her feet again.

There was a short intermission after which my grandmother returned to the stage wearing that long chestnut-colored wig. I pointed at the picture.

I described how with an uncontrollable tremor, she delivered half-remembered lines of Desdemona's, pasted together in a monologue.

After her performance my grandmother had linked her arm with Tomaglio's and monopolized him the rest of the night. My aunt told me that she snubbed Tomaglio's wife, Massina, a famous mezzo-soprano. Massina eventually got sick of it and swept her heavy arm across a table of champagne flutes, sending them flying, showering everyone nearby with champagne and shattered glass. She made a dramatic exit, throwing her cape over her shoulder and cursing my grandmother in Italian.

Anton laughed.

As we were leaving the room, he stopped again before the first three pictures. "It's like looking at you, Vera," he said. "As if you lived as an actress in an earlier time."

I focused on glistening Titania with her head tilted upward, the image that disturbed me most because I could so clearly see my own face there.

A few days before my grandmother died, I had gone to her room with my father and while he sat on the edge of her bed, I stood huddled against him, holding onto his arm. I was six. The curtains were open and daylight overpowered the usual red darkness of the room, igniting everything, even my grandmother who leaned back propped against an enormous white pillow, wearing a nightgown much too large for her. In contrast with the delicate French lace at her throat and wrists, her face, neck, and hands appeared gnarled, as if carved of wood.

"She's an actress, Sergei," my grandmother said hoarsely, gesturing at me with a misshapen finger. The balls of her bloodshot eyes shook slightly side to side.

Everyone says she is your miniature, Mama," my father said gently.

She looked directly at me and pleaded with those trembling eyes, "You will keep me alive, won't you, my little actress?"

I whimpered while my father spoke reassuringly to her.

For a while after she died, I suffered fits of spasmodic breathing, imagining her near me, trying to find her way into me. Where would I go if she was successful in taking me over?

“It’s like looking at you, Vera,” Anton said, breaking through the agitation of the memory.

“I am not her,” I said.

“No,” he said thoughtfully. “Of course you aren’t her.”

As we were leaving the house to search for the white deer, Lilia Petrovna told us that she had seen it early in the morning eating bluebells in one of the neglected gardens.

“Anya Leonideyvna said she wasn’t sure if it was a doe or a young buck,” I said.

“It is a doe,” Lilia Petrovna said, “and she appears to be pregnant.”

A surge of lightheadedness overcame me. I grasped the railing as we descended the porch stairs.

“That seems even more miraculous,” Anton said.

“She’s very shy,” Lilia Petrovna added. “I saw her from a distance. We stared at each other through the leaves. I took a step and she vanished.”

“You’re very lucky to have seen her,” Anton said.

“Why? Tell me why I am lucky,” Lilia Petrovna said almost irritably. “What will be different in my life?” She didn’t seem to expect an answer and wandered off.

“What kind of things did your family sell in the store?” I asked Anton as we began our search for the white deer.

He listed a wide range of things: face cream, pen knives, phials of castor oil, lamp wicks, vodka or Santorini wine, sold by the glass. Tallow candles, olives, laxatives, fruit gums, sardines, raisins, Crimean sea salt. He said there were lots more things and searched his memory . . . cheesecloth, string, shoelaces. Even buckles for waistcoats.

"One labor I particularly hated was drying out and repackaging used tea leaves to sell as if they were new."

"Oh!" I said.

"Yes. My father was very cheap and tried to get away with that sort of thing."

"Oh! I imagined from what you said to Father Ivan that your father was a very dignified man."

"No," he said, shaking his head. "It's very true what I said to Father Ivan. My father was successful at making certain his children were well educated. But in almost every other way my father set a terrible example. To important customers my father was servile, but when anyone complained that the tea stank of fish or the coffee of candle wax, he would publicly punch and kick the shop boys."

His father had been summoned to the Taganrog magistrate for excessive beating. And this, Anton reminded me, was the man who put on such a deeply pious face in church.

The family store was swarming with flies. Anton's father persuaded his sons that flies were good, that they cleaned the air. When a rat was found in a barrel of olive oil he was too mean to pour the oil away and too lazy to boil and re-filter it. Instead, he had the local priest conduct a service in the shop and consecrate the oil. This incident drove all the customers away and heralded the collapse of the store and his father's bankruptcy.

We'd been searching for an hour or so when the sky began to rumble. Anton had started coughing occasionally after the meal. I invited him to come back inside if it started raining but he said it was better if he went back to Dr. Mitrofan's. He said I didn't have to walk with him, but I did. When it started raining we ran and laughed as we got soaked, but the running and the laughter caused Anton to cough hard. I wondered if he would invite me in, but instead he offered to get me an umbrella for my walk back to Volkhov. I could see by his face as we stood under the awning of the porch that he was tired. He said he would go early to bed and be better in the morning. He would come around ten a.m. and we'd continue to look for the white deer.

Chapter 7

I had suspected Anton had come to Volkhov the past few days to be with me, and that finding the white deer was secondary, but this particular morning he was quiet and pale, his eyes raking the surroundings. Seeing the white deer felt like a need rather than something he just wished for.

We were on an overgrown pathway, running parallel to a stream, when Anton stopped walking, drawing in a sudden breath, and pointing to something white seen through foliage and half hidden in river grass. We waited where we were, afraid that if it was the white deer we might frighten her away.

But we heard a splash and watched a large white crane arise gracefully, pulling itself up into the air.

"How beautiful," I said, hoping to counter any disappointment.

Anton turned away from me and coughed softly into his handkerchief.

"A crane represents long life," I said.

As he folded his handkerchief and placed it in his shirt pocket he looked at me as if struck by my words.

We searched awhile longer. I could see by his complexion that Anton was feeling worse. When I asked him he said he was fine and he even seemed faintly irritated by the question.

He eventually said he had to leave, that Dr. Mitrofan was waiting for him, and he told me he would probably not be visiting for the next two days, that he planned to go with the doctor on his rounds.

For three days I did not see Anton. I went twice to Dr. Mitrofan's and knocked. Once the door was locked and no one answered. The other time Lika told me that Anton was taking a nap and she would tell him I had come.

It was morning and I had just walked out onto the porch when I saw Dr. Mitrofan carrying his medical bag, walking past, on his way to leave the property. I overtook him.

"Can you stop for a glass of tea?" I asked.

"No, Vera," he said and sighed. "I have patients coming to the house. They could be there already."

I walked along beside him, keeping pace with his hurried gait. He looked tired, the bags under his spectacled eyes heavier than usual, his frizzled hair uncombed.

"Were you here to see Uncle Boris?"

"Yes," he said. "He is suffering a hemorrhage."

"I thought he was doing so well. I see him sometimes riding one of the horses."

"He's been warned against riding." He shook his head. "Tuberculosis is a trickster of a disease. You see how unpredictable it is sometimes, going very suddenly into remission so he feels much better, even healthy. That sense of vitality makes him arrogant. He swims in the river or rides a spirited horse. He's a foolish man, thinking he can beat his illness."

"But he takes his medicine, doesn't he?"

"When he's feeling vital he stops drinking the Obersalebrunen, and has hot soup and hot foods. He smokes and takes quinine, all things I have repeatedly warned him against." Dr. Mitrofan walked with purpose. "Then he has what he's having now! Hemorrhaging and attacks of difficult breathing, and he has to inhale fumes of turpentine." He made a frustrated noise. "He was getting better but is worse today than when he arrived last summer."

One evening at the end of the previous summer, I had been walking on the pathway near the avenue of birch trees, the sun on the horizon lighting everything a brilliant red, and saw a man on the road I was sure was a vagabond, his dark shadow preceding him. He walked with a lurch, large as a bear, clothes worn and dusty looking, a pack and a gun slung over his shoulder. I could not even see that he had blond hair, beneath the mats and the filth, and the leather of his boots had lost their structure, raveling like beaten cloth around his ankles.

The man had stopped walking and stared at me, his breathing labored and audible. I'd had the uncanny sensation that the moment had occurred before, and then in the fraction of a second his face felt familiar, as if I had been looking at it all my life.

I followed and was a few yards away from him when Aunt Marya descended the front stairs and approached. He dropped his pack and gun, and though his shoulders were hunched, his head hanging, he towered over her. Struggling for breath he said in a raspy, low-pitched voice, "I am here to see Pelegaya Alexovna Belenovskaya."

My aunt asked if he meant Madam Denisova. When he remained silent she asked what business he had with her.

"She is my sister," he said.

He was taken to the bathhouse for a long steam. Dr. Mitrofan examined him in the small annex house where he now lived. On my aunt's orders, a servant carried most of his clothes out on a stick to one of the fire pits and burned them.

There had been no clothes in the house that would fit such a large man, so my aunt opened a trunk of my grandfather's, an archaic collection of military jackets, old-fashioned white blouses, and silk Tussar pants. My grandfather, who had died twenty-five years before, had been, in his youth, a very large man, ostentatious and dramatic in his attire.

I never knew before he came that my mother had a living brother. I knew she'd had two brothers and I thought both had died in Siberia. He asked for my mother but she refused to see him then and still refused to see him now.

In the first months he was here, Uncle Boris had sometimes lurched to the house and stood in front looking up at the windows. He knew which one was my mother's room. He must have seen her looking out once. My aunt often had a servant bring out a chair and my uncle would remain there for hours.

One night a servant brought out a little table and a lamp and placed it near him. He looked so different from when he'd arrived. I was fascinated by him. His clean hair, like filaments of gold and silver metal, caught any light and reflected it, confusing the moths, so they circled his head instead of the lamp.

I looked down from a window once and saw that he had fallen asleep, his head lolling forward, the nape of his neck exposed, his shoulders wide and lonely.

"Anton was still sleeping when I left this morning," Dr. Mirtofan said. "His coughing kept him awake."

"I heard Anton say something curious to my aunt and Father Ivan. Something to the effect that by becoming a doctor he would make himself immune to illness."

Dr. Mitrofan nodded. "He is a very interesting fellow, smart and scientific-minded. And formidably self-reliant. You can see what a perceptive and compassionate fellow he is. He will make a great doctor but I think there *is* a little of that belief that the role of the doctor will put him on the other side of illness."

"And," I added, "he insists on how practical-minded he is but seems determined to glimpse the white deer for the good fortune it symbolizes."

"Ah," he said. "The White Deer. It's so interesting, Vera, that there is a white deer on your property now while Anton is here. You've seen the talisman he carries?"

"Yes."

"The Vanquisher of Illness."

"What?"

"The white deer is the vanquisher of illness."

"He told me that seeing a white deer at a time of change in one's life was a good omen for the future."

"That, too, is likely true. But for Anton, I can guarantee you he wants an encounter with the white deer because it is the vanquisher of illness. He wants to see it, I am certain, for the same reason he thinks that becoming a doctor ensures his good health. The charm he has is actually a Siberian talisman from the northern oblast where a friend of his family spent three years in prison. His friend brought the charm back with him to western Russia and gave it to Anton's sister, Masha, because she thought it was pretty. When Anton was fourteen and very ill at my house I sent for his family, worried that he was going to die. His mother and sister Masha came and that is when Masha gifted the charm to him. Anton recovered quickly after that and I think he equates the charm with feeling better, though he would never admit to that."

We walked a little slower and for a while in silence. "To actually see a white deer, the vanquisher of illness, is hailed to be the most potent form of healing magic."

"Do you mean he wants to see it because of his bronchitis? That will soon pass."

When the doctor said nothing, a nerve tightened in my chest. "Anton is such a big robust fellow."

"Well . . ."

"Isn't he?"

He turned his face in my direction, still keeping his pace, and looked at me gravely. "He mostly appears that way."

He seemed to be weighing whether or not he should say something. "When he first arrived two weeks ago, Anton suffered a bout of pleurisy. He's getting better so I am mostly hopeful, but there are certain things I see that remind me a bit of the way your uncle's illness behaves."

"But how is Anton's health similar to my uncle's?"

The doctor looked at me earnestly, his brow furrowed with feeling. "I cannot diagnose tuberculosis at this stage in Anton, but there are moments when his breathing or the sound of his cough distresses me, and I worry."

"Anton told Father Ivan that when he was a child his father made him and his brothers get up before dawn in the winters to sing in the chorus of an ice cold church."

"Yes, that constant cold and lack of sleep! And his father beat them on their backs, which weakened their lungs. Anton told me that his father believed that one beaten boy was worth two unbeaten ones!"

"Poor Anton," I said.

"There has been quite a bit of tuberculosis in his family. Anton's brother, Kolya, he may have told you, suffers a serious case. Kolya is a young man but I would say his case, from the way Anton has described it, is as bad as your uncle's." The doctor's own breathing was audible and fast, not only from the exertion of walking and speaking, but from rising emotion.

We stopped when we reached the road that separated our properties. An expression I could only read as fatalistic appeared on the his face as he went on to say that the seeds of illness were very much there in Anton, that since the peritonitis that almost killed him five years before, illness was a constant threat hanging over him, and that he suffered periodically from migraine, abdominal maladies, and malarial fevers in hot weather.

"I'm surprised. He talks about traveling through Siberia."

The doctor took a deep breath and seemed to be trying to quell agitation that had been building as he spoke.

"It was when he was healing from the peritonitis that he developed a preoccupation with Nicholas Przhevalsky, the Far East explorer. He wanted, he said, to follow in his footsteps."

That, the doctor explained, was when Anton first talked about traveling through Siberia, and that the desire for dangerous adventure is characteristic of a man of fragile health.

"And when he is feeling well he has some of the denial and even arrogance your uncle displays. He is not ready to give up any of his hard won selfhood."

The doctor stared down to the ground, color coming into his face, looking vaguely guilty for having spilled out so much about his houseguest.

"Sometimes I share things that maybe I shouldn't. You understand, though, Vera, don't you," he asked, tilting his head and looking at me with a plea in his damp brown eyes. "He is like a son to me. I know you haven't known him long but I think you like him."

"Yes," I said.

"I want you to understand the challenges he lives with."

He put down his case and took both my hands in his. "Anton doesn't like to talk about his health, Vera. It's best that you not mention any of this."

"I won't," I promised.

He gave me a tender look and nodded.

"My patients are probably already waiting for me."

He picked up his bag but just before he left he said, "I hope he sees the white deer. I'm so glad, Vera, that he has you to search for it with him."

He rushed off in the direction of his house.

I had believed Anton when he told me it was bronchitis but as I recalled him struggling not to cough, his entire body sometimes in convulsions, it was clear there was a deeper malady. I thought of the shadows under his eyes.

Taking a shortcut back through the trees, I overheard a conversation in a woman's muted voice. "Champagne and crates of oysters don't just materialize out of nowhere. There has to be money."

A man's voice interrupted at the word *money*. "I tell you, the family is in financial straits."

I thought of the Dolzhenkos, but they had already sold their property. It struck me that they were talking about us. But my aunt was too practical for this to be true, and it angered me that guests who were being so lavishly entertained would gossip about their hosts.

Chapter 8

I had thought I might not see Anton the next day either, but he arrived around eleven o'clock and we sat for a while on the veranda, drinking glasses of tea.

His posture was slightly stooped but he hardly coughed and when I asked, he said he was feeling better. He seemed distracted, looking off onto the sunlit grounds, watching the exuberant birds departing and returning to the trees.

"Anatoly Slezkine arrived late last night," I told him. "If Prince Miranov comes any time today, chances are the performances will be tomorrow evening."

"And you and Sasha will do your scene."

"Yes."

"Are you feeling ready now?"

"No. I am not feeling ready, Anton."

He gave me an indulgent smile then gazed off again at the chattering birds, flying from the ground to the trees and back. Dr. Mitrofan's revelations made me look more closely at Anton. His color was so much better, but a light film of perspiration shone over his cheeks and forehead, though the breezes on the veranda were cool.

It was subtle, but I could sense the presence of illness like an aura around him, a lucent but barely visible cloth, rumpled and fragile.

We wandered along an overgrown pathway between poplars and linden trees, yellow butterflies trembling as they floated past.

We made our way for about half an hour in silence. I sensed he was melancholy and that feeling infused me and seemed to change the atmosphere around us, intensifying the shadows that fell from the trees. Even still, there was pleasure in sharing silence with Anton. The feeling on the air between us quickened the sense of my pregnancy, made me feel it as a kind of deepening of everything. We moved as we always moved when looking for the white deer, gingerly and with bated breath, expecting to come suddenly across her.

The future was something unknown, for both Anton and me, but when we searched for the white deer, life became filled with possibility. It would probably be two months before anyone would be able to see that I was carrying a child. For now, though Anton didn't know about it, it was something I was sharing with him. In his company, I had started gradually accepting my condition and now, today, I felt myself embracing it.

Petya was with me, I told myself, in the presence that was powerfully but gently remaking me. My body had become softer in places, slightly swollen in others.

I saw in my mind an image from a book of old engravings in my aunt's library. Mercury, with wings at his temples and long waving hair, smiling a womanish smile and leaning forward as he walked waist-deep through a river, wild with currents, holding on his cupped palm a mysterious ball with a cross on top, which was said to represent the world. I felt like I was Mercury. There was a new tightness, a pleasant sensation low in my belly where it was beginning to swell, a kind of pressure. The pregnancy made me feel that, like Mercury, I was walking waist-deep against water.

Out of nowhere, Anton spoke, interrupting my dream. "I would like to talk with your Uncle Boris," he said.

"Why?"

"Because, as you know, I plan to go one day to Siberia."

"But, Anton," I said, impulsively pressing a hand to his upper arm, then quickly withdrawing it. "No one goes there voluntarily."

"You said that to me already, Vera, but don't you think it's barbaric that we abandon people there?"

"Yes, it's barbaric. I agree, of course. But going there is a form of suicide."

"Perhaps I will be able to speak with your uncle after the performance, tomorrow or whenever it is."

"He won't be there. He is profoundly antisocial."

I wandered off ahead of him a bit, but Anton caught up with me and asked for directions to Uncle Boris' annex house.

It occurred to me that anything Uncle Boris might say about Siberia would only discourage Anton from his deranged idea of going there.

"You shouldn't go alone. He doesn't know who you are. He's been ill and his behavior is hard to predict."

"I'm not afraid, Vera."

"No, I'll go with you. He might be willing to talk to you. We can try."

We shifted directions. "He barely talks to me, Anton. My aunt says it's because he doesn't like or respect women. Even still I pity him."

Continuing to watch for the white deer, we headed to the annex house.

I wandered ahead of Anton.

About twelve years ago, long before Uncle Boris came, my mother received a letter from Siberia, a letter in a yellow envelope. Something happened to her after she received it. She started feeling cold all the time and that is when she started keeping a fire going in her room, even when the weather was warm. It lasted for a while, this illness of feeling perpetually cold. It was around this time that she asked my father to move out of their rooms. He put all his things into another room on the other side of the house. He didn't understand what had happened, but he reassured me, saying it was only temporary, that when my mother felt better he would be moving back in. One day near that time, Madame Gabinskaya came to see my mother and the two of them sat close together on the red velvet couch, whispering.

A framed photograph of Sasha's father holding her as a baby had always hung on the wall in Sasha's room, a source of fascination to me, a strange, shadowy brown and beige image. Ilya Iunoshev was a tall old man with long white hair and beard, peering at the camera lens with kind, serious eyes. My mother was in the picture also, smiling and standing beside him, looking so young, younger I was sure than I looked now at nineteen. It was after the letter in the yellow envelope came that Sasha knocked the framed picture off the wall and the glass cracked. She insisted the broken picture stay behind her dresser and would not allow any of the servants to remove it or put the picture in a different frame. But a few months after that she displayed the picture again on a shelf near her bed, insisting the cracked glass remain.

I was seven years old, but my tutor had started coming when I was six so I was a precocious reader. I tried to sneak off with the yellow letter, taking it from the drawer where my mother kept it. But my sister caught me before I could read it and grabbed it from me, infuriated and in tears. With my mother's approval, Gabinskaya threw the yellow letter onto the fire and I watched with them as it turned to ash.

After the burning of the letter my mother stopped feeling so cold all the time, but she never allowed my father to move back in with her.

When Uncle Boris appeared the previous year, eleven years after the arrival and burning of the yellow letter, my mother felt cold and started sitting again before the fire in her rooms, even when the weather was beautiful. She did not want my uncle driven from the property. She knew he was ill and wanted him cared for, but still wouldn't see him. I had asked many times why she wouldn't see him and never got an answer. I was sure Sasha knew, but it was something she would never share with me. The two of them, my mother and sister, had secrets.

My uncle's annex house appeared behind a gathering of Russian olive trees. The door was ajar and orchestral music resounded from inside. My aunt had given him a gramophone and recordings of Glinka, which I had heard him playing over and over. We stopped outside the open door and looked in. The music was loud enough that he did not hear us as he leaned back on a settee listening with his eyes closed and his mouth open, like a man being given an infusion of much-needed oxygen. As he breathed slowly and deliberately, he shook, and every few seconds, something like a hard shudder ran through him.

I knocked on the doorframe, Anton standing close behind me, but Uncle Boris did not hear. Finally I called out his first name and he sat up with a gasp, something like a wild hope flashing in his eyes. When he saw it was only me and some unknown young man, a silent rage animated his face, which had gone as pale as clay.

"Uncle," I said.

He gestured for us to go, and when we didn't he slammed his fist down on the table near him.

"Go!" he growled, with barely enough strained breath to give the word volume.

We walked back to where we'd been earlier on the property.

"I'm sorry for his rudeness, Anton."

He shook his head. "Dr. Mitrofan told me he hasn't been well. It was a bad idea to disturb him."

After a silence, I said, "You seem far away today, Anton."

He nodded and told me he had received two letters from Moscow.

"One from Aleksander?" I asked.

"One from Aleksander, yes. The other from my poor mother."

He told me that his mother revealed something to him that she hadn't written about in any of her letters before. Since they moved to Moscow, his mother, father, sister and two younger brothers had been living in a dark, one-room basement flat in the Grachiovka District. "I knew they were not in a particularly nice area of town but I assumed the flat was sufficient. I didn't know it was a single room and the only thing they can see out the window, which is near the ceiling, are the feet of passersby." Anton went on to describe the disgraceful poverty they'd been living in. His mother said that she wanted him to be prepared.

"I hope you don't mind me unburdening myself this way."

"No, Anton! Of course I don't mind."

He went on to tell me that Aleksander and Kolya, his two older brothers, lived in a different flat, but according to his mother, they came around drunk and yelling and upset everyone. Kolya was sick but he drank and yelled. He got commissions to do paintings and he started but didn't finish them. He dropped cigarettes on the floor and stepped on them or left them burning on the edge of a table or a counter. He and Aleksander boasted about socializing with Moscow's demimonde and frequenting the Strelna Pleasure Gardens, a terrible influence on Ivan, their younger brother, who was now drinking too, and failing his examinations.

"My mother reminds me that I am the one member of the family who does not shout, hit, or weep. She says I must hurry, that my influence over everyone else is needed. She believes my presence will change everything. I stayed behind in Taganrog to finish school and tutored so I could send them money every week and now all family members, even my father, who was a brutal tyrant when I was growing up, cast me in the role of savior. A role I *do not want!*" he said with emphasis.

"My mother urged me repeatedly in this letter to hurry and get there. I don't know what she thinks will happen with me there, Vera. She expects me to fix everything, but how? She has set up a space for me in that basement flat until I can get them all out of there.

"I have just enough money to go back to Taganrog, gather my mother's icons and various other articles of furniture, hire a cart, and go to Moscow. And then I will be in medical school, but I am also expected to rescue everyone from these dire circumstances?"

"Oh, Anton!" I said. "That's not fair."

"And Aleksander," he said, smiling ironically, "Aleksander started his letter with his first priority, that I should send cigarette papers and tobacco right away, a demand rather than a request, which he repeated later."

"But what did he say about what you've written?"

"To put it plainly, Vera, he didn't think much of my play or my story."

Regarding Anton's story, *Rainy Days*, Aleksander had been impressed by his use of language but said his plot was shallow, that there was no insight or observation and no experience of life in the writing. "He asked me why anyone would want to read it."

"That's cruel!" I half-whispered.

"He was being honest, not cruel. He meant for me to ask myself that question."

Regarding Anton's play, *Fatherlessness*, Aleksander said it did not come together into anything cohesive. He said that while Anton handled a few of the scenes with some skill, as a whole it was an awkward enterprise, that from beginning to end felt like a lie.

"Your mother said Aleksander was drinking and yelling and causing unhappiness. I doubt if you can rely on his words, Anton."

He shook his head. "I *can* rely on his words. Aleksander is a brilliant writer and Kolya is a brilliant artist. Each of them sells his work and is respected for his talent. In spite of their failings, they are my big brothers. I miss them. I want badly to impress them, so I am disappointed."

"I'm sorry, Anton," I said, and resisted the urge to touch his arm.

"I knew the play was more difficult. It's a harder form to master, but I thought I'd achieved something with the story at least. I'm only trying to write a short, silly entertainment."

"Maybe he isn't right."

"He *is* right. His words have already sparked ideas in me about how the story might be improved."

"I'm glad you won't take this as the final word on your talent."

Looking preoccupied, he gazed off past my shoulder.

We were nearing the carriage road when we heard harness bells and the clomping of horses.

"Is that your father?" Anton asked as an elegant maroon coach appeared and moved in the direction of the stable.

"No," I sighed. "That's Sasha's Prince Miranov. He travels in that ridiculous carriage. Now chances are even better that the performance will be tomorrow night or the next."

Anton said he needed to get back to Dr. Mitrofan's, that he wanted to look again at his story.

"Whenever the performance is, Anton, remember I am not an actress. In the past whatever I did on stage for was fun."

"So why are you so resistant now?"

I didn't answer but his question set me to thinking. *Resistant.* Yes, that was the right word. Maybe it was resistance that made my performance feel so flat and false. I would not give myself over to it.

"One year," Anton said, "I must have been thirteen, my two older brothers and I were cast in an amateur production of Gogol's *Government Inspector*. I was very stiff and self-conscious. The second week of rehearsals, the director was ill, and to our frustration, much-needed rehearsals were canceled for several days. We bribed a doorman to let us into the dark auditorium. We passed a lit candle back and forth as we said our lines. I played my role better after that experience and I don't know why."

"Maybe I need to rehearse in the dark with a lit candle," I said.

Anton smiled, but quickly became pensive again.

Coming from the direction of the summerhouse, a large, hunched figure carrying a massive chest of drawers appeared on the carriage road.

"Who is that?" Anton asked with interest.

"That's Nickander," I said. "As you can see, he is very strong. I used to call him Nickander of the Hard-to-Climb Stairs because of the way he carries drunken guests up the stairs."

Anton let out a soft laugh and focused thoughtfully on Nickander.

"I saw him once carry a piano!"

Anton shook his head in amazement. "The Atlas of Volkov," he said with feeling.

We watched for a few moments as Nickander passed.

"He does that so gracefully," Anton marveled and appeared fully absorbed by the wonders of Nickander. "He carries that massive weight like someone unencumbered."

"There is so much to Nickander, Anton, but no one really looks. He is probably one of the gentlest people I have ever met. And he is pious, always praying under his breath, the prayers of the blessed Filaret. One day when I saw him weeping and touching his forehead to the icon in the downstairs kitchen, I started to think of him as Saint

Nickander. I always wonder how someone can be so large and yet so invisible?"

"To others he is invisible, but you, Vera, can see him." He gave me an affectionate smile that sent a shiver of pleasure through me. "You who are always engaged with the invisible!"

"I'm sure you will witness it this summer, Nickander calmly rescuing a guest who has overindulged, and carrying them back to the house and up the stairs."

"Nickander of the Hard-to-Climb Stairs!" Anton said with a thoughtful smile.

"Don't forget how pious he is."

"The Pious Atlas of Volkhov," Anton said, his smile intensifying. He reached over and gently squeezed my shoulder.

"And there is one other thing. I think he is in love with Vova. You know, the maid, the summer hire who talks to herself. I've seen him listening to her with his head bowed and one hand on his heart. I don't know if she knows he exists."

Chapter 9

As I approached the house, I heard the whistle of a mockingbird then a hoot like an owl, and knew my father had arrived and was looking for me.

"Ver-ooooushka!!" he called out musically, then whistled again like a mockingbird.

Coming through the trees, I saw him standing on the veranda.

"My darling!" he said with nervous expectation as I climbed the stairs to the porch. I could see from his expression that he was ready for my inevitable rebuke for his lateness, but I held back.

He was, as always, debonair, a carnation in his lapel, his sweep of dark wavy hair oiled and combed. But his beard was gone. I had never seen my father without a beard, except in photographs from decades past, and it startled me. In a way it made him look younger, but he was also thinner and less robust.

"Oh, Vera, forgive me!" He pressed his hands together as if in prayer.

"What happened to you, Papa?"

"I'm so sorry but I lost track of when I was meant to come." Without the beard even more of his face went pink when he twisted the truth.

His ordinarily gray sideburns had been blackened with some kind of dye, a black that did not quite match his hair.

"I needed your help," I said, trying to temper any resentment in my voice, "but now it's probably too late."

"Tell me how to help you, my little nestling," he pleaded.

When I did not answer, he looked at me with a heartbroken expression. "Please come in here, dearest one," he said. "I have something for you."

I took a step forward and followed him inside where he ushered me in the direction of the parlor.

A package wrapped in shiny sky-blue paper sat on the coffee table before the dark blue brocade sofa.

"Sit, sit darling," he urged.

I sat down before the present but did not touch it.

"Tear the paper, Veroushka," he pleaded. "Tear it!"

And so I tore the paper slowly until a large, colorful carousel with painted horses was revealed.

"It's a music box!" he said.

"A carousel, Papa? I'm not a child anymore."

He gave me a wistful look, his eyes wide and shining. "Are you not, my little pinwheel? Isn't there some small part of you that still is a child?"

He bent over and wound the back of the carousel, tiny bells playing a bright repeated measure. "Tchaikovsky," he said. "From the *Marche Slave.*" I gazed at the horses going up and down, and could not hide my delight with the color and the music.

"Oh, there she is, my little girl."

He knelt near the couch taking my hands and kissing them. "What will become of me if my little girl grows up? I cannot allow it."

I took a deep breath and sighed, and as I did, a tear trickled down my face. I often cried in my father's presence, every vulnerability rising to the surface. He was the person I trusted more than anyone else, the person who indulged me everything. I opened my arms for him, wishing I could tell him the truth about my feelings for Petya and my disappointment and grief that he had not returned to Volkhov. I imagined telling him all of it, even about the child, and I imagined him taking me in his arms and murmuring that it was all right, that he would love my child as much as he loved me. But I couldn't tell him. Not yet. Not until I had to. So when he asked what was wrong I directed all of my emotion into my dread of the performance.

"It's hurting you this much?" he asked with an astonished whisper. "You always had fun on the stage," he said softly, his eyes gleaming in earnest. "You were always so playful and natural when you performed."

"It's become more serious."

"Why is that, Vera?"

"I don't know. I feel false. My acting feels flat, Papa. I am only myself, not Viola. The audience will see that I am not Viola, that I don't know how to be Viola."

He made a noise of protest. "The actress, Rozonova, who played Gertrude, Hamlet's mother, to my Hamlet, used to say that she and Gertrude were one being. She said that sometimes Gertrude was more Rozonova, and sometimes Rozonova was more Gertrude and that was just the nature of acting.

"So if you are feeling more like Vera than Viola while performing the scene, according to the brilliant Rozonova, that is all right. You have her blessing. And you have mine, darling."

He bent his head forward, his brow wrinkling with the efforts of his thoughts. "Everyone, the whole world becomes silent for you when you are on the stage. Everyone barely breathes, they listen so closely. They take in their breath when an actor speaks. I miss it, Vera. How I miss it."

"Oh, Papa. For some reason I am resisting. It's the words, I think."

"Ah," he said, his eyes lit. "You are resisting Shakespeare's language. It has the power to so easily break your heart. You will suffer less if you give yourself to it. It is one of Shakespeare's most moving speeches of unrequited love."

Those last two words sent a soft shock through me.

I did not want to believe that my love for Petya was unrequited. But maybe that was the truth of it, the thing too painful to face. My resistance to the monologue was simple.

"Rosonova said something else I will never forget: An actress must drive her own suffering like she is driving a team of horses."

A chill rose up over my shoulders and head, like a cold twinkling veil.

My father had also brought a gift for my mother.

"Is that woman up there with her?" he asked, referring to Gabinskaya.

"Most likely," I said.

"How can I get a moment alone with your mother?"

"I can go in and ask," I said.

He wanted to show me the gift so I followed him to his room where his bags sat on the carpet still unpacked.

After he'd moved out of the rooms he shared with my mother, he had returned to his childhood bedroom, the room that had been his since he was a tiny boy and first moved out of the nursery. Over the years it changed with him as he became an adolescent and then a young man, but there were still signs of childhood, beloved relics left in place: a small painting he'd done on a tile, a boy before a dark blue background with his arms raised and stars circling his head. A stuffed toy turtle. A framed photograph of a dachshund chasing a ball.

From a large cloth shopping bag he brought out another music box, smaller and quite different from mine, black and lacquered with brightly painted pictures on it.

"It's beautiful, Papa," I said.

He wound the back and it played a faintly familiar sounding melody.

"A song from *Ruslan and Lyudmilla*, the opera I took your mother to see in Petersburg before we married."

"And these illustrations?" I asked, examining the box.

"From an old Baltic tale."

I recognized the skating figure as Little Marusia, from a story of a girl performing pirouettes on the ice. On almost every side of the box Marusia was depicted spinning in a different position. But on the back she was not there, only the trees in the background and the frozen lake, marked by scratches from the blades of her skates. In the story, Little Marusia had spun in so many circles that she had eventually disappeared. It bothered me that my father had been so oblivious of the metaphor and had chosen this for my mother. A part of me wanted to tell him, to point out that it is the story of a girl who disappears in the end, but he had put so much thought into the gift that I couldn't. I kept looking at the beautiful paintings but I found myself focusing mostly on the back panel, the air where Marusia vanished swirling with particles of ice.

"Why are you frowning? Don't you like it, Vera?"

"I told you, Papa. It's beautiful."

He turned to the mirror and as he adjusted his tie I asked, "Why did you shave your beard?"

"I shaved to look more as I looked when I played Eugene Onegin. Your mother fell in love with me when she saw me perform that role."

"Is that why you put the black dye on your sideburns? You want her to fall in love with you again?" I asked.

"They've grown very gray lately. Doesn't it look good?"

"No, and a little of it is smeared on your ear and some on your neck."

"Hmmm. It's very warm today," he muttered offhandedly.

"You look sad, Papa."

The comment caught him off guard. "I miss your mother."

I poured water from the ewer into the large bowl and dampened a cloth. "Try and wash some of it off. You'll look better without it."

"All right, Vera, but I want your mother to see a younger man when she looks at me."

"My mother is no longer young either, Papa. Do you think she stands still in time while the rest of us do not?"

While I knocked, my father stood a few feet back from the door in the hallway outside my mother's room, breathing deeply and slowly as if to calm himself. There was a silence before the approach of firm purposeful footsteps that I knew belonged to Gabinskaya. She opened the door, looking down at me with a territorial glare. Past her, my mother sat on her red couch wearing her fur coat, turning her head and looking cautiously in my direction.

"Maminka," I called out. "My papa would like to speak with you. He has a gift for you."

My mother and Gabinskaya exchanged a look, before my mother lowered her eyes and seemed to be considering. She looked up again and gave her friend a single nod of the head.

I beckoned to my father to come. As he walked in through the doorway, Gabinskaya, almost as tall as he was, remained where she was, standing like a guard in black. When my father saw that she was clutching the long barrel of her rifle, which stood up beside her, butt to the floor, he reared his head back. "Madame," he said with controlled indignation, "this is my house, not yours. Put that gun away."

Gabinskaya hesitated, blinked, then leaned the gun against an armoire.

My father breathed harshly through his nostrils, looking at the floor, gathering his wits. When Gabinskaya showed no sign that she intended to leave, my father told her he wanted to speak alone with his wife. "You may go off guard duty now, madame," he said with a light note of sarcasm, his face flushed.

"It's all right, Maxima," my mother said to her friend.

When my father tried to close the door, my mother told him to leave it open. He left it ajar.

Gabinskaya moved past me in the hall and sat in a chair, her jaw clenched, while I remained on my feet, drifting back and forth near the open door, sometimes looking in.

My father pulled a chair closer to the couch and began to speak in a quiet voice to my mother, who I could only see from the back. Now and then she would nod her head or make a sound in response to something he said.

She made a gesture with her hand and my father, still speaking quietly, unwrapped the music box and wound it until the music began to play. They both sat awhile in silence listening. The back of my mother's head was very still. But I could see my father's face, his eyes filled with light as if enchanted. There were moments when my father's eyes scanned the room, as if for something particular.

But other moments he looked directly at my mother as if to access her response. She'd murmur and nod.

The music slowed almost completely and they spoke quietly. When there was a silence, my mother stood, the cue to my father that the meeting was finishing. He got to his feet and when she reached for the music box he handed it to her carefully.

"My dear Pelegaya," he said.

Holding the music box away from her body with both hands she looked around the room, clearly for a spot to place it. She carried it to a bookcase, and holding it against her chest with one hand, she moved something on the shelf with her other hand, and as she attempted to place the music box on the shelf it slipped and fell to the floor near her feet with a crash. A little mechanism broke free of it and flew halfway across the room past the carpet and landed on the floorboards. As it turned in a feeble automated circle, it played the tune with a wavering dissonance, as if heard through water.

While my mother remained a few feet back, looking at it with distress, my father stood over it seeming to wait, as the notes lost volume, distorting, ending in a blur of sputters.

"I will have it repaired, Pelegaya," my father said, picking up the mechanism when it was finally quiet. I will have the finest expert in Kiev repair it and I will bring it back to you for you to enjoy."

"I am so sorry, Sergei," she said in a quiet voice full of feeling, the reserve she'd been maintaining throughout the entire meeting gone.

My father pressed a palm to his heart. "Dear, dear Pelegaya," he said with emotion. "May I come again to see you? In a few days, or in a week?"

When she gave a small nod of the head, he took a step toward her. She stepped back and he halted. He bowed to her again, and came out into the hallway clutching the pieces of the music box.

Chapter 10

When the hour arrived, I walked with my father, our arms linked, along a winding pathway that descended to the outdoor stage. We could see Sasha hastening ahead, also on her way there. She had raided the carefully preserved wardrobe of our grandmother's costumes and was wearing a long white and purple satin gown with a chiffon scarf. She had the role of the beautiful Olivia and I was playing Viola, disguised as a messenger boy, wearing pants and tunic, my hair pulled up and stuffed under a green felt beret.

When I complained that I would have rather been wearing a beautiful gown, my father told me that many of Shakespeare's best women disguised themselves as boys. "Viola is a more interesting part than Olivia."

"I'm still jealous of the beautiful dress," I said. "If I was wearing a beautiful dress I could gesture gracefully and let the dress act for me. But in boys togs, I cannot rely on posturing."

He said nothing to this as if he hadn't heard it. He looked despondent, far away. After a silence he said, "She still wears a coat and sits before a fire, Vera, but she is perspiring the entire time. Perspiring. I will never understand, Vera."

"I will never understand, either, Papa."

"And the photograph of me in the role of Eugene Onegin, the photograph that has always been on the little side table, is gone."

"Maybe she put it in a different spot, Papa."

"No, I looked. It wasn't displayed anywhere in the room."

My parents had met in Petersburg where my mother saw my father perform the role of Eugene Onegin.

She had always, even after my father had moved out of their rooms where they'd lived together as husband and wife, kept a little framed picture of my father in the role of Eugene Onegin, a votive candle burning before it.

I didn't tell him that the candle she'd kept lit in front of it had always bothered me, as if it were before an image of the dead.

"I believe now that she fell in love with Eugene Onegin and not with me," my father said. "She never got over the fact that I was someone other than Eugene Onegin. But now it seems she's discarded the picture, probably under that woman's influence."

We followed a descending path through olive trees until we could see the outdoor stage ahead. Performances were ordinarily given on the bare wooden platform, but at Slezkine's request, curtains had been rigged up around the entire perimeter of the stage. He had told my aunt he needed privacy before performing.

"Papa, listen, don't praise Maestro Slezkine too much after his performance."

"Of course I must praise him if I am moved to do so."

"But don't do it too much. Aunt Marya said he likes discretion when he is praised."

"I am always *discreet*, Vera," he said, emphasizing the word and looking hurt at the suggestion that he might not be. "But I suspect he is not sincere about that. All performers crave adulation!"

"But listen to me, Papa. Don't be too effusive. Aunt Marya was adamant about it."

He nodded, but a maudlin shadow hung over his brow, and I was not sure how well he was listening.

As we reached the back of the stage, which was set on a clearing between a cluster of gnarled mulberry trees and a stand of poplars, he asked if I wanted to listen to Slezkine from the audience but I said I preferred to go backstage and begin to prepare. He kissed my forehead and proceeded around to the front. I climbed up the two stairs onto the back of the stage, and stepped between curtains.

In a dim corner where the side and rear curtains met, I could see the back of a small figure of a man, balding and slumped at the shoulders. He sat very still in a chair, violin and bow lying across his lap. I was sure he heard me there, but he did not turn and I knew better than to break his concentration by saying hello.

I took a few more steps in the backstage darkness and saw Sasha far stage left, standing at an oblique angle. She turned briefly, glanced at me, then turned back again and continued whispering her lines.

I peeked out between the brocade curtains at the gathering audience. People milled about talking around a motley group of chairs, some wooden, some upholstered, set out on uneven ground facing the stage. Along with my father's siblings, Aunt Marya and Uncle Pavel, Victor Victorovich and Anya Leonideyvna stood laughing with a few newly arrived guests.

Lilia Petrovna appeared, wearing red, her bosom on full display, a bird of paradise in her hair. "Isn't Father Ivan coming?" I heard her ask Uncle Pavel, who shrugged his shoulders.

Dr. Mitrofan and Anton appeared, Anton dressed formally, too formally, as if he were attending an elegant event in Kiev. He wore a stiff white cambric shirt and an elegant morning jacket, which was snug at the shoulders and must have been borrowed from Dr. Mitrofan, who was a few inches shorter. It moved me, the sweetness and awkwardness of it. Anton stood there, beautifully out of place among the other men who were neatly but more casually dressed. Dr. Mitrofan wore a tight dark blue dress coat and had trimmed his voluminous sideburns, oiled and combed his dry, gray, frizzy hair back away from his face, and topped his head with a crimson-colored fez, a black tassel hanging down on one side. Proudly introducing Anton to different people, he smiled and nodded. My father bowed and reached for Anton's hand.

I wouldn't tell Sasha, who remained in her circle of concentration, that Prince Miranov was nowhere to be seen.

I dropped the curtain and stepped back into a shadow. As I mouthed my lines, a dull ache in the pit of my stomach grew sharp. I tried to think of the things my father had said to me but even Rozonova's words, which had hit me with such clarity earlier— "An actress must drive her suffering like a team of horses," —now *felt* nebulous.

An old servant with a red, weather-beaten face, Volodio, had been charged with the opening and closing of the curtains. He stood near the pulley and I hid a few feet behind him in the makeshift proscenium. Slezkine approached from his shadowy corner and gave a nod to Volodio. As the curtains squeaked slowly open Slezkine rested his cheek gently against the chest of his violin, his eyes closed as if in a trance. When the first note sounded, a flock of noisy, chattering birds in the nearby trees went silent. The emotion in the music was immediate, infusing everything, every early evening shadow, every green fragrance from the foliage, with its generosity, with its tender melodious suffering. Some locked chamber in my being unbolted and the dread that had tightened my every nerve released. For seven or twelve minutes, however long the music pervaded the atmosphere, so too did my passion for Petya, along with my certainty that what was between us was not finished, could not possibly be finished.

The maestro held the last note until it was quiet. When he lifted his bow from the strings his audience rose to their feet with applause. Still in the grip of a serious emotion, Slezkine did not tolerate the adulation for long and disappeared again into the shadow from which he had emerged.

When at last the applause quieted, Sasha, carrying a chair from the opposite proscenium, sat down center stage, her back to the audience. She lifted a hand mirror, a prop of her character, Olivia's, and gazed into it. But I could see that with the mirror, she was surveying the members of the audience, looking, I was sure, for Prince Mironov, who was still missing.

I stepped onto the stage and the two of us exchanged dialogue and went through the rudimentary blocking Sasha had created for us. Still vibrating from the emotion of the adagio, I had lost much of my self-consciousness. There was also something new and uncertain in Sasha's posture, something more present about her, which drew me in and made the interaction fresh. I would not understand until later that this affect was due to the fact that the prince was missing.

When the moment came for the monologue I turned and faced out, past the audience into the trees that were growing shadows in the first reddish light of the descending sun. Phrases of the adagio, measures of building music were alive in me, at one with my own yearning. And I saw a shadow there, beyond the audience, a shadow between two poplar trees that formed itself into a figure, one I was certain could only be Petya. I began to recite Viola's speech. "Make me a willow cabin at your gate and call upon my soul within the house."

The audience emitted a supernal silence.

"Write loyal cantons of contemned love and sing them loud even in the dead of night . . ." I concentrated on the shadow that moved slightly. The words that had felt awkward in my mouth while rehearsing them came out with an ease and sincerity that surprised me.

"Oh you should not rest between the elements of air and earth . . . but you should pity me."

At the end of the scene, the clapping audience broke the dream. My father, Anton, and Dr. Mitrofan stood up from their wooden chairs. "Brava!" my father cried. "Brava!"

Even the crude Víctor Victorovitch had a look of damp elation in his eyes.

As Sasha and I held hands and bowed, I searched the trees for Petya's figure but no one was there.

Different guests clasped my hand or Sasha's, offering sweet words of congratulations. Bottles of Veuve Clicquot were popped open and poured.

Anton approached Uncle Pavel, but Pavel turned and walked away from him. Anton stood very still a moment, seeming to absorb the rebuff, then went and joined Sasha and Dr. Mitrofan.

I overtook my uncle.

"Why do you behave that way to our guest?" I demanded.

For a moment he had no answer, then said calmly, "He is a revolutionary, Vera."

"Uncle!" I corrected, "Anton is a student, not a revolutionary."

"Same thing," he said, sipping from his glass.

"It is not the same thing! Dr. Mitrofan was once a medical student. Would you call him a revolutionary? Be polite to Anton!"

He looked unmoved and walked away.

I was going to follow him but my attention was drawn by a worrisome tableau, my father holding his chest with both hands and bowing before Slezkine. The maestro looked irritated, his face pale. My father had been warned, yet kept intensifying his praise, going headlong into his own humiliation.

"Please Sergei Mikailovich, enough!" Slezkine muttered.

My father apologized, bending even deeper before the maestro, who shook his head and turned away.

My aunt sailed over, taking Slezkine by the arm, talking quietly to him about the chanterelles and champignons cooked in butter and waiting at the dinner table. "And there will be mushroom caviar and black bread."

He nodded enthusiastically.

"And fried potatoes with wild forest mushrooms."

I approached my father who stared glassy eyed into the trees.

"He is such a genius, Vera."

"Yes, Papa, but that was rude of him."

Victor Victorovitch and Anya Leonidevna came and congratulated me. When they got into a conversation with my father I broke away and joined Anton, Dr. Mitrofan, and my sister. Sasha, I noticed, was focusing with a particular intensity on Anton.

"Volkhov must be a very old estate," Anton said.

Sasha concurred, tilting her head and pointing her chin in Anton's direction as she smiled, a flirtatious, choreographed movement I'd seen her use before with other men, though never with Prince Miranov, who always made her feel self-conscious and cowed. But there was something strained about her, a stricken determination. I understood all at once that this flirtation with Anton was driven by the fact that the prince had neglected to arrive to the little performance Sasha had orchestrated specifically for him. Had he left the estate? Had he lost track of the time?

I sensed Anton's fascination over my beautiful sister's attention.

To break what felt like a spell between the two of them, I told Anton a story Sasha hated about the ancestor who had built Volkhov.

"He was kicked out of the Winter Palace by Peter the Great himself for his abysmal manners. Apparently he was cleaning his teeth with a hunting knife at the dinner table."

Sasha's cheeks bloomed with uneven blotches of bright pink. "My sister," she said, "is part of that bloodline, and clearly inherited that barbarous lack of manners."

"I'm not being rude, Sasha! I'm just sharing with Anton some interesting facts about our family."

"*Your* family," she said, as if she had not made this clear already with the comment about my bloodline. "Vera and I have different fathers. I am Alexandra Iunosheva and my sister is Vera Denisova."

"Yes, *my* family. I am from the side with the abysmal manners." I waved my arm ostentatiously and bowed, causing Anton to restrain a smile.

Sasha looked irritated.

My heart beat hard. "It's humorous, Sashenka," I said. Sasha rarely showed interest in anything funny and always felt impatient with a joke or a laugh. So it was the form of an attack to involve her in something humorous because she was so out of her element. I felt guilty about it, my heart pounding even as I maintained a smile, but Anton was my friend and she was taking steps to be the focus of his attention.

"There are better things to talk about at a social occasion, little sister."

"But people are interested in such things, Sashenka!" My father's father had been a contradiction of a man who wore a silk caftan and bast shoes at home, but insisted his footman wear a powdered wig and walk backwards bowing his way out of a room. "This family comes from despots torn between Asia and Europe."

Sasha shook her head and looked at Anton as if for sympathy. But I saw her eyes flash to the pathway searchingly and I could feel her managing a mild hysteria.

Dr. Mitrofan, who had been standing quietly nearby throughout it all interjected in a polite, mollifying tone, "Peter the Great confused all Russians!" Through the smudged lenses of his gold wire frame glasses, his moist eyes twinkled.

Chapter 11

It was probably ten p.m. when a servant girl appeared in the distance between two trees and rang the dinner bell.

Sasha linked her right arm with Anton's left, and the two of them led everyone slowly toward the house. I walked behind them, only half hearing the smatterings of idle conversation and laughter from those who followed.

A new layer of clouds drifted in above, charged with the glow of the late day sun, which was lowering itself on the horizon but would not set, these late June days, until after eleven.

"In the height of summer, Anton," Sasha said, "peacocks scream to one another at this hour." Her posturing and falsely modulated voice set me on edge. I wanted to call out to her that she was no longer on the stage.

"And when the wheat is tall, you can hear the quail running in it. On windy days it's hard to know if it's the quail or the wind stirring the grain."

I wanted to say that I knew the difference, but I swallowed the impulse when I noticed how her gloved hand fidgeted, hiding itself as best as it could behind her. I allowed myself to consider how hurt she likely was that Prince Mironov had never arrived to the performance while he was probably still on the property somewhere. I worried that she would not take him to task for his negligence and the thought of that bothered me almost more than her monopolizing Anton.

It was often Sasha's habit to charm men then throw them away. Though Anton looked sophisticated in his fine clothes, a cream-colored silk handkerchief peeking from one breast pocket of his jacket, he was younger than she was and had no money. How long would she need his attention?

Since the scene had ended I kept feeling pulled back into the feeling of it. I had been so absorbed in the intensity of those minutes, so given over to the urgency Viola was feeling. It amazed me. I wanted to relive it completely. I felt it still in my body like another state of being, a heightened focus. An organized dream. But there was too much going on around me, too many noisy interactions, too many exclamations. A part of me was waiting until I could be alone and sink into the memory of being Viola.

Watching Sasha, still in the costume of Olivia, speaking to Anton, it was as if she was saying lines. She'd lift her head displaying her long neck, and the little jewels in her hair sparkled blue and cold. She was presenting a happy demeanor, but I could feel her struggling to keep her upset at bay. When I thought of how I'd resorted earlier to humor to make her uncomfortable, a rush of guilt opened and spread like a fan in my chest.

There were times, lying back on my bed with me, she would spill out her frustrations with various suitors. Once she told me she wanted to chop off all her hair, go into a monastery, and live behind high stone walls. Other times she would come in, lie down beside me, and simply take my right hand in her incomplete left one. At such moments I knew she loved me. Fueled by that tenderness with her, I went along with most everything else.

We all found our places at the table on the terrace, the chair beside Sasha, meant for Prince Miranov, left empty. A rumble sounded in the sky and Uncle Pavel, taking on the role of master of ceremonies, went into a sudden treatise on the weather, and the prevalence of thundershowers. He wore a jubilant air, smiling and humming. "This is the time of year we most often see the *Australias Marmette*." The hair he had combed over his bald spot lifted in the breeze.

It always startled me to look at Uncle Pavel next to my father. No one would have ever taken them as brothers. My father, Sergei, the youngest of the three siblings, was handsome and tall, his thick black hair threaded with silver. Pavel was shorter. Perhaps he would have been just a plain, average-looking man if not for the bulbous forehead which made him strange-looking. While Pavel smelled of caraway seeds, my father smelled of cedar and sandalwood, and his finely tailored clothes, like a confectionary.

"Have you ever heard the song of the *Australias Marmette*, dear Maestro?" Uncle Pavel asked.

The maestro shook his head indifferently. Soup had been served to him and he did not wait for the rest of us.

"It is called the Stradivarius of birds!" my uncle went on. "Usually we hear them in the birch trees, but sometimes in the peach orchard."

"They sound lovely, but they do eat the peaches," Aunt Marya remarked.

"But that is little price to pay for their songs!" cried Uncle Pavel, the worst kind of hypocrite. Two summers before, he'd had servants start small, contained fires between the trees in order to smoke out the birds.

"If it rains there will be no croquet tomorrow," Victor Victorovich said mournfully.

"We can play whist tonight, but if we tire of it I can always perform my monologue from *Hamlet*," my father offered with sincerity, though he often suggested this in company and rarely followed through.

"Heaven help us!" Uncle Pavel said. "Twenty years later and this aged Hamlet still hasn't made up his mind."

Only Victor Victorovich laughed. My father blushed and looked offended.

The sky went suddenly overcast and crickets began to sing in the cool grass.

When a breeze taunted the flames in the lamps, crystal and silverware flickered. In this exalted light, Anton looked particularly handsome in his white cambric shirt and soft silk bow tie.

Sasha shot him the occasional smile as she ate. And I noticed, much to my dismay, that he too stole glances at her.

From the other side of the house came the strains of my mother's voice, something melancholy in Italian. The French doors on her balcony were clearly open. For a few minutes no one spoke as my mother's voice quavered, but she stopped short of a crescendo, repeating the one expectant phrase before it, again and again, never advancing in the song. My mother's voice put my father into a mild trance. His eyes were glassy and his skin pink. He had several glasses of champagne after the performances, and now at the table had quickly drained his first glass of Lafite and was on his second. But for others around the table, the effect of the repeating phrase was frustrating and put a vague psychic irritation on the atmosphere. Shadows formed between the maestro's brows and his nostrils flared as if there were a bad smell.

My mother's voice was never perfectly in tune but its soft dissonance had always been pleasurable to me. Its imperfections were, for me, part of its beauty, but as she sang now I felt embarrassed for her and for myself. She was completely unaware that she was being listened to and by people who likely did not find her occasional flat note charming.

"She's practicing," I said by way of apology. "Vocalizing."

Uncle Pavel began to speak, one of his usual monologues for filling silences or awkward moments when guests were present, listing the many stars of the Italian opera who had visited Volkhov. There was a distant sound of a French door closing and after that my mother's voice was muted, too quiet to be objectionable but still there, like a persistent gust of wind outside a window.

When Pavel paused in his list of luminaries, Anton asked if Felice Varesi had ever come to Volkhov.

"Of course!" Pavel snapped then left off talking about the Italians and segued into a list of Russian artists who had been guests.

His dislike of Anton was so marked and so curious I found myself remembering a night when I was thirteen or fourteen. We had guests and were eating on the veranda. My aunt summoned Petya, who was passing, and spoke with him briefly, dispatching him on an errand. The pianist and composer, Mikhail Robkovsky, casually remarked that the young servant had a remarkable face. The actor Streptakov agreed and said that it was an aristocratic face. Uncle Pavel had smiled, excused himself, and gone inside. I followed quietly and saw him standing between two dressers in an empty room, his fists tense, as if struggling to contain his upset.

At my uncle's snub of Anton, Sasha glared at him disapprovingly. She then offered Anton a conciliatory smile. My heart sped. Sasha's interest in Anton brought my own feelings sharply forward.

My father, also aware of the snub, turned and faced Anton, singling him out. "You may have noticed, Anton, that we have a very large house but we do not have a butler. We once did, a man named Popov. From my birth, he was here in this house, part of this house and these grounds, this Eden of my childhood. Popov grew to be very old and suffered with terrible arthritis."

"Do not tell stories of Popov, Sergei," Uncle Pavel said, rolling his eyes.

"You do not care to remember the dead, Pavel, but I do."

"We are at a meal!"

"There is no wrong place to remember the dead."

Uncle Pavel shook his head and began speaking to Victor Victorovich and Anna Leonideyvna about a time one of the artists accidentally broke a Chinese vase.

But my father focused on Anton and me. "Popov had a little overweight dog named Potemkin. Vera remembers Potemkin." My father described the dog's flat, wrinkled, scowling face, a dog that never wagged his tail. Every morning, Potemkin would waddle into the front hallway and wait for the door to be opened, then go outside and do his business. But the last month he was alive he would hesitate at the open door. Instead of going out he would turn around, come further into the house and leave a puddle on the floorboards.

My sister, sitting in the proximity of my father's voice, made a quiet sound of exasperation.

"And every day, slow-moving old Popov would clean it up. He never admonished Potemkin."

My uncle had stopped talking and everyone was listening to my father.

"After Potemkin died, Popov would not come out of his bed. I could hear him crying through the door. A few days later, Popov himself died." He sighed.

I had been watching Anton as he'd listened with polite interest, holding his fork suspended. I'd been memorizing his features so that I could consider them without staring at him. If that mustache were shaved off, I wondered, would he have Petya's upper lip? The full lower lip was remarkably similar in shape.

"That, children, is a story of attachment of an exceptional nature," my father said, wiping the dampness from under one of his eyes with his dinner napkin. He looked at Anton and then at me.

"No," Uncle Pavel said with a soft, contemptuous laugh, "that is a story about a servant and a dog."

"It is a story, Pavel, about two hearts bound together."

My father was used to my uncle's attempts to humiliate him and usually absorbed his insults calmly. He had told me once that he pitied his older brother. It was so clear when they were young that their mother did not like Pavel. She was fickle in her feelings for Aunt Marya, by turns affectionate and indifferent, but loving and complimentary to my father who had been painfully conscious of this as a child. Thus, he continued to endure my uncle's dislike. But in this moment I noticed that my father looked hurt. And quietly indignant. "Dear, dear Popov," he muttered, gazing off into the distance. "Even near the end, before he took to his bed, he used to put on his green livery, simply to prepare coffee."

A breeze rushed in, causing a set of tiny hanging bells to ring softly. Anton looked up as if charmed by the sound then met my eyes and gave me a smile suffused faintly with sadness.

"What wonderful performances this evening," Anton said when there was a lull.

"Yes, Vera and Sasha, you each did a beautiful job," my father added. "And Vera, you instinctively understood the nature of the downstage monologue!"

"It was not what we had originally decided," Sasha said. "Vera was meant to address the monologue to me."

"But it was affective, Sasha," my father said. "Quite affective."

Sasha nodded and looked distractedly toward the grounds.

"A downstage monologue is outside the flow of normal time," my father continued. "It is the interior made exterior."

"Yes, I was also thinking of that," Anya Leonideyvna said. "If you had performed this in a theatre, all the lights would have gone out but for one shining on you downstage."

The noise of voices at the table blurred and I felt myself back on the stage, addressing the shadow between two trees. The sensation filled me even now, something so exquisite I could hardly name it, a different state of being, one of openness and receptivity. My father had said that the world goes quiet when an actor speaks on stage.

My reverie was broken when Prince Miranov materialized on the terrace, head and chest held imperiously high. Sasha took in a little spasm of breath, put down her fork, and stood, reaching out one arm and gesturing to the chair next to her with the other.

As he moved past to take his seat, he emitted a heavy perfume, a redolence of amber and saffron.

I had met the prince once in the bright of day but he was even stranger looking in lamplight. A tall narrow-chested figure in a tight turquoise tailcoat, maroon ruffles at his throat and chest. His face, too, was odd, a short snub nose and overly long jaw, dark forelocks plastered to an inch above his brow.

He made a vague, insincere-sounding apology for being late to the meal, saying he'd been wandering in the gardens and that he found the flowers so distracting, particularly the blue hollyhocks and the purple gentian. He never mentioned missing the performance. Something deliberate about his manner suggested to me that he had purposely missed it to taunt Sasha, to play with her feelings.

Sasha introduced him to those at the table who had never met him.

"Let me ask you, Pavel Mikailovich," the prince said, addressing my uncle. "Doesn't anyone prune the trees in your orchard?"

"I believe that the trees are growing fine, Prince Miranov," my uncle said in a magnanimous voice.

"I know nothing of orchards," Victor Victorovich interjected. "Do they require human intervention?"

"They do and they are being neglected," the prince responded.

"Thank you for your concern, Prince Miranov, but we do have a crew of men working for us in the orchards," my aunt said.

This, I knew was not true. At the end of the previous summer, my aunt had greatly reduced the staff, including any that would have tended to the orchard. She had only hired two temporary maids for the current summer to clean the guest rooms. She used to hire four.

And Nickander and Osip now filled various positions. They repaired everything on the grounds and mucked out the stable, and one night had been made to serve at dinner, each looking awkward in a swallowtail coat.

"Well, Marya Mikhailevna, the men you hired are doing a very poor job of it. I would speak with them directly."

"Please do not concern yourself, Prince Miranov. What they might be doing shabbily, Nature herself will take care of."

"It does not work that way. An orchard is not the same thing as forest or wild meadow. The fruit on your trees is being eaten by aphids and Japanese beetles. And there are diseased and damaged limbs that need to be cut back."

The maestro, who had been quietly focused on his food, never raising his eyes from his plate, suddenly spoke in a small, nasal voice, and the whole table went silent to listen. "Everywhere I go, orchards and forests are being cut down. Forests catch fire or dry up and there is no new growth. What does grow is cut down right away. We do not think of nature as fragile, but it is. It is wrong to take it for granted."

Everyone had paused eating, except Victor Victorovich who cut noisily into a piece of meat.

"The world is not meant to last forever," the maestro continued.

Vague mumbled responses sounded around the table.

"Things have changed, it is very true," Dr. Mitrofan said. "On my estate and here at Volkhov. There were once geese, cranes and black grouse. You never see them anymore."

"What happened to them?" Anya Leonideyvna asked.

"Well, marshes dried up and some of the ponds. And the rivers are lower. They were once filled with pike. The pike are still there but much less plentiful and harder to catch."

The maestro had listened with interest to Dr. Mitrofan, but now picked up his fork and disappeared again from the conversation, giving his attention fully to a second helping of mushroom julienne in sour cream.

"Your orchard, though," Anton said. "It could survive if properly cared for. It is too late for a full crop this year, but there is always next year."

"Shamefully neglected," the prince said offhandedly. "What are the enemies of an orchard? Frost, of course, hares, certain birds like cockchafers. But most of all human negligence."

"You are aristocracy, Prince Miranov," Uncle Pavel ventured. "Why do you concern yourself with such mundane things?"

"An orchard is not mundane! Besides, I am a modern man. Modernity will overtake tradition."

"Yes, yes, I have heard this," Victor Victorovich mumbled. "The middle class will rise and the aristocracy will fade."

"Well," Prince Miranov said, puffing out his chest. "We will not *fade!*"

"Oh no! No! Apologies," Victor Victorovich said.

"We certainly will not *fade*."

"Sasha told us you were recently in Petersburg," my aunt, always excellent at diverting a subject, said to the prince.

"Yes, yes!" He wiped his mouth with his napkin, then said, "We all know the story of the Ice Palace and Empress Anna of the Romanovs." While in Petersburg, he said, he had heard the most "wonderfully detailed" version of the story.

"Reportedly, it was architecturally extraordinary. Tall and pinnacled, cornices and columns, all made of ice, harvested from the frozen Neva. They say it rivaled the size of the Winter Palace itself.

"Empress Anna had it built during the extreme winter of 1739. She was a terrible practical joker, and simply to entertain herself, ordered her jester, Mikhail Golitsky, a fallen nobleman, to marry one of her servants, a very ugly Mongol woman. Empress Anna organized the whole wonderfully monstrous event with processions of animals: pigs, goats, and camels. She wanted the whole affair to be as bizarre as possible. The couple came to their wedding riding in a cage on the back of an elephant.

"After the wedding feast the newlyweds were transported to the palace made entirely of ice. Everything inside was made of ice as well. The chairs, the table, all the furniture, even the marriage bed. The empress stayed in the room with them while they consummated the marriage on the bed of ice. Then she left, and from the warmth of the winter palace, she kept watching their antics through the transparent ice walls. It's a marvelous story. What an eccentric Anna was!"

"You know that the jester and the serving woman died, don't you?" I said. "It's not a marvelous story. It's a story of cruelty."

Sasha pinned me with a warning look.

"All history involves cruelty, my *young* friend," the prince said, emphasizing the word *young*.

"Didn't Anna herself suffer a terrible death?" Lilia Petrovna asked. "I remember something about her growing morbidly depressed under the influence of her lover, Count Basis."

"Legend has it," Prince Miranov said, "that one night she was walking in one of the dim mirrored rooms in her palace and saw a horrible figure, obese and elaborately dressed. She recognized it as herself. Some say she died of apoplexy right then and there."

"Extraordinary!" said Victor Victorovich.

"How grotesque," I remarked.

"Yes, well, I am interested in the grotesque," the prince said, and shot Sasha a brief but weighted glance, which horrified me. Sasha froze slightly and looked down at her plate.

When the meal was over and people were getting up from the table, I heard Sasha tell Prince Miranov that she would like to show him more of the estate in the morning.

He said something to her under his breath, which I could not hear, something which left her looking unsatisfied and confused.

Chapter 12

My father strolled with Anton and me along the pathway leading away from the lights of the veranda. "I don't like listening to all of this nonsense about forests being cut down," he said, inhaling the evening air. "In spite of what Dr. Mitrofan pointed out, the marshes that have dried up and the birds that are gone, this is still my childhood home, Anton Pavlovich. Vera's also. So many familiar and beloved trees here! Poplars, birches, willows."

"And linden trees," I added.

"Yes," my father said. "And all the bushes, wild lilac and flowering magnolias! It is still a kind of paradise. And in the dark you can really feel the presence of all the trees. You can smell them in a way you don't smell them in the light of day, and if you listen, you can hear them making a beautiful sound." He stopped walking, raised his head, and seemed to be listening. He let out an uneasy sigh. "I say all of this . . . I hear the trees, but it is as if I am only remembering them."

"What do you mean, Papa?"

"I am separate somehow from the feeling. I cannot feel them the way I once could. I miss this house and these trees, even as I stand here. How can that be? I am here in the presence of the house and the trees, breathing the very air and yet I miss this place as if I am not here at all. Can either of you explain this to me?"

"Papa, you had too many glasses of Lafite and you barely ate your dinner."

"You see, I lived here long before I brought Vera's mother here and little Sasha." He shook his head. "Time is devilish. The two of you may be too young to understand. We live inside time. It carries us and we cannot see it or get free of it. In a play, time is organized in some ways. You feel you can grasp time in a play better than the way it moves in life. Even though years can pass between acts in a play, or even between scenes."

"Yes," Anton said, "and whole areas of time might disappear and only be referred to in dialogue. Yet it feels possible to chart time in a play."

"Anton writes plays, Papa."

"Do you, Anton?" my father asked with interest.

Anton mumbled a soft laugh. "I write plays, but very badly."

My father stood still again and took a deep breath, facing out into the near darkness. "This was my childhood nest, my nursery. But where is the little boy I once was? Where is he?"

"Dear Papa! Go downstairs to Aniuta's kitchen and ask her for a strong cup of tea."

"Am I embarrassing you, Vera?"

"No, Papa. Well, yes." I smiled. "A little."

He kissed my hand then bowed to Anton.

"I am going to have a strong cup of tea, as my most beloved one has instructed me to do. Although I do not believe it will address the problem."

He started walking toward the house but turned and called me over to him. He squeezed my hand. "Vera, how long should I wait before asking your mother when I can visit her again?"

"I don't know, Papa, a few days more?"

He nodded. "Yes, alright."

I rejoined Anton. My father took a few steps toward the house, turned again suddenly and cried out, "The air is humid tonight. If you go near the fountain, watch out for mosquitoes!"

When he was no longer visible on the pathway I told Anton that my father seemed to have grown older since I'd last seen him. "He's sadder than he used to be."

In response, Anton made a quiet sound and went thoughtful.

As we strolled along the pathway, he said, "I think you found the right door to enter the scene. You performed so well."

I thanked him.

"Seeing you on the stage, it's clear that acting is a passion of yours."

I hid my pleasure at his words. "Acting has always been only a summer game for me, like croquet," I said.

He smiled. "Croquet?"

"I guess I have always thought of the profession of acting as self-indulgent," I said.

"I understand. But the theatre should not be about the cult of the actor."

"The actor should be at the service of the play, correct?"

"Yes."

I wondered if I was guilty of not having served the play.

"It's interesting, Anton. I was thinking tonight that the actress has to know the arc of the story in every particle of herself, and yet she must not know it."

"What do you mean?"

"Because she must believe that something else could happen, that the play could end differently. Don't you think?"

"Yes," he said. "That the doors of fate remain open. Such an interesting observation."

"Another metaphor about doors," I said and we both smiled.

"You were so tied in knots over this scene. It was wonderful to see you set yourself free the way you did."

"I confess, Anton, if I did well tonight, it was because of Slezkine's performance. Because of the beauty of the adagio. Since he stopped playing, an invisible orchestra has been following me."

"If that is what music does for you, you must always listen to it before going on stage, even if you only hear it in your mind."

"But when will I go on stage again?" I asked. "Maybe next summer in a short scene? I am not really an actress."

Anton furrowed his brow and was about to respond, but before he could speak, Prince Miranov's voice sounded nearby, commanding that Osip bring him a lamp. He and Sasha stood in silhouette near a tree.

"My sister gets irritated with me, Anton, but we really do love each other. She deserves better than that snake."

I had seen the prince treat Sasha dismissively before and asked her why she put up with his cruelty. She had told me that he could see the truth of her, that he understood her in a way that I didn't. I'd asked her to please explain what she meant. "He knows what I am," she'd said and refused to say more. I told all of this to Anton and he shook his head, as baffled by it as I was.

We heard footsteps behind us. It was Uncle Pavel on the pathway. When he saw us he turned around.

"I'm sorry my uncle is rude to you, Anton." We continued on our way to the fountain, away from the lights of the house and deeper into the darkening evening.

"He seems determined not to like me."

"My uncle disliked Petya, too. He tried to prevent Petya's internship from happening. I think he dislikes you for reasons similar to those that he disliked Petya. Because you were born into poverty and yet you're making something of yourself. Petya was born into the serving class but is handsome and gifted. Such things seem to bother my uncle. Perhaps because he was born into wealth but can make nothing of himself."

"But as an aristocrat, does he really have to make himself into anything?"

"Well, my grandmother lionized my father for his good looks and talent and she was dismissive of Pavel, who she said had neither."

"Father Ivan offering me all of that undeserved praise at the meal the other day, that must have made your uncle dislike me even more."

"Yes. Probably," I responded.

We strolled a little while in silence.

"Now, after seeing you act, I feel that you should play Desdemona, and repair your grandmother's damage to the role. I cannot imagine a better Desdemona than you."

I smiled.

"I'm serious. And I think I shall call you Desdemona Denisova."

"Well, if you're going to do that, then I'm going to call you Antosha Chekhonte. And if I'm mad at you, I will call you the Man without a Spleen!"

We both laughed.

"You know, Anton, I didn't tell you this before, but you look a lot like Petya. You are just a little taller and your hair is darker."

He stopped walking and faced me.

"He had blue eyes and you have brown."

"Petya is my doppelgänger?" he asked with enthusiasm.

"The two of you are very different in personality. But physically you are alike."

"Tell me more about how we are alike."

"You both have the same heavy eyelids. Even when you're wide awake you look a little sleepy."

He made a soft, surprised sound, this observation seeming to give him pleasure.

The darkness deepened as we progressed along, but soon we could see the gaslight burning in its lamp, a lugubrious flame, somewhat weak and mostly blue. As we came into its circle and sat on the wide marble edge of the fountain, it cast its deep cobalt aura over both of us.

A chorus of nightingales was engaged in an exuberant back-and-forth, repeating a certain melody as if in answer to other birds in the distance, the songs echoing in the darkness.

"And what else? How am I like the gifted Petya Fyodorovich?"

"Sometimes when we are quiet and searching for the white deer, I feel so content. I know I am with you, but I feel in a way as if I'm with Petya."

"Maybe I've been sent in Petya's place."

"By whom?"

"I don't know. Some mysterious force. Maybe by Eros."

The words sparked a pleasurable chill over my shoulders. I laughed softly, more breath than sound.

"The monologue you performed," Anton said, his voice seeming to brush against my skin, "you addressed that to Petya. I almost turned around to look and see if he was there."

His words left a bright aftershock on my being. I was too moved to form a response.

"I am right, aren't I?" he asked. "It was as if you were speaking directly to him."

"Yes, I saw him, or I . . . imagined I saw him in the trees. I'm just stunned that you could perceive that. It's strange," I said, barely audibly, "to be seen so . . . clearly."

"I felt as if you were speaking the monologue to me. But that was because it was such a strong performance. I felt like I was Petya, or I was wishing I was."

I laughed softly.

"In the drawing Petya did of you . . . did he see you clearly?"

My breath paused.

When I didn't answer he asked, "Does the image do you justice?"

I remembered it had produced many different responses in me, and in the months since I'd looked at it, its impression kept changing in my memory. Sometimes I felt afraid to look at it again, remembering the shock of vulnerability in my expression. Other times I'd resisted looking, nervous of the sexual swoon it might induce, and afraid of missing Petya too violently. But I couldn't say any of that to Anton.

"He did capture something."

"Did he often draw you when you were young?"

"No. No, he never did. I had to ask him to draw me. And he did only once."

The flame in the gas lamp began to flutter and dim and all at once extinguished itself in a huff. The sky was nearly fully dark.

"We better go back," I said.

"Wait," Anton said. "Listen." The wind blowing in the rushing birch leaves made a soft throaty sound. "That's what your father meant by the trees at night."

"Yes," I said.

We stood unmoving as the trees stirred and breathed. Though the night air was raw and black it smelled deeply green like clover and the musk of poplar leaves. Anton's fingers touched my wrist. He took my hand in his.

We walked carefully in the darkness back in the direction we'd come from.

"So you had to ask Petya to draw you?" Anton's face was all shadow, but his curiosity was palpable in the dark.

"Yes."

We heard footsteps and saw light moving on the pathway between trees.

It was the half dark figure of Dr. Mitrofan, carrying a lamp, and calling out to Anton, who explained to me that they had planned an early-morning fishing trip together.

We walked toward the brightness, a few fluttering moths circling the lamp.

"Would you show me Petya's other drawings?" Anton asked.

"Yes. Tomorrow."

"I'll be back from fishing before noon, I think."

When we reached Dr. Mitrofan, I let go of Anton's hand and he bowed and said goodnight.

An hour or so later I heard voices near the stable. Looking out my bedroom window I saw Osip preparing Prince Miranov's carriage for departure. I was surprised to see

Oleg Radzitsky, in his mustard yellow jacket, standing illuminated by the carriage headlamps, which Osip had just lit. Prince Miranov emerged from a shadow and approached Radzitsky. When Osip disappeared momentarily into the stable, the prince stepped very close to his friend so they stood facing each other. The prince touched his friend's shoulder and slowly ran his hand down his arm. Leaning into him he spoke while the other listened and smiled.

When Osip emerged from the stable, the prince took a step back and dropped his hand to his side. Radzitsky climbed into the carriage, followed by the prince.

I went to Sasha's door and stood there, hesitating. I knew I could not tell her what I'd just witnessed.

I heard her sniffling, quietly crying, and knocked.

She went silent.

"Sasha," I said as I opened the door.

Still wearing the costume from earlier, she was sitting on the edge of her bed looking distraught, her face red and damp. "What do you want, Vera?"

"What's wrong? What did Timofei say to you? What did he do?"

"Nothing. I just asked him not to leave and he left anyway."

"He's awful to you," I muttered.

"Why do you hate him so much, Vera?"

"Because he's cruel to you," I said incredulously.

"No," she said.

"Yes! You know he is! He missed your performance. Probably deliberately to hurt you. And he didn't apologize for that when he arrived at dinner. He behaved as if your performance meant nothing. It meant so much to you!"

She seized up slightly, recoiling at my words.

"Why do you tolerate his cruelty, Sashenka?"

"Because," she paused and breathed audibly. "Because he understands who I am."

"What do you mean when you say that?"

She blew her nose and folded the damp handkerchief on her lap.

"How can you say he understands you? You think he understands you better than I do?"

"Yes!" she cried and stood up. She ushered me from the room and started to close the door but I held it forcibly open.

"You're fooling yourself about the prince! So many men would treasure you, but he never will."

"Maybe that's the way it should be," she said and pushed the door hard, driving me back into the hallway as she closed it.

Chapter 13

The mild, black night looked into my room through the open window. I sat up against my pillows, wrestling with questions about my sister. She said enigmatic things about why she was drawn to the prince, but never explained them. I remembered the way the prince had run his hand down his friend's arm, with a tenderness I could not imagine him showing to Sasha.

In those few moments that I'd witnessed their intimacy, I'd felt an equal affection between both men, something understood. Who was Sasha really to him?

It hurt to think that she did not expect tenderness from a lover. Why did she choose mistreatment and humiliation? Why deliberately live in such pain?

The night air entered through the screen, stealthily and in soft rushes.

I gave up trying to understand my sister, and let my mind go back to Anton's interest in the drawing that Petya had done of me.

The single time I'd looked at the drawing, it had produced a shock. Though I could not see it clearly now in my memory, I could feel it, a confusion of danger and sensuality, an experience so heightened but full of such unsettling sadness, I had been unable to look a second time. Sometimes I remembered it as being beautiful, and yet it had hurt me.

I got up, lit a flame in my lamp and retrieved the drawing from where it was hidden in a dresser drawer, rolled up and wrapped in a mauve silk slip.

I unrolled it, and my heart began to quietly throb. I felt as if I was turning a corridor in a dream, coming upon a shadow figure of myself. Petya had admitted me into the textured, windy atmosphere of his inner life.

I was, in the drawing, as I had been when I stood half naked before him in the ballroom, but he had taken liberties. My hair was loose and blowing around me, not partially pinned up as it had been in the ballroom. My upper arms were at my sides, but my forearms lifted away from my body, palms open and facing up, as if offering some kind of supplication, the posture of a saint in an icon, a contradiction in my nakedness. There was the impression that I was moving forward, that I was trying in some way to step out of the confinement of the paper.

My skin was so palpably realized, nuance in every shadow, my mouth slightly open and my tongue and the edges of my teeth finely, patiently drawn. Deep shadows filled the dips at my collarbones. I imagined Petya bent over the page, the soft strokes of his pencil, and his finger smudging the shadows at my waist and under my breasts. I imagined him carefully, patiently drawing each nipple. Even the texture and folds of the dress were almost too finely done. Anyone would have been able to see that the rumpled fabric was velvet.

He had, in the drawing, pushed the dress down farther than it actually had been, exposing my belly and the curve from waist to hip. He had drawn this an hour or so before we made love, so he had not yet seen that part of my body. He'd drawn it as he imagined it. Any sexual feelings from adolescence that had been repressed or hidden, were set free and incarnated here.

My eyes in the drawing troubled me. The expression I could only describe as blighted desire, whereas in Yulia's eyes, he had seen intelligence and confidence. And she had not been drawn in shadow but in clear direct light. He had not labored over the texture of her skin, as he had in the drawing of me. Nor had he drawn the brooding atmosphere as he had in the drawing of me, but had left the background blank.

My mother's room was right next to mine, and through the wall I heard her hum the first measures of a song she used to sing to me when I was small.

My eyes dampened. I felt a deep sadness, which seemed to originate from my womb. I imagined my baby listening from her little ocean of water within.

The sound of my mother's voice gradually faded. She did this sometimes, woke in the middle of the night and started humming or singing something, usually repeating a single verse or incomplete phrases from a song, and I'd wake up as if receiving a visitation, a message of feeling, something lost and longed for. Then, abruptly, silence.

I remained still, waiting for her to sing again, but she didn't.

Music was powerful but so ephemeral. It dissolved except in memory, and in memory it was broken, incomplete, only phrases returned. The drawing was solid and in its own way, physical. The paper smelled like Petya. I held it against me. Petya's warmth, his fragrance and his breath, were all over the rough paper.

I imagined handing Anton the rolled up drawing, watching as he removed the slip from around it and unrolled it.

I imagined his silence as he looked at it, his eyes flashing to meet mine, then darting back to the image.

The drawing had left its gray silvery dust on my fingertips. And if Anton held it, if he unrolled it and touched it, it would leave the same gray, silvery dust on his.

I did not sleep all that night, one palm pressed low on my belly. My body glowed like a lamp in the dark room.

Chapter 14

The next morning, I gave extra care to my appearance. I put on a lace blouse and my favorite yellow silk skirt. I brushed my hair and left it long, tying a scarf, embellished with little amber beads, around the hairline as a kind of headband.

I left for Dr. Mitrofan's around eleven thirty. I had placed the three rolled-up drawings that I owned in a cloth bag. One was of Count Orloff the stallion, one of the linden tree. And the one of me.

I was not sure if or how the moment might come that I would show Anton the drawing of me. I would have to feel everything out. I vacillated between a thrill at the thought of it and the certainty that I would never show him, that it would remain hidden in my bag while he looked at the other two.

The doors were open again and Lika was snoring on a kitchen chair, her head back against the wall, her mouth open. Standing on a sideboard near her, a robust samovar exhaled wisps of steam.

The house was quiet. Anton and the doctor had probably not yet returned from fishing. I wandered up the hall looking into rooms, then climbed the stairs and knocked softly on doors, opening them and looking in. In one room I spotted Anton's shirt from the day before, draped over a chair. A large window overlooking the gardens was open and morning sunlight came spilling in. Everything in the room seemed to be stirring, from the white covers on the unmade bed, to an errant sheet of the *Evening Gazette* that rose up like a cobra with every new breeze, crackling and writhing, before collapsing again onto the rug. I stepped in and quietly closed the door.

On the nightstand I found a novel: *In the Land of Mantillas and Castanets* by Bezetsky. I sat down on the bed and opened it. Inside was an unsealed letter, the envelope not yet addressed. I resisted taking out the pages, but my curiosity was too great. The letter was not yet signed, clearly left unfinished. It was dated the night before, 11:45 p.m.

My dear brothers, it began. Much of the first long paragraph was about the area of the river that ran through Dr. Mitrofan's property. He mentioned a huge pike he had seen eyeing him from the shallows. *I am after him in the morning*, he wrote. *That grandfather's hour is about to come.*

In the next paragraph he described the neighboring acreage, *Volkhov*, as *the grand though dilapidated and doomed estate of a theatrical family*. My heart paused at the word *doomed.*

Once great orchards are sad, rundown now, and neglected, though everything that grows wild is thriving in the summer weather. Old trees of every kind, an Eden of sorts, only waiting for the apple to fall and the appearance of the serpent.

The matriarch, now dead, was the bombastic actress, Dashkova. She came through Taganrog in a Schiller play before any of us were born but left her reputation behind her, the worst kind of mannered actress, it is reported, with all the grace and sensitivity of an alligator.

The room went four shades darker.

Anton's character here was so at odds with his gentle, earnestly polite manner.

I thought of folding the letter and putting it back, afraid if I kept reading, he might fall further in my estimation. But I took a breath and continued.

The squire of Volkhov, Sergei Denisov, is reportedly a talented actor who hasn't worked in more than a decade. An overly sentimental man, so sincere I find myself suffering for him. When praising Anatoly Slezkine, who performed on their summer stage, he froze in a deep, spasmodic bow, bent so far forward I thought he might touch his forehead to the ground.

My heart raced with indignation and my throat tightened. But the sentence that followed was even worse.

He is a handsome figure of a man and I am told that he is quite the hound with the women and travels about living the life of a playboy.

I stared at the words and they smeared together on the paper.

I threw the letter onto the bed beside me and waited for my heart to slow down. When I picked it up again my eyes were drawn to the mention of my mother.

Sergei's wife is a mysterious soprano who lives like a hermit in some unknown area of the house and who I have heard vocalizing in the distance but have yet to glimpse. Her brother, who spent years in a Siberian prison camp, wanders the back acres in turn-of-the-century military regalia, carrying a rifle.

There are two delightful young women in that house, Sergei's daughter, Vera, and his stepdaughter, Sasha. Sasha is the older of the two, though it is difficult to say how old she is. I cannot quite describe the effect her beauty had upon me when I first saw her. I felt a painful though pleasant sadness, undefined as if in a dream. But she is not somehow at ease with her beauty and tries in strenuous ways to show it to effect, and I am afraid I find that tiring, as if she's attempting to use any man she engages with as a mirror to somehow see herself.

The younger girl, Vera, is quite different.

I watched Vera and Sasha perform a scene from Shakespeare on an outdoor stage. The breathtaking Sasha delivers her lines with adequate charm, but Vera is a genuine actress. There were a few moments as she stood there when I would have cast her as Joan of Arc having a vision, a radiance about her head. There were no false notes.

Any sense of wonder I may have felt over Anton's words about my performance was eclipsed by the sensation of nausea over everything else I'd read. Polite, gentle Anton had been judging us every moment. We were transparent to him and apparently ridiculous, and the worst was what he'd said about my father, which caused a hard, pulsating pain in my chest and stomach.

Through the large window I saw movement in the distance, Anton and Dr. Mitrofan returning with their fishing gear on a path between trees.

I skimmed the remainder of the letter to see if he had written anything of what I had shared with him about Petya, but there was no mention of him. The rest seemed to be focused on questions about his own family.

With a shaking hand I put the letter carefully back.

I intended to escape out the front door but as I was passing the kitchen I heard something shatter. I found Lika crying, standing before shards of a broken glass.

"Let me sweep that up for you, dear Lika," I said, and got the dustpan and broom. In a trembling voice she asked me if I would please put out the glasses for tea. So I swept up the rest of the glass and set the table. At this point, the samovar was steaming so hard it shook on the side board.

"Thank you, Vera Sergeyevna," Lika kept muttering, looking at me through wet, rheumy eyes. She smelled faintly of onions and stale urine.

Lika had been with the Mitrofans for decades and had a permanent room downstairs where she had been invited to stop working and stay on as a family member. Though her hands shook she insisted on continuing to work, and Anton had shared with me that since he'd been there Lika had dropped or broken something every day.

I disposed of the broken glass as Anton and the doctor took their boots off noisily on the porch. Anton appeared in the doorway smiling, his hair windblown, his skin pink from the sun, gleaming with sweat. He said my name and my face burned.

"Have you been in the sun too long, dear Vera," Dr. Mitrofan asked as he came in, "like the two of us have been?"

I touched my hot cheek.

Anton spotted something on the table. He picked up a tiny amber bead and handed it to me. "There must be a loose thread on your scarf. There's another one of these on your sleeve."

He started to reach for it and I withdrew my arm and shook it off.

I said I had a little bit of a headache and had to go home.

"Do you want a powder for it?" the doctor asked me.

"No, I have something at home."

Anton eyed the rolled-up drawings in my cloth bag and asked if I would wait for him to have a quick steam and change his clothes.

"You should both help Lika," I said. "She isn't feeling well."

When he turned his attention to Lika I went quickly out the door.

I was near the road when Anton called out to me. "I will come see you in an hour, Vera Sergeyevna."

I rushed, crossing awkwardly through the high grass of the shortcut, horrified that I might have shown Anton the drawing. I had imagined telling him the story of the drawing, how it had come about, bringing him further into the intimacy between Petya and me. I'd been willing to make myself vulnerable to him.

From a distance the house looked less solid. Closer up it looked eroded in places. Decrepit paint peeled on the banister up to the porch, the scuffed stairs unsteady and complaining. Going in through the main door, I noticed that the green and gold brocade curtains in the windows were faded and, in places, threadbare. The paint on the windowsill was cracked, a fragile cobweb quivering in one corner.

As I stepped into my aunt's study where she did the bookkeeping, a floorboard groaned under my foot. That floorboard had groaned for as long as I could remember, but at this moment, the sound of it alarmed me.

I heard it mentioned often, the orchard going to seed, but had deliberately not asked. I had not let myself think too much about what it might mean. Still, I had often felt, especially at that amorphous hour before daytime ended, an overarching atmosphere of uncertainty around Volkhov, a disquietude so palpable it produced a din.

And I had dreamt of deeply rooted trees rising from the earth, floating up into the sky. I had dreams of the house missing a wall or an area of roof, rain pouring into the dining room, the downstairs kitchen flooded in near darkness, old Aniuta treading the water, lit icon candles floating around her. Even when I wasn't dreaming, strange sensations woke me up at night, the feeling of things coming loose of each other, like the bed might collapse beneath me or the door disengage from the bolts that held it to the wall.

I had to have known but had managed to keep it all at bay because nothing could threaten Volkhov. Volkhov had to hold together.

But Anton had called the estate of my childhood *doomed*, and that word kept repeating in my mind, tolling hard like an iron bell.

I opened the ledger on the desk, large pages, each filled completely with numbers and notes in very small writing. I extracted from between two pages a wrinkled, slightly discolored map of the property that might have been more than a hundred years old. On it, areas of the estate were drawn in fading, brown ink, charting the location of the orchard, acres considered forest, acres considered meadow. Drawn in, too, and marked as such, were lines indicating the river and its tributaries, the main house, the summerhouse, annex houses, and the stables. Pencil marks that had been erased were still visible over areas of the map.

A square of bold ink, clearly recent, was drawn over an area of back acreage where Anton and I had been walking in search of the white deer.

I opened the ledger again to the most recently filled out pages, all crowded with calculations, scribbled and scratched out entries, and columns of numbers, but I could make little sense of any of it. I turned the pages back to years before where all the notes and calculations looked neater, more organized. There were notations about the yield each year from the orchard, profit made from peaches sold by the crate.

I leafed through an open envelope on the desk, thick with bills and receipts for fish and meat and all kinds of provisions, and for cases of champagne and crates of oysters.

"Vera!"

I jumped at the sound of my aunt's voice. She stood in the doorway looking at me with dismay.

"Aunt Marya, is everything all right with Volkhov?"

She came in, closing the door and lowered herself heavily into an upholstered chair facing in my direction. "No, it's not all right."

"Why have you allowed the peach orchard to become overgrown?"

She let out a heavy sigh and looked at the floor. "The world has changed so much. I am very glad for the emancipation, but it's no longer realistic to properly manage that orchard."

She told me that since Petya's father, Fyodor, had suffered an injury the year before, then eventually left the estate altogether, it had become impossible for her. Fyodor had been good at directing the laborers to graft and prune. He'd had a sharp eye and cared for the trees, and then when it was time, he'd organized the packing of the peaches in the hot house. "Taking care of an orchard is a massive amount of work." Each tree, she explained, had to be thought of individually. Each had to be constantly pruned and monitored against caterpillars and other infestations and watered extra when it was hot. And each tree could not be allowed to grow too high, every canopy had to be opened to allow for airflow and sunlight. Even if she could afford enough laborers to care for the entire orchard, she could not afford to hire someone to oversee.

"I would have to oversee everything and my heart is not in it. Pavel's heart certainly is not in it, nor your father's. It would, as with so many other responsibilities, be left to me. One must love the work and give oneself over to it completely and if one is not disposed to do that, it could drive a person mad."

"You say you can't afford to hire someone to oversee everything, but . . ."

She interrupted. "The money is not there, Vera."

"But Aunt, you are spending so lavishly on oysters and champagne and all the other food and labor to entertain so many for so long!" I picked up a receipt I'd just looked at. "A thousand rubles alone for oysters? And this is only one shipment."

She put her hand over her face as if to hide it from me, but lowered it after a moment, sighed, and looked at me with resignation.

"My mother left the house and the estate with all its debts and troubles to me. These past thirteen years since she died, any money she left me has been poured into the upkeep of the house and the orchard, and of course into the summer parties. She left the most money to your father and over the years he has been giving me money, and maybe things would have been all right another two years at least, but your father made an unsound theatrical investment and lost a great deal. Maybe I shouldn't be telling you this, but he won't tell you himself because he is having difficulty facing his mistake. He is insisting it will not affect Volkhov and that nothing will change. I could be angry with him for having been so reckless, but what is the point of that, Vera? It's done."

"When did you know about my father's loss?"

"A month or so ago."

"So why did you still have the summer party? So much expense!"

"People would have come. We would have had to turn them away."

"Yes, and why could you not have done that? Or, you had time, you could have written to people."

She winced and averted her eyes from mine.

"Why, Aunt Marya?"

"Tradition," she said, but still would not look at me.

"Tell me why, please, Aunt."

"My brother, your Uncle Pavel. The summer parties are important to him. He looks forward to them."

"It's not because of Uncle Pavel. What are you not telling me?"

It was the way she turned her head to the side, the softness and gravity that overcame her, that told me it had something to do with the priest.

"Father Ivan?"

She froze momentarily.

"Aunt, I know how you feel about him. You don't have to pretend."

"I could lose him, Vera." She paused then added, "If he is in any way mine to lose."

"Why? What do you mean?"

"He sees me and this estate as one. He believes that things here are well grounded and steady, and he compliments me on how well I run everything here. He teases me about the lavishness of what is offered at the parties but it is because it is all so pleasurable to him. When we speak privately he praises me and kisses my hand and tells me Volkhov is a sanctuary for him, that he misses Volkhov when he is not here in the colder months. He equates it with summer and leisure and happiness. I want to uphold the illusion that all is well, at least for the rest of the season."

I was dumbfounded. I had always admired my aunt for her practicality. I had always felt secure at Volkhov because of her. "It makes no sense, spending the last of the money on champagne and oysters and summer help because you think it pleases Father Ivan."

She sighed and rubbed her forehead.

"Aunt, are you hoping he will make a proposal?"

She blinked, then looked at me with wide, sad, hopeful eyes, but did not answer the question.

"If he sees the family as impoverished, I think he would be less drawn to me. I don't think he wants to come here and find sadness. He is always around sadness, the poverty-stricken, the ill, and the dying. The summer parties, the buffets, and the oysters, those are all part of what is between us. As long as I have the summer parties, he will feel that the world is steady."

"What about Volkhov?"

"We are going to have to sell parcels of the land. Dr. Mitrofan was right when he said that this estate and his own have changed. Nature on her own is slowly reducing everything. Wild ducks used to winter here. But the marshes and the ponds have dried up. The maestro was right, Vera, when he said that things are not meant to last forever."

"But, Aunt! Things could have been done differently!"

"Even if the orchard produced as much as it once did, that wouldn't save us. We have long accumulated debts, Vera."

A long silence held the air as I tried to absorb the shock of all of it.

"I didn't know the situation was so bad, Aunt."

"We have been juggling things for a while. You are the last one in this house to know this. You, out of all of us, don't want new things. You don't spend money. Your mind is elsewhere. You don't even travel to Kiev. You stay here and wear the same clothes. You don't notice because your mind seems always to be on something else. And you are always outside somewhere wandering the grounds."

Lying down on my bed, I cried. Volkhov as I'd always known it was doomed, as Anton had written, so perhaps it was also true what he'd written about my father. I had always believed that my mother banishing my father from their private rooms had been unfair and I still believed it. This revelation, true or false, did not change that. In some essential way that was difficult to describe, my mother had withdrawn her heart from me, too, and I did not know why. My father's behavior with other women, if what Anton said was true, could have been the result of my mother having closed him out. In the time he spent away from me, was he "wandering around, living the life of a playboy"? Did he arrive late all the time because he didn't want to part with his latest conquest? I fantasized about punishing him for this by refusing to see him, but the certainty of how hurt he would be made some of the anger fall away. And I needed my father, who, with his myriad failings, his absences which always hurt me, cared what I thought of him and had the most acutely tender feelings for me. I could not indulge a fantasy of punishing him without being stopped by the great reservoir of love for him that lived in me.

And, I reminded myself, he had so often invited me to Kiev to stay with him, but I had not gone. I had not wanted to be away where there would be no chance of running into Petya or seeing him from my bedroom window as he walked with Count Orloff.

And even if I wanted to leave now, I couldn't. I touched my tightening belly. Petya would come back. He had always been inseparable from the trees, the air, the light of Volkhov. He would come back, I told myself. He had to.

I curled up with my pillow and cried until I dozed off.

Part 2

"Better the illusion that exalts us, than ten thousand truths."
—Pushkin

Chapter 15

The smell of gardenias startled me awake. My mother was singing in her room, the first measures of *In the Grove Near the Danube*, something she had sung when I was little. Waves of bliss seized me, the notes long and pleading, and I experienced the sound of her voice with such intensity in those moments, as if she were traveling on the air through the wall and infusing herself with me. When I was little, this song had been my favorite, and she had said, affectionately, that I was an odd little girl to prefer such a sad piece to the other merrier ones.

No more than an hour could have passed since I lay down but it seemed dark. When my mother went quiet the smell of gardenias faded, replaced by another fragrance coming in through the screens: the promise of rain. I thought of Anton and the pressure of tears stung in my chest and throat. He was not who I had at first perceived him to be, but coarse, judgmental. The sweet young man I befriended had dissolved into the ether.

I stood up and went into the hall. One of the servants had lit the wall sconces early.

When I opened the door to my mother's room, Sasha was lying on the sofa, her left hand wrapped in damp linen. The smell of a pungent concoction of herbs sent a shock of unhappy nostalgia through me. Many years had passed since I had smelled that or had seen Sasha's hand wrapped this way. The two of them seemed to have reverted to an old, more elemental state, some strange magic they thought they were performing against the missing finger. I wondered if I was still on my bed, dreaming. Sasha looked unhappily at me as if I were intruding, her lips clamped tightly together, her white-blond hair spread out all over the red velvet pillow.

My mother stopped singing when I came in. She was sitting in the green wingback chair. On the small table near her was the box she kept her tinctures and medications in.

"Veroushka," she said in a soft voice full of hesitation.

The weather was warm but a fire was burning.

"Where is Prince Miranov?" I asked Sasha, remaining near the threshold.

She waited a moment before responding. "He left. He will be back, though, and I expect you to be nice to him."

I stepped further into the room. "I only said that Empress Anna was cruel. Which she was."

"You should have just let him tell the story. You didn't have to say anything."

"I could have said more, Sasha, but I held my tongue. Empress Anna did not die of apoplexy seeing her image in a mirror. She died of kidney stones."

Except for the crackling flames the room was silent.

I remained standing. I wanted to somehow make myself a part of their togetherness. I thought of bringing up what Aunt Marya had said about the slow demise of the estate, but felt silenced by the way the room shifted in the firelight.

As I took another step into the room, a branch in the fire fell loudly as if in protest, sending up a shower of sparks. My mother and sister looked at it with alarm. Their figures seemed to shimmer with impermanence. They knew things about impermanence that I didn't know and it struck me that there had always been something temporary about my mother's refuge in this room. It was like she was only taking shelter, waiting something out.

I wondered if they saw the old woman in the flames, shifting perpetually side to side like a crab.

My heart pounded. I wanted to demand their attention, accuse them of leaving me out. I could tell them about the baby and risk my sister's anger and disapproval. And how would my mother react? I imagined her retreating even further, to the point of disappearing.

Still, the urge to tell them was tearing at me. If I told them, all their attention would be on me, even if just for a while.

But I held back and in those moments of loneliness, while my mother and sister shimmered in the firelight, I touched the tightness of my belly and felt suddenly sure that my baby would be a girl. A blissful sadness overcame me. I could imagine her, my own daughter, a warm little creature I would hold close in my arms, whose forehead I would cover with soft kisses.

I put my arms around myself and closed my eyes. It was better that I not tell them. My baby's presence in my body was, for now, a miraculous secret. She and I belonged only to each other.

When I opened my eyes my mother was looking at me uneasily as if she could sense something. She began searching through the box of medications which she now held on her lap, sorting through packets of dried herbs.

"Rhodiola," Sasha said, referring to the herbs. "Or Eleuthero. Either would help me."

The two of them were engaged in something Siberian, and I was a foreigner here.

I left, closed the door, and stood in the hallway outside the room. I was right. My mother had stopped singing because of me and now that I was gone she sang again, a more vigorous song but one that rang with melancholy. My eyes filled with tears as I listened.

Footsteps approached from up the hall. Maxima Gabinskaya looked at me impassively as she opened the door to my mother's room without knocking. When she was inside and the door closed again, my mother continued singing. Why was Gabinskaya included when I was not? I remembered her throwing the yellow letter from Siberia onto the flames, all four of us mesmerized as it rose up, turning thin and black and breaking to ash.

It didn't rain. I watched the avenue of birch trees from an upstairs room. The dark clouds moved away and a mild sun appeared.

"Veroushka!" I heard my father down the hall, knocking on my door. "Veroushka?" he asked. I heard the door creak open and a few moments of silence before it creaked closed again. His footsteps came in the direction of the room I was in. I hid to the side of an armoire and heard him hesitate at the door before his footsteps retreated and he went downstairs.

I went to the window and watched for Anton, whom I also planned to evade, but I did not get the satisfaction because he didn't come.

That night I had trouble sleeping and spent the first hour of the five-hour darkness at my window listening to the crickets and the nightingales, chiding myself for having opened my heart to Anton.

New guests arrived and I could hear them in front of the house, laughing and talking with my father. When there was a lull in the conversation, my father began to lightly, distractedly sing: "*Now everything is gone. I am under the wedding crown . . .*"

"Sergei Mikailovich," a new guest said, "your brother, Pavel, brags that this house has twenty-three rooms, but you do not have a butler."

"Our dear old butler died four years ago and my sister has never replaced him."

"It makes sense," the man responded. "The world as it once was will be gone soon enough. I feel it like the ground slowly being pulled away. It is all disintegrating around us."

My heart pounded.

"Nonsense, my friend," my father laughed. "Nothing is disintegrating."

I slept and had a dream I was on a dark indoor stage lit by a single weak lantern. I was speaking the monologue into the darkness. I knew there were dozens of people listening, but I couldn't see them. I had the feeling again that I'd had on the outdoor stage, a feeling of complete absorption, of living in a state of beautiful intensity. Very quietly the roof and walls of the theatre dissolved and I was standing outside, under a vast night sky filled with stars. The audience was still there in the darkness, listening. I woke with my heart going fast, wishing the dream had not ended.

I got up and carried a lamp to the other side of the house where my grandmother's rooms were preserved.

I remembered her telling my aunt that she was plain and the chances of her ever marrying were not good. My aunt had not shown a strong reaction, but even as a small child I had felt that she was injured and I lashed out at my grandmother. I'd called her some kind of childish name and she'd started to cry, her wrinkled bosom heaving under diamonds. It made me unsteady, the power I had over her. She died a month later, and for years after I felt guilty for not having returned her affection. I found myself now, in spite of the terrible things I had heard about her and what I had witnessed myself, worrying that I had forfeited an opportunity to be loved.

I opened the massive double door, and in the penumbra before me, saw two long rows of costumes displayed on dress forms. Some of the feeling I'd had during the scene and in the dream, the heightened moments of life in a play, urgency made graceful, was thick in the dim air around the figures.

I stepped in and the massive doors closed with a soft boom behind me. The dress forms stood like an army of ghosts, many of them headless, some with faceless cloth heads. Some wore veils or wigs or hats on those faceless heads.

A few figures stood outside the lines in strategic places, as if enlisted as guards: Helen of Troy's purple and gold gown, Joan of Arc's armor, Hecuba's dark robes, and others from roles I didn't readily know. I started walking between them and held the lamp close to some of the more fragile constructions, with areas of fabric beginning to disintegrate. Others were enclosed in glass vitrines while others still wore loose tents of cheesecloth as protection, as if spiders had enmeshed them in webs.

The air smelled of stale potpourri and of something burnt and sulfurous, as if a match had just been lit and blown out. The redolence of dead flowers smelled like the past, faded and distant, more memory than smell, but that scorched and faintly sulfurous odor seemed alive, like a presence.

Once or twice I turned to look mistrustfully at one of the dresses as I passed it.

I saw one that had terrified me when I was small: a stiff, gray dress with ballooning leg-of-mutton sleeves displayed on a form with a bald, blank-faced head covered in cloth and stitched up the middle. It leaned slightly forward from the waist in what I, as a child, had perceived to be a threatening manner. It used to stand in the doorway outside my grandmother's room. I thought she'd said it was from an Ostrovsky play. I was sure that it used to move as I walked past it.

There were others, though, that captivated me, postured dramatically, with stuffed sleeves bent and formed as if gesturing or reaching out.

I entered the dim chamber of my grandmother's old bedroom with its dark red velvet walls, gilded wall sconces, curved Louis XIV furniture and vermillion brocade fainting couch.

The window was sealed shut behind a heavy curtain, the air close, odorous of stale flowers, dead for over a decade. Maybe she was still here. She had offered me a legacy that I'd refused.

I tried to think of excuses for her cruelty. Maybe as a small child I had misunderstood what she'd said to my aunt and the tone she'd taken with others. Maybe the young farrier who she had had sent to Siberia actually *had* tried to steal her jewels. But then I remembered Petya telling me what he'd heard about the Krasnoyarsk Saltworks where the young farrier had been sent and had escaped from after three years. He'd described haggard, wretched men, half starved, who spent twelve hours a day incarcerated in cramped and poorly ventilated cells, many of them rat infested, the other twelve hours bent in the low light of the fires and unbearably hot ovens, ribs shining on their bare torsos. The unclean conditions and stench of open sewage. Petya had described the dim towers and massive rusted machines with which men pumped water from below the earth's surface. Others, at deep wells, pulled up water in buckets. In the dim, overheated rooms, men tended to boiling brine, the air heavy with evaporation, while other men separated and sifted salt from large flat pans.

I held my lamp to her amber headboard.

Numerous insects, suspended in the clear brown gold appeared almost poised, spiders that looked like jellyfish, legs trailing beneath them. But there was also a spider with some of its legs broken away and a dragonfly with one wing detached and floating near its head.

With trepidation, I moved a small pillow and saw the delicate bird with the broken wing, something my grandmother had shown me because she thought I was going to like it.

"It's hurt," I'd said.

She smiled. "It's dead, Vera."

Heat had built in my stomach. "But it was hurt," I told her. "It still looks hurt."

"Creatures that small don't feel anything," she said and waved her hand dismissively. I was little but I knew she was wrong.

Every night my grandmother slept on her silk pillow with her head near a tiny bird, petrified in its suffering.

I had been right, I told myself. I had been right to turn away from her.

Walking slowly again through the procession of costumes on the way back, I tensed, feeling certain that one of them would lift a sleeve and touch me.

The maids said that this wing was haunted, that things moved inexplicably from one place to another. But my aunt told me that Uncle Pavel came in here sometimes alone in the middle of the night and moved things. I'd asked her if he did it to scare the maids and she'd said, no, that he did it to prove to himself that my grandmother was dead and no longer had any control over him.

"So Uncle Pavel is my grandmother's ghost," I'd said to my aunt offhandedly and this had, for some reason, horrified her.

As I closed the massive doors, I felt all the dresses watching me.

Early the next day I set off for the Zemstvo School in Ilyakin to help the teacher.

Chapter 16

When I got home, no one mentioned Anton. I thought of his enthusiastic promise to come the day before. I asked numerous people, but no one had seen him.

I was still upset by things he'd written, but there was silence around his absence like there was around Petya's and that made me feel an ache similar to what I felt waiting for Petya. I wanted release from the feeling. I wanted him to come as he'd said he would.

It was almost ten but there was still a streak of red light in the sky. Tired of waiting for a sign of Anton, I took a lamp with me to look for Proskovia. I found her sitting in the upholstered chair on the hill. She offered me bread and cheese wrapped in a handkerchief, but I said I wasn't hungry so she nibbled on it herself, then tossed each dog a small wedge of cheese.

The air was particularly sweet, soft breezes stirring from the leaves. Dog violets burned like blue embers in the shadows beneath bushes.

"Do you sit out here all night in complete darkness?" I asked her.

"The moon!" she said, surprised by the question. "It's been very bright the past few nights. The flame in your lamp will barely compare to the light of the moon."

I put the lamp down in the grass and sat.

"Have you ever met someone and felt sure that you understood them," I asked her, "and then discovered that there was something else to them? Something you never would have suspected?"

"Oh, yes. No one is simple. We can never really know another person, can we? I listened once to a lecture by Madame Krylovskaya. Do you know who I am speaking of?"

"She has followers among the guests here," I said.

"Oh yes, I believe that. She is a spiritual guide with great authority. She believes that we don't completely know ourselves either, because we are afraid of silence. It was a few years back when I heard her, before I came to live with dear Maxima, who offered me freedom and shelter from the world on her estate. I had very little money. I still don't, but it doesn't matter anymore. It was a hot day and the doors of the auditorium had been left open. I snuck in the back. Madame Krylovskaya had one simple instruction against all forms of suffering: to pay attention to silence. In silence, she said, is everything. It is a very enigmatic thing to say, and I still do not know what it means. She said that the most sacred hours in the cycle of the day are the hours before dawn. Since I am awake anyhow, I try in those hours not to think about the past and not to think about the tedium of the day to come, but to listen to the silence. When one is alone one can hear the silence better. It is still difficult, though. I distract myself constantly."

"Why did you come here with Maxima?"

"The cards told me to come. They said there was something for me here. Perhaps it was simply for the pleasure of meeting you, dear girl."

"Do you spend every night outside?" I asked.

"Sometimes, if it rains or if I'm not feeling well I will stay inside. Otherwise I prefer to be outside. The sky is my ceiling and the trees are my shelter. Look how they arch over us so tenderly."

"I feel that way, too, Proskovia. I am at home with these trees. To lose them feels unimaginable. Maybe these here with us now will survive. I hope so. But in the back acres, trees will be cut down."

"That is a tragedy."

"Volkhov is heaven on earth."

I lay down on my side, leaning on one hand and elbow, and gazed up at the coming darkness broken by moonlit clouds. "I once heard a guest say that Madame Krylovskaya had a theory that the living have ghosts. She said that these people were stuck in the past as if in amber, unable to move beyond it."

"Ah, yes," Proskovia said vaguely.

"This guest that I overheard talking said she believed my mother was stuck in such an afterlife."

Proskovia became noticeably silent.

"Do you think that is true, Proskovia?"

"It's possible," she said.

"Why does Maxima bring the gun with her when she visits Volkhov?"

"She often has her gun with her."

"Maxima must have said something to you about my mother."

Proskovia looked up thoughtfully at the sky. "What I do know is vague, dear girl, and I cannot betray Maxima's trust. She is my generous friend, a friend who offers me a peaceful life. She has rescued me from poverty and uncertainty."

"Do you live alone with Maxima on her estate?"

"Oh no. There are three other women living there, too, and four serving women who are treated very, very well. There are no men there. It doesn't matter to Maxima if you have money or not. She is as rich as Croesus. It is an ideal world at Maxima's. Everyone lives in luxury. Everyone eats beautiful food and sleeps in silk bedding and we can choose between privacy or community on any given day."

"How wonderful."

"It is a shame all of Volkhov's marshland has dried up. There is still marshland on Maxima's property, filled with water lilies. Maxima's property is a haven for water lilies."

"They must be beautiful," I said.

"Yes, they are. They say water lilies were once girls who jumped into the water to save themselves from men in pursuit."

"Why aren't men allowed at Maxima's?"

"We are a society of women who reject men."

"But why? There are kind men."

"Yes, there are," she said wistfully.

"My father is a kind man. He never did anything bad to my mother."

"I know from Maxima that your father was always kind to your mother."

"And he is not a philanderer."

"As far as I know he is not."

"Why did she make him move from their rooms?"

"That is not completely clear, at least not to me."

The sky had grown dark and a bright three-quarter moon peered down at us. The trees were wide awake, nocturnal presences in the wind, their leaves shivering intensely, the branches all leaning in one direction before shifting to another. Back and forth slowly they moved as if in a state of rapture, the leaves a chorus of dry-throated voices, going quiet at moments before rushing again at an exultant pitch.

I went back and forth in myself wanting to open up to her, to share everything. I blew out the lamp and its weak circle of yellow brightness dissolved.

"It is late, dear. Are you not needing to get home to your bed?"

"No one will notice, Proskovia."

Sadness filled the air between us.

"Do you miss Petya Fyodorovich?" she asked. Her gentle face was illuminated by the blue white of the moon. "He has been eclipsed, has he not, my dear?"

"Anton said he would come yesterday, and I don't think he did. And he didn't come again today."

"Ah."

"I am still in love with Petya. I always will be, but right now I am thinking of Anton. I am so fickle."

"No! You are resilient, blessedly so, like any young person."

Kingfisher lay at Proskovia's feet, gazing at me, dewy eyed as a fawn. The branches waved slowly, shifting directions in the wind and Feokta lifted his head, sniffing at the air.

"I have told you before that Petya is stuck in my heart like a splinter. But when I think of Anton, I feel the pain of that splinter. They are so different in so many ways, and yet they have confused themselves in my mind. They both hurt me."

"How has Anton hurt you, dear child?"

"I want to tell you, Proskovia, but I will have to admit to something I did that I'm not proud of."

"You can say anything to me, little Veroushka. I live in the half light. I am like a moth on a lampshade, just a shadow."

And so I told her that I had read his letter and about the tone of it and things it said that had shocked me. "I don't know that I'll ever think of him the same way as I did before. In my mind now, his face looks different."

She watched the shadowy branches as they shifted, leaning and bowing.

"What does Anton actually know about your father? He clearly heard that from an unreliable source."

"Those were the hardest words to read, but he also said things about my grandmother. I had difficulty with her, but reading his awful words about her made me angry."

"She is yours to criticize. Not his." She shook her head. "But you are right. None of this sounds like the Anton whose company we enjoyed a few days ago." She made a soft sound. "Each person has many sides. I am someone different when I am with Maxima than I am when I am with you. It does not mean that the Anton you know is not also real."

"Yes, but he feels elusive to me now. I don't quite know him."

"I understand," she said. "Perhaps you don't. Perhaps few people do."

After a thoughtful pause, she asked, "Have you ever noticed that much of the time we can only see parts of the moon? It is often mostly or partly shadow. Sometimes it is almost completely dark. Perhaps we are each like the moon in some way. We find a face that suits us with certain people. The rest we protect or keep hidden. Perhaps it's so startling to find this out about dear Anton, because the face he has shown us is so charming."

This made me smile.

"It is all unsettling, but it doesn't sound like there's anything unforgivable in what he wrote."

I felt a kind of union with her as we gazed mesmerized by the graceful movements of the trees. The wind nudged and brushed against me. It lifted my hair so strands caressed my face and neck, as if urging me, palpably, to tell her I was carrying a child.

From an earlier conversation, I knew the answer to the question I was about to ask, but I wanted to hear her say it again. "What is your strongest wish, Proskovia?"

"To be mother to a daughter, as I told you once."

"Why?" I asked, hoping the conversation would lead naturally into my sharing my secret.

"A daughter would anchor me to the earth."

A slow elation filled me at these words.

"As you probably can see," she went on, "I am not anchored to the earth. You see how restless I am. Perhaps when I find my daughter I will sleep like a normal person. Until then, I will stay awake as much as I can. Because I live in a constant state of waiting for her."

My heart paused a moment, and then went quickly. The subtle tone of desperation that had come into her voice caused me to change my mind about telling her. I was overtaken by a fear, perhaps irrational, that she would want to mother my daughter. Proskovia spent too much time aching for a daughter of her own. But this was my child.

For a while neither of us spoke as we listened to the trees, glorying in the wind.

My mind went back to Anton's written words about my performance.

"Before you met Maxima did you live an itinerant life?"

"Yes."

"Anton mentioned me in that letter to his brothers. He said that I am a natural actress. In a way that unsettles me."

"Why, Vera?"

"An actress is a kind of itinerant, don't you think? Moving from one role to another."

"Yes, I see what you mean."

"I don't want anything to happen to Volkhov. It will be like the world coming to an end."

I shared with her what my aunt had told me and started to cry. Proskovia leaned forward in her chair and opened her arms for me. I got to my knees and embraced her. "*Sssshhh cchhh ssshhh*," she whispered softly as she ran a gentle hand through my hair. My eyes grew heavy.

When I yawned, she took a shawl out of her carpet bag, got up, and covered me with it. When she sat down again she reached deeper into her bag, dug out a small music box, and began to wind it. It went its rounds working a soothing magic over me, and Feokta let out a deep sigh, lay his head down, and closed his eyes. The melody had a familiar ring and she told me that it was from an old Baltic song called "The Seven Swans," based on a fairytale. "When you rescued Petya Fyodorovich from a life of toil, I thought of the girl, Ludmilla, in this story. You are so much like her." As she told me the tale, which she said illustrated the power of silence, I was no longer able to keep my eyes fully open. Somehow all I would remember of the story was that a selfless girl had to rescue her seven brothers who had been enchanted and turned into swans, but I must have been asleep when she said how the girl had managed it. I would remember something about self-enforced muteness, and something about stinging nettles shredding the skin on her fingertips as she sewed. I came close to consciousness several times when the music slowed to a sputter followed by the tightened grinding as the box was wound and the notes began again at a quickened pace.

I woke fully when Proskovia exclaimed, “Oh look! So few hours of darkness tonight! Dawn is beginning. I’ve missed the silence through my own fault. Talking on and on, or filling the quiet with the tinkling of a music box. I will never understand myself.”

Chapter 17

It was still so early, the sun hardly risen, as I left Proskovia and headed toward the house. It was an hour when the air smelled green and sweet and slightly damp and no one but servants would have been awake. Sometimes in the spring or early fall when there were no guests on the property I used to come down in my nightgown at this hour and stand barefoot on the porch stairs where Petya would see me as he walked by. Usually he'd smile or lift a hand to wave, but there were times when he was far away in his mind, and he'd look shaken when he saw me. I had remained willing to disobey the rules that separated us, but Petya had not. After that day when we were fifteen, when we'd run off together and seen the dead bird, he observed a formality with me. He became elusive.

I was about to cross the avenue of birch trees when I saw a distracted-looking Anton coming from a distance, the first morning light igniting a nimbus of red around his hair. He didn't see me watching him from between two trees. A flood of feelings rose from a depth within me. I thought of calling out but hesitated. I was too fresh from slumber and too confused, my hair uncombed and tangled, my clothes wrinkled from sleeping in the grass.

I kept hidden, planning to continue on my way home once he passed. He focused on the ground as he walked, his brow fraught, clearly preoccupied with something that upset him. On a sudden impulse I stepped into his field of vision and called out his name.

We walked toward each other.

"Are you here to look for the white deer?" I asked.

"I didn't think you . . . I didn't think anyone would be up this early."

I ran a hand through my hair, pushing it back from my face. "Proskovia told me a story late last night and I fell asleep in the grass."

He looked at me expressionlessly. I sensed a coolness, a shadow of judgment and felt a flux of discomfort in his presence.

"You said you were coming, several days back," I said.

He reached into his shirt pocket, took out a tiny piece of folded paper, and proceeded to unfold it. He stepped closer to me and showed me that inside was an amber bead. "One like the ones you were liberally shedding a few days ago."

"Yes?"

"I found it in the envelope of a letter I was writing to my brothers."

My heart deafened me for a few moments. "The book it was in looked interesting to me and . . ."

"And so you decided to read my letter, too."

I winced.

He looked sternly beyond me, took a deep breath, and let it go.

"I'm sorry," I uttered.

"Once I got over my surprise . . . and my anger, I had to consider what you read. I am always flippant in tone when I write to members of my family, particularly my brothers. They are coarse and enjoy irreverent remarks. Any . . . unflattering sketches of your family were merely rough shots at entertaining the reader."

My heart raced. "I doubt my father would invite me so often to stay with him in Kiev or to move there, if he was living the life of a playboy," I said with quiet indignation.

"As I said, a rough shot at entertaining my crude brothers. You were never meant to see that and you wouldn't have if you had not trespassed that way. I haven't quite gotten over my shock that you would do something like that."

A fresh wave of shame washed over me.

"Was that what you were thinking about just now before you saw me?"

He narrowed his eyes momentarily as if trying to recall. "No. No, why?"

"You looked upset."

He nodded slightly. "I was thinking of something else."

I sighed, part relief, part humiliation and a tear trickled over my cheek. "I'm sorry about the letter."

He reached into his breast pocket and handed me a pressed and folded handkerchief.

I wiped away the tear. I worried that he wanted to go and hoping to delay him I held onto the handkerchief dabbing my eyes with it. "For days I thought I lost your friendship."

He was silent.

"Have I lost your friendship, Anton?"

"I was upset with you for reading my letter. And I wanted to study."

"You should have come and shouted at me. You shouldn't have stayed away."

I handed him the handkerchief reluctantly.

He started walking again slowly and I stayed where I was, resigned to the fact that he wanted to go. But he turned around. "Do you want to come with me to look for the white deer?"

I said I would and asked him if he would walk with me to the house first so I could change my clothes.

He nodded and we started slowly in that direction.

He asked me if his was the first letter not meant for my eyes that I'd ever read and I told him that I had grown up in a house where no one ever told me anything. "Maybe it's a reflex that I've never learned to suppress."

A jaunt came into his step and he smiled. "I suppose if the envelope had been sealed, you would have steamed it open over the samovar or some such method."

I laughed, relieved by the smile and the shift in his tone. "Of course I would not have done that!"

"I fully intend now, for as long as I am within a few versts of you, to keep all private correspondence on my person."

I restrained my smile but my face grew hot. "My sister and mother keep secrets."

"You felt I was keeping a secret from you?"

"No, with you I did it out of curiosity."

He looked at me sidelong, a faint smile on his lips.

I told him that after reading his letter, I looked at my aunt's bookkeeping. Anton had heard her say to Prince Miranov that someone was caring for the orchard, but she said it, I explained, because she was ashamed that the money that could be used to hire people to prune the trees and to smoke out the pests was being poured into this summer party.

"She has plans to portion off the land and sell it so dachas can be built on it. I am trying still to take in the fact that parts of Volkhov are doomed to fall under the axe. Apparently I am the last to know how bad the situation is."

"I'm sorry I wrote that," he said.

"It is always better to know the truth, Anton."

He smiled. "No matter what devious way you come by it?"

I pretended not to notice when his hand inadvertently touched mine, sending a shock of warm excitement rushing up to my heart.

He said he'd wait for me near the fountain, taking a piece of paper from his pants pocket, unfolding and refolding it into what looked like a paper boat.

I went upstairs, changed my clothes, combed my hair, and put the drawings of Count Orloff and the linden tree into my cloth bag. I hesitated about bringing the drawing of me, but decided to bring it, telling myself I didn't have to show it to him, though a part of me still imagined I might dare to.

Sasha's door was ajar and her bed was made. She was rarely up at this hour.

I peeked into my mother's rooms. No one was in the front room and no fire was lit. I went further in and looked into the bedroom. My mother and Sasha were sound asleep together, each curled up on her side, facing the other, like mirror images, a thin rumpled sheet covering them both, their pale hair spread out and intermixed over the pillows.

I went up close and looked at them. They breathed slowly and in sync as if they were having the same dream.

I touched my mother's arm. "Mama," I said softly. "Maminka."

She barely stirred. They were so deep together in slumber, as if they had vacated the room, even the house, and gone together to another place only the two of them knew about.

I left quietly, ran down the stairs to the kitchen, and put my arms around old Aniuta, clinging to her small, frail figure. When I let her go, her pale blue eyes, set into her soft, wrinkled face, swam with dampness and light.

She gave me some bread with cheese, two small cakes, and a bottle of water to take with us.

I found Anton sitting sideways on the marble edge of the fountain, looking serious as he watched the little paper boat trembling on the water.

I knew he was thinking of Kolya.

He unrolled the drawings, one at a time, admiring each one quietly. He didn't comment on them. He saw the third drawing in my cloth bag but did not ask for it and I did not offer it.

We'd been walking half an hour or so, looking for the white deer, when Anton said that he could still see Count Orloff and the linden tree in his mind's eye. "Petya's drawings are remarkable."

"I know. I know," I said wistfully.

I told him that before Petya had left for the apprenticeship, he had promised that when he was back in six months he would come and visit me. But after he was back on the estate for three days he still hadn't taken the initiative to come see me. I had to seek him out. "Instead of bringing us together, Anton, the apprenticeship put more distance between us."

The sound of rushing water grew louder as we walked in the direction of the river. I told Anton about seeing Yulia, the blacksmith's daughter, touch Petya's hair. "He had done a drawing of her. I saw it in the summerhouse where he was helping with the construction."

I described how I'd lured Petya into the ballroom and we'd danced.

"I told him to draw me." I didn't look at Anton as I described lowering the straps of my dress.

Just as I'd said this we heard a female voice and followed the sound of it around a stand of Russian olive trees.

Two ladies who had arrived the night before leaned on the rail of the little footbridge, looking fretfully down at the river. Osip, who had taken off his shoes, stood with his chest puffed out, unbuttoning his shirt. He threw it to the ground and dove into the water. Instead of the woman's handbag, which when I asked, she said had slipped from her hand, he came up spitting water, squeezing his eyes shut, and holding something in the air, a waterlogged ermine hat wrapped in river grass.

"That's probably been down there for a decade," Anton laughed.

Osip had to go under again and seemed to be down there a long time before splashing to the surface, gasping and shaking his head. He had found the cloth bag but everything had fallen out of it.

"Do you see how Osip's hair is now," I whispered to Anton, "plastered to his head? Even when it's dry it always looks like he just broke the surface of a lake."

"Then we should call him the Sea Lion of Volkhov."

"Ha! Yes. And he is always the one called upon to fetch things that fall into water."

Osip dove down again and as we stood there waiting to see what he would bring up now, Anton asked me, "If you were a white deer, where on this estate would you go?"

"We saw it," one of the women said. "Half an hour ago."

"Yes," the other woman said. "Up that way. It was far away but it looked at us then it was gone."

Anton asked for precise directions but the paths were winding from there to the back acreage and she could only point in a general direction.

I led Anton to a little pathway I had not been on for years, our eyes raking the surroundings. We walked awhile in silence, listening to the rustling of birds and other movements in the leaves.

"You were telling me about asking Petya to draw you," he said.

My heart pounded.

"Please tell me."

I described what had happened, how Petya had left the ballroom and how, when I saw him go to the stable, I went in after him. I looked at Anton meaningfully. "I asked to see the drawing. I knew he had done it because the dust of the pencil was on his fingertips and it hadn't been earlier in the ballroom. But he behaved as if he had not done the drawing. I touched his hair the way I had seen Yulia do it. And I kissed him. Then something happened between us." I held Anton's eyes and quickly looked away. A significant silence hung on the air. It seemed clear he knew what I was not saying.

I told him that it snowed that night and Petya left Volkhov in a sled.

"I found the drawing the next day in the summerhouse where he'd been working."

"So now you've told me your secret."

"Well, not quite everything."

He looked at me expectantly.

"I am carrying a child." I'd said the words with surprising ease.

A muscle in his lower lip flickered almost undetectably.

I told Anton how we'd talked that night in the stable about marriage, that I'd said that once Petya found work as a draughtsman I felt strongly that I could convince my father to approve.

"Petya didn't say anything, but he kissed my hands, and I took that as him saying yes. But since that night I keep thinking about how he'd been forbidden to even see me for so many years. And how his father tried to terrify him out of any feelings he had for me. I don't think Petya believed it was possible."

"When will you tell your family?"

"A time will come when they'll see it for themselves, but right now, I have decided not to think of that. It is summer. Volkhov has not yet been divided and sold. And you are still here, my dear Antosha Chekhonte."

He looked at me with feeling but I could see that he was stunned.

"Life is as it should be for now," I said, but my voice shook and the statement sounded more like a question.

He glanced again at the third drawing accompanying the other two in my cloth bag. But he did not ask to see it.

Anton followed my lead as we walked. Each time I looked at him, he appeared pensive, his focus far away. I worried that I might regret having told him. I had told no one else, knowing that I would only make everything more painful for myself, but I had told Anton so effortlessly, and now I worried that I should have held back.

Once when I turned to look at him he was gazing in a different direction but then turned and met my eyes. I looked at him with an expression I knew pleaded for reassurance. He seemed to recognize this and offered me a sympathetic smile. It was clear from his eyes that he had been thinking about it and had accepted it. He reached over to me and touched my shoulder and the tension in my chest melted. After that, even the green trees we walked among seemed to offer me solace.

When the sun was high above we found a place on a hill at a high incline with a wide vista before it, a willow at the summit providing shade. We ate, then stretched out and leaned back on our elbows watching a parade of clouds, white embankments, some built to majestic heights, traveling gradually across the light blue sky.

"What do you think, Vera?" he asked after a long silence. "Little Vanya or little Katya."

"Little Katya. I am sure she is a girl."

"She may surprise you and be a he."

"No, this is a girl. She inhabits me the way I inhabited my mother."

He turned and looked at me. "You don't remember that, Vera!"

"I do remember. I dream about it."

"Maybe you imagine you remember."

"No, Anton. I remember."

"Mystical Vera, who remembers when she was invisible."

We were quiet for a while watching the clouds.

"Maybe an hour ago," he said, "those same clouds were drifting over Siberia."

I described to him how when I was a child, a letter in a yellow envelope arrived from Siberia, a letter that changed my mother and made her distant. "I mark a change in my life from the arrival of that letter. I overheard my mother whisper to her friend, Maxima Gabinskaya, that it was a letter from the dead."

Not long after the arrival of that letter, I heard a conversation from my bedroom window on a summer night, an antagonistic conversation that involved three or four guests walking past. I was not even certain who they were. In the midst of voices contradicting each other, one phrase stood out: *the separation of birth*. Maybe those words had not actually been said, but that was what I heard. I told Anton that while I would never understand what was being argued, those words floated up above the conversation, articulating something mysteriously sad, telling me something about what my life would be like now. Someone else said the word *catastrophe*.

"I asked my tutor the next day what a *catastrophe* was and she told me it was a disaster, something that caused damage.

"On occasion, ghosts of those voices still awaken me on summer nights."

Anton quietly repeated the words: *separation of birth*.

"My mother's Siberian story haunts her. Sasha is part of that story. But I was born here, so she thinks of me as separate from that time in her life. That must be what it is. My father and I have no part of her Siberian story. But I want to tell my mother that she has always carried the premonition of me with her. I am still part of her, and have always been inseparable from her, and because of that, I too lived in Siberia. But it feels like an impossible thing to say."

We watched a new front of clouds moving slowly, transforming before us.

"You know, there are three of us here today," Anton said. "Me, you, and little Katya." He reached for my hand and held it.

The words had power over me.

"All this time, since you and I first met, she's been with us," I said.

"And so has Petya," he added.

"Well, then there are four of us."

He brought my hand to his mouth and kissed it.

"There are stories where time stops," Anton said out of nowhere.

"Or where one season can last a hundred years," I added.

"I have read that if ever time would stop it would be in summer, that in some ways summer is outside of time," Anton said.

"Do you remember what Anya Leonideyvna said about the downstage monologue? That it stopped time. Maybe the sun this summer is that downstage limelight."

He smiled at me. "We can dream."

"Let time stop with you never leaving for Moscow and Volkhov never bending under the blows of the axe."

"And what of little Katya?"

"She will never suffer the catastrophe of separation."

After Anton left, I looked up as I was returning to the house and saw my mother at a third-floor window looking out, focused on something or someone she saw. She had an overview, while my own perspective on the ground was limited and blocked by a front of trees. She moved her head, and seeing me, dropped the curtain. I walked in the direction she had been looking, passing through the trees. In a partial clearing Uncle Boris was standing, eyes trained on the window where my mother had been. When he saw me, he looked down at the grass.

"Uncle," I said. "Uncle, can I speak with you?"

He turned and walked away.

Chapter 18

In the afternoon, Anton and I went to the house to eat. I felt a twinge of guilt as I surveyed the buffet: a roast goose with apple stuffing, a marzipan pyramid studded with colored fruit, and little square blue and pink cakes that looked like lacquered boxes. I couldn't help but think that the luxurious food was purchased with money that should have been used to save Volkhov. But I was hungry. I served myself a slice of roast goose.

The large conservatory dining area was empty but the glass doors were open onto a garden where a group of guests sat talking. We paid only cursory attention to their conversation as we ate, something about bad investments. I rolled my eyes and Anton smiled.

After we finished our lunch, we went back to the buffet for dessert. I took half a pear in madeira, and Anton took two slices of fruit halvah covered with cherry syrup.

The conversation outside had shifted to a more interesting topic. In half-hushed voices they spoke about the disreputable behavior of a certain woman, a guest. At first it was not clear who they were talking about but when there was mention of a scandalously low-cut dress,

I guessed it was Lilia Petrovna. One woman mentioned an affair Petrovna had had with a man at a spa outside Yekaterinberg, and right under the nose of his spouse.

Anton and I could see the gathering through the open door if we leaned our heads at a certain extreme angle. It was Anya Leonideyvna, Victor Victorovitch, and Tolskaya, an actress who wore bright colors and had a manner I found abrasive. There was another woman there who I didn't know, older and thin, wearing a crisp, pale green silk dress.

"We talk about Petrovna as if she was the only one involved. The man at the spa took part in this, too. Men are rarely compromised when they indulge in such trysts," this older woman said, "and rarely consider what it will cost the woman."

We were sure they were oblivious that we were listening. I gave Anton a conspiratorial smile.

"We aren't scandalized by his behavior, but we are by hers," the thin, older woman went on.

"True," Anya Leonideyvna said. "Men pay less of a price for such behavior. It is expected of them. They are the cruder sex."

Various stories were exchanged in which women who had committed transgressions ended up suffering in one way or the other. I avoided Anton's eyes when a pregnancy was mentioned.

"Men consider women they have trysts with their conquests," Anya Leonideyvna added. "Why would any woman allow herself to be considered simply a conquest? To be so lowered?"

I wondered if Anton thought that I might be Petya's conquest. A warm flood of embarrassment filled me. I considered trying to explain to Anton that I had initiated the encounter with Petya, but the outspoken actress, Tolskaya, saved me by playing the devil's advocate and saying something outrageous. "Madame, have you ever heard the cry of a man in the throes of sexual climax? He sounds like the one who has been conquered. The French do not call it *la petite mort* for nothing. The woman has conquered him. That sad and terrible cry comes out of a death agony."

Anton smiled as he looked down at his dish of halvah. I felt the urge to laugh.

Anya Leonideyvna made a huffing sound as if appalled. "The troubadours had superior ideas about romance. It is so much more interesting between people if they do not give in to their animal natures."

Victor Victorovich emitted a short, atrophied laugh. "My animal nature is my finer nature."

"No it is not, Victor Victorovich!" Anya Leonideyvna retorted. "I have seen your animal nature in your eyes. It is disgusting, maybe even more so than most men's."

Anton wrinkled his forehead, half-smiling, half-scowling in disbelief.

"I see. I see," we could hear Victor Victorovich mumble.

"You are too English, Anya Leonideyvna," the woman in pale green said. Perhaps she pitied the befuddled Victor Victorovich. "We Russians are more like the French."

"You think we are a nation of libertines!" Anya Leonideyvna balked.

"No, but we are not like the English," the woman in pale green chimed in.

In the mix of argument, Petrovna's pursuit of the priest was mentioned.

"Father Ivan is a widower and that makes him fair game," Tolskaya said.

"I'm stunned by what I'm hearing!" Anya Leonideyvna said.

"Having a lover does not destroy a man's reputation," Tolskaya added. "It should not destroy a woman's."

More adversarial words were exchanged and soon the group dispersed.

As we left the house I quietly told Anton that I did not like hearing that Lilia Petrovna seemed set on pursuing Father Ivan. "He and my aunt have a special closeness. I think they are moving toward an understanding."

"I noticed how Petrovna spoke to him at the meal we all shared but I cannot recall him showing any interest in her," Anton said.

We turned onto a path in front of the house and found ourselves walking a little behind Sasha with two of her paramours, each of their profiles visible as they addressed her.

The shorter, more muscular man, whose hand seemed to cup the air beneath Sasha's right elbow, spoke intently to her. "Alexandra Iunosheva, my friend, Georgiy, and I are engaged in a heated discussion about the viability of scientific research. My own position is that what is called modern science is just a newer form of alchemy. Nature is as elusive to us now as she was in the Middle Ages."

"And I disagree with my dear friend, Dmitri," the taller, more casual-mannered one said, smiling widely as he leaned closer to Sasha. "I feel that modern scientific research is just beginning. One day, dear Sasha Ilyevna, all the secrets of nature will be revealed."

The shorter, wide-shouldered man spoke again, looking stern in his convictions, saying that man was not intended to master nature. "My position, and I suspect you will agree with me, dear Alexandra Iunosheva, is that mystery is necessary to the survival of the human soul."

"I maintain," Georgiy, the tall one said, challenging his friend, "that science is no threat to poetry and certain mysteries. But it will cast light," he said with great enthusiasm, "so mankind will no longer live in the Dark Ages." He breathed audibly, almost giddy with the idea, and looked at her with expectation. "And war will no longer be necessary!" On what appeared to be a sudden bold impulse, he grasped Sasha's left hand. She pulled fiercely back from him and they all stopped in their tracks.

She seemed in her expression to be feigning indignation, but I recognized it as a mask for a deeper upset. She had suffered a momentary loss of control. That hand, she always made sure, was never touched. And I knew she was already barely holding herself together. Whatever had happened with Prince Miranov had unbalanced and upset her. Her indulgence of these two young men had been, I believed, her attempt at distracting herself until his return.

The tall one muttered profuse apologies, bowing his head. She broke from them and walked quickly back to the house, leaving them conferring in quiet voices.

As we were taking a pathway away from the house to continue our search, Anton asked me if I understood what had just happened.

"My sister . . . is very self-conscious because she is missing a finger on her left hand."

He was quiet a moment.

"The strange thing is, that the missing finger is related to Siberia somehow."

"But there wasn't an accident in Siberia, was there?"

"No, she was born without the finger."

"How then could it be about Siberia?"

"I don't know. It is something I am excluded from. Her hand seems to represent something to her and my mother. Please never let her know that I have told. It tortures her."

"Of course I won't tell her. But I confess, I already knew about her finger. Remember that Dr. Mitrofan has cared for her since she was small, and you since you were born."

"But that is private!" I said.

He smiled, clearly thinking of my breach of his privacy.

I looked away. "Dr. Mitrofan knows how much she suffers over it."

"We weren't talking about your sister, per se, but about nature and the human body. That is when he mentioned Sasha and her missing finger and said something I would keep thinking about. He said that it was as if nature was trying to compensate for Sasha's otherwise perfect beauty with that small deformity."

I would never have described to Anton the very light blond hair on Sasha's hand, and the strange aspect it had in its nakedness, that it was smaller than the other hand and had less mobility. Talking about this would have been too much of a disloyalty. To say she was missing a finger felt almost mundane. But the other details were more personal and sadder somehow.

It had all happened so quickly, so the tall young man had likely not had time to feel the odd stiffness of the gloved hand, its lack of dexterity and atrophied gracelessness. He might not have encountered the deadness of the stuffed finger sleeve. But maybe he had.

I wondered how much Dr. Mitrofan had described Sasha's hand to Anton.

"So how could Sasha's hand be related to Siberia?" he asked.

"I'm not sure. It's as if it involves some kind of painful legacy that she and my mother share. I can't explain it any better than that."

Sasha had always been a cipher. She had told me often that she disliked men, but she flirted shamelessly with them. She encouraged proposals and had had several, but in the end she always broke them off.

"I think she likes conquering men. Once they are her devotees, she finds them tiresome."

"Maybe that is why she likes the terrible prince. She cannot conquer him. So she is not bored."

"You are likely correct about that, Anton."

After a pensive silence, Anton said again that he wondered how Sasha's missing finger might be related to Siberia.

"I wish I knew." I described to him how when I was small, back when I had been part of everything and we were a trio, my mother often told Sasha and me about the Holy City of the Children of the White Czar, a place of safety. She imagined her mother waiting for her there in a swan-shaped sled.

I told Anton about the arrival of the yellow letter and how I was closed out after that. "Things between my mother and sister became more intense and sad. For a while my sister was angry and I don't know why.

"She is still impatient with our mother, but closer to her somehow. It's something awful, whatever they share."

We stopped when we reached a hill with a steep incline and a great vista of sky before it. With our legs stretched before us we leaned back on our elbows and watched as a front of reddish cirrus clouds passed very slowly. Anton said they looked like flames in the wind.

I told him about the old woman in the flames who, if you focused, you could see treading in a burning fire. "She's one of the Siberian elementals. I've seen my mother throw little pieces of bread into the fire for her. And you have to be very careful with the flames. If you want to stir the fire with a poker you must do it gently and respectfully. If you are not kind to her, she will not be kind to you."

"What will she do?"

"I don't know." I smiled. "I suppose instead of keeping you warm, she might burn you.

"And there is the Vorsa, a monster that rushes through the forest, causing the trees to bend." I told Anton how our mother used to point out the Vorsa on windy nights, as the three of us stared from the dark of her balcony, out toward the birch trees across the park.

Up until around the time my father moved out of the rooms they'd always shared, my mother had lit a green glass lamp every night and placed it near the window, so that her mother, who had died in Siberia, would always know where she was.

"And I saw her mother's spirit once in a violet dress, just a glimpse of her through the birch trees."

"For you, Vera, there's so much mythology connected to Siberia. It is not the Siberia I think about."

Anton gazed a while at the clouds as if lost in thought, then turned to me. "You've made me so curious. What could the secret be between your mother and sister? The Siberian secret."

"I have tried for years to find out."

He nodded then looked back at the clouds. "Do you believe in the old woman in the fire?"

I hesitated. A part of me wanted to say no, but I thought of how carefully and softly I always stirred the embers, always afraid to hurt the old woman. To say I did not believe in the old woman would have been like separating myself even more from my mother. In a soft, adamant voice I answered, "Yes. I have seen her."

He raised his eyebrows and looked away.

"Why do you pretend that you think such things are ridiculous, Anton?"

He narrowed his focus on me. "Not *ridiculous*," he sighed, taking issue with the word.

"You carry a little talisman of the white deer. You are spending long hours in search of her. You believe in magic, Anton."

"Not *magic*," he said.

"What do you call it then?"

"How many opportunities does a person have to see a white deer?"

"But you said that seeing her was a sign, an invitation to leave an old life for a new one."

"Yes, I did say that."

"Why is that not magic?"

"Maybe it is, Vera. Maybe I am a hypocrite."

We lay against the hill about two feet apart in silence. Anton reached for my hand and held it, as we watched the slow drifting and transformations of the clouds.

Chapter 19

Anton sent a note that he would be joining Dr. Mitrofan on his rounds. For the three days he did not come, the weather was dark and overcast, soft rumbles from the clouds. Afternoons were blurred by rain. Guests filled the front rooms with laughter or arguments. Some played cards or chess under the patio awning. A few went outside with umbrellas, but there was no croquet or catching butterflies.

I looked at old books of poetry in my father's library, or took naps. I went downstairs when I heard Gabinskaya playing the piano, Mozart's Fantasia in C MINOR, something she'd played repeatedly the previous summer before Petya had gone to Sevastapol. I sat on a stair in the hallway outside the empty ballroom, leaning my head and shoulder against the wall and closing my eyes as I listened. The music flooded me with memories of Petya, which kept giving way to thoughts of Anton.

On the third day Anton arrived at around seven p.m., and we went to the buffet and ate pate and oysters. We each drank a glass and a half of Rhine wine and shared a champagne glass full of red wine sherbet. He was quiet while we ate, but every time I looked at him he was focused on me, his eyes lit with what I could only read as affection.

"I missed you," he said.

We wandered together into a shady narrow pathway through olive trees. He picked a small yellow flower and put it in my hair.

We laughed as I studded his beard with tiny purple asters. Giddy and a little drunk, we walked for only about half an hour before going back to the hill where we'd rested the last time he'd come.

We leaned back on our elbows and looked at the vista. It was after nine and the sky was still lit but the first hint of nighttime was in the air, banks of dark reddish clouds hiding the sun.

"The last few days away from you," Anton said with a half-smile, "I kept thinking about what we'd said, that there are four of us when we are together, not two."

"Yes. It's too easy to say someone is not present just because you cannot see them," I said, and his smile deepened.

"You may detect a fleeting fragrance or a rush of heat!" Anton said dramatically. "A shadow might loom over you a moment."

I laughed.

"When we talk about little Katya, my dear little stepdaughter," he said, "I imagine a tiny girl in a white dress and white kerchief holding your hand as you walk together in a garden. I imagine little Katya with black hair like yours."

"She will have very pink cheeks and will smile when she is only two weeks old."

"Everyone who sees her," Anton said, "will weep with happiness."

"And you will sing to her, Anton!"

"Yes, I will always be here. I will never leave Volkhov and I will sing to my little stepdaughter always, starting now." He leaned over my belly and sang in a slow, quiet voice: *Bayu-bayushki-bayu.*

Then he embraced me, his heart beating near mine. Very easily, as if it had been a casual hug, he moved back from me.

After a silence, he said, "My dear Desdemona, I see there is a third drawing in your bag."

I nodded.

"Is it the drawing you said you would never show me?"

My heart skipped and began to race. "Yes."

"You said you only looked at it once."

"I looked at it again. I think it shows a truth about me, but perhaps not a beautiful truth."

"I am very curious what you mean by that."

I reached into the bag, slowly brought it out, and handed it to him. As he unrolled it I turned and lay on my side on the inclining hill, facing away from him.

A nightingale alighted on the grass a yard or so away from me. Looking in my direction, it began to sing, the song ending in a lilt as if it was asking me a question.

I heard the sound of the rough paper being rolled again. I turned and faced Anton. He placed one hand gently over my hand and grazed my inner wrist softly with his fingertips. A quiet explosion of feeling took me, a pleasure so consuming I closed my eyes.

After a few moments he withdrew his hand. I opened my eyes to see the nightingale noiselessly ascending, vanishing. I could feel the memory of Anton's touch burning on my skin. Sunflowers standing near us in the evening sun gave off a dark and musky fragrance, as if they were sweating. I reached for Anton's arm and he pulled me softly toward him.

It was almost strange how hot his skin was. But more interesting than the heat was the vibration, something subtle yet dynamic, like bees buzzing steadily and quietly under his skin.

As we kissed, a long sustained moment full of pleasure and something like hypnosis, some of the tiny purple asters fell from his beard, which had a silken feeling on my lips.

He broke from me, smiling, rolled onto his back and closed his eyes, and I lay my face against his chest. My heart jolted with empathy and affection as I listened to his lungs working, creaking like the opening and closing of a door on an arcane cabinet. His body was telling me something that Anton himself could not hear, his lungs working as if on hinges. He turned on his side and faced me again, and we shared a slow, extended kiss, while quail cried in the distant orchards.

I wondered if the seeds of illness that the doctor had diagnosed were being passed from Anton's mouth to mine. Would it make me part of him somehow? Would I carry something of him with me when he left, a shadow of him always mine? I felt a kind of greed for that shadow, for that part of Anton that he resisted and denied.

"I am only little Katya's stepfather," he whispered, his mouth close to my ear, as if he had to remind me and himself. "In this foursome, my dear Desdemona, I am only number four."

We lay with our arms around each other, and soon the caresses intensified between us. The fabric of the dress I wore heated and softened with pleasure, becoming as sensitive as if it were my skin. As we held back from amorous congress, the grass beneath us, the garments that kept us chaste, shuddered with sensation.

The sky had grown darker.

We brushed the grass and leaves from our clothes and our hair, then walked, keeping our separate counsel, and on the air between us, sadness and desire kept shifting places, like key changes in a piece of music.

When we reached the avenue of birch trees, we stood facing each other.

"It's summer, Anton. Time is supposed to stand still."

I went near enough to him to rest my face lightly on the breast of his shirt, and just as gingerly, he rested his warm palms on the wing bones of my back. And the feeling was there again, like a swarm of bees calmly but steadily buzzing under his skin, as if an excess of life force was challenging his illness, eclipsing it, but with too much vivacity, threatening to burn out too soon.

A lone nightingale cried out from the bright nocturnal orchard.

Chapter 20

Around half past ten the next night, the sky almost dark, Anton and I headed toward the hill where the fireworks were going to be.

On a path flanked by olive trees and wild bracken, we ran into a despondent Proskovia, the dogs walking behind her, their dark, melancholy eyes seeming to appeal to us for answers.

"Oh! My children!" she said. "All day I have been pursued by the scent of violets! And the sensation that I have missed my chance. That I am always missing it."

"What do you mean, dear lady?" Anton asked gently.

"The violets are the daughter I have never met. They pursue me. She is all around me, do you understand? Yet I cannot see her."

"Come with us to see the fireworks, Proskovia!" I said, touching her forearm.

"Oh no, no," she said definitively. "Too many people are spiritually restless. I cannot be around it. I am like a sponge, without defenses. I will only give my time to children like both of you."

"I wish you weren't sad, dear Proskovia!" I said.

"I am tuned to the sense of my daughter like an animal is tuned to the earth. She is there yet she eludes me! It is as if she has been torn from my womb. That is how much I feel her. She too is wandering in a kind of twilight, lost as I am and perhaps in search of me." She closed her eyes and leaned her forehead on her hand, then looked up again suddenly and cried out, "This scent of violets!"

"Should we stay with you, Proskovia?" Anton asked. "We do not have to see the fireworks."

"No! You are children. You must see the fireworks!" she said. "Besides, Aphrodite is still presiding tonight over Volkhov!" Proskovia pointed up vaguely at the sky then walked away, the dogs following dolefully after.

We'd only been walking a few minutes more when we heard noise and saw branches shaking in a dark thicket of trees ahead. Anton squeezed my hand. We were certain we were about to see the white deer light up the dim pathway.

After further rustling of branches, a human figure emerged, Lilia Petrovna holding her white velvet hat, her hair unpinned and hanging down her back, covered with bits of leaf and twig. A louder commotion and the breaking of branches heralded Father Ivan who came forth half bent as he wrestled with the bushes, holding his ministerial hat against his chest with one arm. He stood on the pathway, his long black robe rumpled and spotted with torn blossoms.

We had already stepped back, camouflaging ourselves behind a clump of bushes. I stood open-mouthed, looking at Anton, one hand on my chest. They spoke to each other under their breath in soft conspiratorial whispers, then headed quickly along the pathway.

"My poor Aunt Marya."

"Proskovia was right about Aphrodite presiding over Volkhov tonight," Anton said.

We continued along and heard a woman crying. We searched for the source of the sound, looking through various pathways between trees, but could not find it. Soon it trailed away.

"Drama and trysts in the dark forest," Anton said quietly. "It's like *A Midsummer Night's Dream.*"

"My poor aunt!" I said again.

We could hear voices and see lamplight as we came to the hill where everyone was gathering. A few lamps hung on branches. Some people stood while others had spread out blankets and sat on the grassy incline. I looked for Aunt Marya but didn't see her.

Nickander walked past us, carrying a drunken guest in the direction of the house.

Anton and I found a place to sit on the hill and my father wandered up to us, squatted down, and showed Anton his pin of the Russian Greater Coat of Arms, which had been presented to him by Czar Alexander II. He angled it so that it caught the light from a swaying lamp behind us. "The sweet liberator, the emancipator of the serfs, was moved to tears by my portrayal of *Hamlet.*"

"Such an honor," Anton said with feeling and my father's eyes filled with tears. I guessed he was a little drunk.

"It seems to me, Anton Pavlovich, the play should not take place in Denmark but in the oblast of Poliakov. Hamlet is Ukrainian by his very nature, wondering whether to go on living."

"Papa!" I cried softly.

"I am only talking, dear one. But like so many of us, Anton, Hamlet bewails his sensitive nature! I received such acclaim in the role," he said, a dampness gleaming on his eyes. "Such acclaim as I will never again receive."

"Oh, Papa!" I squeezed his forearm. "Stop!"

I was not sure he knew about Aunt Marya's feelings for Father Ivan. If he had not been tipsy, I might have explained the situation to him and told him what I'd seen. Trying to contain my distress, I kept scanning the area for Aunt Marya.

A few yards away, I saw Sasha, flanked by her two suitors who both followed her lead in everything. If she stood, they stood. If she sat on the grass, they sat on the grass. She moved her forearm and right hand gracefully as she spoke, even as she hid her left gloved hand much of the time behind her, though it made the occasional choreographed gesture so as not to draw attention by being too absent. While the shorter, muscular man kept talking, the tall young man was quiet, as if still chastised from the incident days before. He looked both wounded and lovelorn as he watched Sasha from beneath his brow. I wondered if he had some sense of her secret, and was moved that a woman who presented herself as perfection itself had a malformed hand. Did this endear her to him? He seemed mysteriously closer to her, in the way that I had imagined Anton was closer to me for having found me crying in the doctor's consulting room. He was handsome, although awkward and perhaps too sincere for Sasha. Still, I found myself hoping that something deeper might develop between them and she would take her heart away from the prince.

Lifting her head on her long neck she postured so that they might regard her. She kept them enchanted. Now and then she turned and looked at Anton and me, but mostly she scanned the periphery. Was she expecting Prince Miranov or only hopeful that he might appear?

"Do you know, Anton," my father said, "what a wonderful girl our Vera is? She is the kindest girl, so filled with compassion. She once saw a prisoner being carted to Siberia on the road to Eliade-Luria, and it changed her. She wept for this man and worried for him. She thought of him constantly, this kind girl."

"She *is* very kind," Anton said.

"I am happy you realize it. I find, dear Anton, that most people pay little attention to the suffering of another, and few people revere kindness as they should. My little pinwheel," my father said, then kissed my forehead three times. "I am giving you a crown of kisses!"

"Stop it, Papasha," I said softly.

"Vera helped one of our servants, a talented young man, to a position where he learned a trade, and that young man is now working in the north for an ecclesiastical iconographer."

My heart stopped. "Working in the north?" I asked.

"I keep forgetting to mention it to you. Petya came to see me in Kiev months back. I gave him a letter of introduction to a man I know, Mr. Radish Kiriak, who has a business near Petersburg that employs draughtsmen. Mr. Kiriak was very impressed with Petya's drawings, particularly those of icons."

My heart galloped hard, an ache of pressure building in my temples. Phantom smells of wood smoke and hay came to me, smells that always conjured Petya.

"And Vera, Radish Kiriak wrote to me to express his gratitude for the introduction and told me that Petya just got married."

The words, like a thunderclap, momentarily deafened me.

"He married the blacksmith's daughter from Korablin. After he found work he left Kiev for Korablin and married her and they went north."

Nickander, who would have known this, had not told me. I always suspected he knew about my feelings for Petya, and perhaps Petya had confided in him. He had likely been afraid to hurt me.

I had helped Petya away from me. He was married and lived in the real world, while little Katya and I did not.

My father, oblivious and a little drunk, struggled to his feet and regarded the sky. A succession of fireworks went up with soft explosions, white and pale pink starbursts expanding across the panorama, before disintegrating, falling in lit crumbs to the earth. He moved off to talk to Father Ivan who was sitting under the low branches of a mulberry at the top of the hill with Lilia Petrovna.

I sensed Anton sharply aware of the effect of my father's news on me.

"Desdemona Denisova," he said softly.

In what felt like an attempt to console me, he got to his knees from a sitting position and came closer. He reached for my hand and held it a moment before I extracted it. "Please, Anton, don't!"

He retreated, sitting back where he had been but a little farther away. I turned my back to him and faced out into the blackness in tears.

Pink light burst in the sky, a giant flower expanding and breaking slowly apart, dissolving as bits of light fell to the earth.

We sat in silence through the rest of the fanfare and then stood when the fireworks were over. People began to disperse, many of them carrying lamps. When I turned, Anton was gone.

My father, holding a lamp, approached me.

"Where is Anton?"

"He left," I said.

I linked arms with my father, who sang distractedly, "*Now everything is gone. I am under the wedding crown . . .*"

A melancholy warble sounded from a clump of tall bushes and we stopped a moment.

"That is a bittern," my father said sadly. "The bittern is a bird that is always alone. No other bittern ever answers its call."

"Papa, you are being dramatic. That can't be true."

"It is true," he said. "And no one ever sees the bittern."

"It doesn't even sound like a bird," I said, "but some sad person hiding in the trees."

A soft rumble resounded in the sky.

"It is funny you say that, Veroushka. When I was a boy, a woman was often heard crying in the trees on the property. My brother, sister, and I used to go out looking for her, but never found her. It remained always a mystery, the woman in the trees. Now I think it was only a bittern crying. Magic leaves when childhood ends."

I was too despondent to tell him that Anton and I had heard crying earlier but no one seemed to be there.

The sky rumbled again and a light rain began to fall. Any stragglers from the fireworks ran past us. Osip appeared behind us on the road offering my father an umbrella, then turned, as the rain came down harder, and ran in the direction of the house.

My father and I headed back together, huddling under the umbrella as the rain intensified, showering down hard. I thought of Anton getting soaked and of his infirm lungs.

My father sang again in that light, far-away voice, "*Now everything is gone. I am under the wedding crown . . .*"

Tears rose to my eyes.

Maybe it was the song, or my father's gentle, magnanimous presence that made me need to confess, "Something has made me very unhappy, Papa."

We stopped walking and he faced me, the rain battering the umbrella we took refuge beneath. "Why, Vera. Why?" he pleaded quietly.

"I am afraid to tell you why."

"You must tell me," he urged in a high-pitched breathy voice, his brow furrowed with concern. "I cannot have this. I cannot have you unhappy."

"If I do tell you, Papa, will you promise not to judge me? Will you promise to love me as much as you do now?"

"I will not judge you," he said as if I should know better than to ask such a thing. "And of course I will love you and help you if you need me to." He had grown less careful of sheltering the lamp beneath the umbrella, and rain rushed down over the glass that protected the flame, quivering shadows breaking up the glow.

"I would not burden you with this, Papa, but it is unbearable."

"Tell me. Oh, my dearest girl. You can share anything with me."

I told him how when I had tried to organize the apprenticeship I had believed it would be in Kiev, and I had planned on going there, too. "I imagined you taking Petya and me to dinner and for carriage rides."

"I will take *you* for dinner and carriage rides."

"No, it's not that . . ."

Another rumble sounded in the sky. The rain now splashed hard around our shoes, my hems and his cuffs getting soaked.

I breathed the damp air fragrant with rain and hesitated.

"I fell in love with someone. I kept it secret a long time."

"With whom, my girl?" he asked sweetly.

Again I hesitated but the thought of finding some relief, of getting comfort from him, won over my fear. "With Petya Fyodorovich."

He peered into my face. "Oh, Vera!"

"I arranged all of those things about the apprenticeship because I wanted him to have dignified work so we could eventually marry. He didn't even know what my plans were. I felt sure that he had not forgotten me, that he would come back, because he knew as much as I did that we were meant for each other, or I thought he did. I thought I understood him. When you said he was married, I realized that there is no hope. My heart is destroyed."

"Vera. Vera," he said quietly in disbelief. "Those feelings will go. Trust me. Such feelings go away!"

"You are not listening to me, Papa."

"This is a childhood infatuation. You fell in love with him because there are so few prospects around you."

"No! That is not why I fell in love with him."

"Petya is a handsome young man, Vera, but he was born a servant."

"He has a dignified place in the world now."

Even in the lamplight I could see that the color had drained from my father's face. In the silence I became aware that the rain had stopped. We heard that strange-sounding bird again. He handed me the lamp, turned away, and closed the umbrella, shaking it out.

"You agree with Father Ivan when he talks about the atrocious treatment of servants, but you think they are lesser beings. Maybe you are no better than your brother, Pavel."

"No."

"Yes. You do not feel that Petya deserves love."

"Of course he deserves love, and he has love."

"My love, Papa."

He was silent, shaking his head.

"You care more about your own pleasures than anything else."

He reared his head back, clearly stung by my words.

"I have heard things," I said. For a few moments I would not look at him, struggling to hold back tears. When I did look at him again he was staring down at the lamplight reflected in a puddle.

"I am sorry I said that. I should not judge you for anything, Papa. Do not judge me."

"I blame myself," he said, his eyes damp.

"Why? You are not understanding."

He held the collapsed umbrella away from us, and embraced me with his free arm. I gave myself to the embrace, too unhappy not to try and take comfort from it.

I knew I could not tell him about little Katya.

"I do not want to be alone now, Papa."

"You will not be," he said.

He had tea sent up. As we spent the next two hours in his study playing cards, I kept breaking into a sweat, nausea coming and going in waves.

I went to my bed but did not sleep. At moments when it felt too hard to accept, I let myself believe that my father was mistaken, that Petya had not married Yulia and that his return was still imminent. But the reality would set in. It was as if Petya had been the vital organ that had kept my blood circulating. I felt a light cramping in my belly as if other organs were struggling to take over the work of that phantom organ. Everything hurt. Everything felt strange and wrong.

After two hours of trying to sleep, I got up. I was sweating and felt weak. Looking out my window I saw a sudden powerful rainstorm driving guests rushing toward the house from around the estate. I got dressed and sat on the landing at the head of the stairs, unseen by some, ignored by others. Some people remained on the porch waiting it out, while others crowded the main rooms of the house. When I heard the faint echoes of a piano, a sad piece of music being so beautifully played, I knew it could only be Maxima Gabinskaya. I followed the music down the staircase to the lower floor and sat in the dim hallway outside the ballroom, listening. The falling rain, audible through the window, added to the spell of the music. Gabinskaya played slowly and with great expression. Her playing was exquisite, like nature herself, atmospheric as the sky, by turns bright or shadowy. The door was mostly closed, open only a crack. I could have looked in but didn't want to. I saw Gabinskaya in my mind's eye, a masculine figure all in black, a gold watch hanging on a chain at her chest pocket. In public her expression was harsh, closed. When passing her outside or on a stairway in the house she carried herself imperiously and did not make eye contact, a stiff figure, inseparable from the long gun she clutched. But when she played music she became an entirely different creature, her arms and neck, her upper body pliable, mobile. I had learned not to watch her as she played because she did so as if in a trance, head bowed low and slowly swaying. Sometimes her head went so low as she played that her lips brushed against the backs of her hands. *Strange. Gabinskaya was strange.* But when I did not watch her, when I did not see the weird way she applied her hands to the keys, her whole body distorting with the task, or her gun leaning against the side of the piano, the music was so generous, so tenderly beautiful, it made life feel like an expansive dream. I closed my eyes and saw the drawing of the linden tree and felt myself moving slow motion through its gray, windy shadows.

The piano went quiet. A jolt shot through my body as my mother began to sing. I had hoped she was upstairs and I could go on listening to Gabinskaya's solo piano. I sat forward with my eyes closed, trembling all over.

My impulse was to get up and run to a different part of the house, but something held me there. The note was from a high octave, the vibrato uneven. She sang with uncertainty, her skills so raw and unpracticed compared to Gabinskaya's artistry. Why would such an artist collaborate with a woman who could not always get the notes right? She clearly felt an intense affection for my mother. I found myself in the grip of wonder over this. She indulged her in music and stood guard over her. I surrendered to staying and listening to the tremulous, childlike voice and saw, in my mind, my mother before Siberia, the girl who had lived on the edge of the Black Sea, a girl with a sun-faded parasol and a goat named Dunya that opened the gate with its teeth. A girl I could hardly bear to imagine, who would go on to suffer such terrible loss.

Overcome with love, I covered my face with my hands.

Cramps, low in my belly, became painful. When I stood, a heavy flux of dampness soaked me between the legs. I made my way to Aniuta's kitchen and told her I was bleeding.

Part 3

"My dreams and I have grown apart . . ."
—Pushkin

Chapter 21

For three days and nights I kept to my bed, attended by Aniuta, who climbed the two flights to and from her downstairs kitchen, bringing broth or black currant tea. My aunt and Sasha had asked me questions and conferred with each other, diagnosing a particularly heavy menstrual flow, one that made me feverish and nauseous. Aunt Marya wanted to get Dr. Mitrofan, but Sasha had been against it.

"What would he know about such a thing?" Sasha asked.

"He's a doctor, Sasha!" my aunt replied.

"But he's not a woman. Vera doesn't need a man poking at her unnecessarily. She's had difficult red days before, as I have, and I'm sure you have, too."

They asked me if I wanted the doctor and I shook my head no, and that settled it.

Aniuta brought me an Icon of the Three Hands and placed it on my nightstand, a little candle lit in front of it, the Holy Mother holding the sacred infant with three arms instead of only two.

And Sasha brought me her old snow globe, something I had coveted as a child but she had always been possessive of. Her Siberian cousin had gifted it to her when she was still very small. Inside was the small figure of a girl in a sled, one of her hands missing, broken off at the wrist. When I saw Sasha standing near my bed holding it, I tried to rise but my head swam, so I dropped back down onto my pillow. Sasha shook the globe and set it on my nightstand. I gazed at it, my heart beating quickly as the snow swirled.

When I was eleven or twelve, I told Petya about the snow globe. The fact that it had traveled with my mother and Sasha from deep in Siberia gave it an aura of danger. I told him that it was not like a snow globe from this side of the Ural Mountains. The water inside was not clear, but slightly dark. "All water in Siberia is darker," he'd said. He had wanted to see it. I hid it under my jacket and brought it outside to show him. Whenever he'd misbehaved as a child, his father had told him he'd end up in Siberia, a place of unrelenting suffering, and regaled him with stories of the Salt Works and the Silver Mines.

We'd sat huddled close and hidden beneath the mulberry tree, examining it. Condensation frosted areas inside of the glass, air having somehow gotten in. The water appeared amber as Petya held it up in the overcast daylight. He shook it and we watched the little figure's severed hand, which must have been hidden under the false snowflakes resting at the bottom, swirling wildly among them.

I had always been careful not to ask Sasha how the hand had broken off, as if it was somehow a question about her own hand.

The presence of the snow globe in my sickroom conjured Petya and made me feel even more deeply the sharp edge of loss, of him and of his daughter, my little Katya.

I believed that old Aniuta knew that I was suffering from more than my woman's malady. My deep, at times convulsive weeping, which I gave way to only when I was alone with her, must have made her certain.

Over the years, Aniuta had been the one person who seemed aware of the depth of my feelings for Petya. She was the one witness to how often I sat in a corner of her kitchen, looking at Petya's drawings. She loved him and had always been protective of him, so I wept openly in front of her. She was not a person for words, and when I was with her, I didn't use words either. She sensed the nature of things, the nuance of my grief. I believed as she gazed at me, small teardrops visible in the depths of her misty eyes, she could feel the loss of little Katya. Like Anton, she could imagine her. As she stroked my damp hair back from my face, humming quietly under her breath, I grasped one of her soft wrinkled hands and held it to my cheek, breathing in its smell of candle wax and lemon balm.

On the third night, still weak but feeling better, I went to Sasha's room and asked if I could keep her company. She looked softly at me, inviting me in, her room dim except for a lamp on her vanity. Her tender manner, which I knew was partly because of my weakened condition, made me want to share everything with her, but I knew it wasn't possible. I was too afraid she'd explode with disapproval.

Maybe it was the slight shadow at the corner of her left eye, or a certain hesitation when she looked at me, but I knew something was preoccupying her. My feeling was that it was about the prince.

I lay on my side on her bed, and though it was a warm night, Sasha spread a lambswool fleece over me, then sat before the mirror and brushed her hair.

There was a peaceful feeling in Sasha's room in the low lamplight, a silver sheen on the pale green brocade wallpaper, the curtains and bedspread darker green and etched with leaves and delicate flowers.

I closed my eyes and drifted off. I awakened to see that she had put down her brush and was sitting now on the side of the bed, her upper body twisting in my direction, holding a letter on blue paper.

"It's from Timofei," she said in a muted voice. She looked at me uncertainly as if considering something.

"Is he coming back?"

"Yes." She looked at the letter.

"Do you want me to read it?" I asked.

For a moment she seemed not to see me, though her eyes were set on me. But then she shook her head and folded it.

"It's not important . . ." As she said these words, energy drained from her voice. She looked down at the folded letter on her lap, then got up and took it to her vanity. She put the folded blue page in a drawer, sat down, then picked up her brush again. I could see that she was looking at me in the mirror. Her eyes unsettled me.

I remembered her asking for my impressions of the prince after the first time I'd met him, and my forthrightness, telling her I did not trust him. I recalled feeling that she'd respected what I'd said, though she'd gone on to have a relationship with him, as if she'd been courting unhappiness. I had the feeling now that she wanted to hear again what I might say. She seemed to be in some kind of quandary over him, torn between the desire to share it with me and the desire to leave it unspoken between us.

"I don't like Timofei's friend, Oleg," she said suddenly, her eyes in the mirror again set on mine. "He was never a cartographer, and he isn't really a surveyor of land. He made that up. His family rose out of serfdom. He pretends to be something he isn't. He's just a businessman."

"Is that letter you were going to show me about Oleg Radzitsky?" I asked.

"What? No, no. It's not." She looked down. "I just don't like him."

It had struck me before that the prince's interest in Sasha was mixed up with his desire to acquire areas of Volkhov. He had brought Oleg Radzitsky with him to Volkhov the second time he had come here. And after that I had seen Radzitsky roaming the back acres. My heart was beating hard. I had, since the disclosures from Aunt Marya, tried to turn away from the truth of our fate, and I wanted to do the same now. Everything hurt too much.

After a long silence I turned onto my other side and from that new position could see the framed picture with the cracked glass where Sasha kept it on a shelf. Even through the web of cracks, enough was visible of each figure in the tableau.

I surveyed the photograph as I had many times as a child when I'd been drawn to the peaceful depiction of my young mother, who was probably no more than twenty-one at the time, standing next to the tall gaunt-cheeked elder, bearded and with long grayish hair, the husband who looked like he could be her grandfather. He held my infant sister in his arms. As a child I had not questioned the oddness of the picture. Maybe it was the loss I'd suffered and the days of fever and weeping, but I felt a kind of clairvoyance when I looked at it now. That picture was not separate from everything Sasha held in silence in this room. And the secret itself was getting tired of staying hidden. It would not hold much longer.

I had asked Sasha in the past why she had knocked the picture off the wall and why she still displayed it broken rather than put it in a new frame, but she would never explain. I had a feeling if I asked her about it now she might tell me the answer. But at this moment, I was afraid to hear it. The pain in my womb was still too fresh and I could not listen to a story of suffering. And I knew it would be about suffering.

In a way I knew the story already. I had lived and breathed it all my life. I felt the chaos of it in my nerves. It lived facelessly in my body.

I could hear the strokes of the brush in Sasha's hair, a dry, repetitive, comforting sound.

I closed my eyes.

The next day Prince Miranov came back to Volkhov. He would not stay in the wing where guests stayed, but in a rarely visited area of the house near my grandmother's old rooms. Whenever he came he brought with him a silver dressing case and a portable bath.

I watched from an upstairs window as he and Sasha wandered the grounds in front of the house. She was quiet, her head bowed, her arm linked with his as he talked to her in a persuasive manner, which caused me to clench my fists.

I wrote a note to Anton.

My dear Antosha Chekhonte, please forgive me for turning away from you the night of the fireworks. I know you understand. Come to Volkhov as soon as you can. And we will have tea, just the two of us, on the veranda. I want to tell you something.

Your Desdemona.

Osip delivered the note into Anton's hands but he did not write a reply. I waited, but the day passed without a visit.

I wrote him again the next afternoon.

Dearest Anton,

My little Katya, your stepdaughter, is no longer with us. I lost her, dear Anton.

I gave it to Osip to deliver and he returned an hour later with a reply.

Dearest Vera, I cannot express how sorry I am to hear this. I know you must be grief-stricken. She will always be a part of you. I see our little Katya in my mind's eye with her black hair and little white kerchief. I am filled with sorrow, my dear friend.

Anton

Another day passed without a visit.

I sat at the window of my father's rarely used study, which had an overview of the road veering to and from the avenue of birch trees, and watched for Anton. But I found myself watching Sasha and the prince as they sat together on the marble embankment around the fountain where Anton and I had sat the night the gas lamp had gone out, the night his fingers had touched my wrist, and a moment later he had taken my hand.

They seemed to be in conversation, though it was the prince who was doing the most talking. He still looked like he was trying to persuade Sasha of something. My heart drummed. Whatever it was, I wanted her to say no.

He gave her a small, slender purple book. I watched them look together at it, Sasha remaining silent as the prince spoke and turned pages. It was clear to me by the way she leaned against him, the length of her upper arm and shoulder pressed close against his, that she wanted to be physically close to him. But she seemed disinclined to talk, something reluctant in her demeanor, and he had to press her, address her as if with questions, until at last she'd nod her head at something he might be pointing to in the book.

From my overview I saw another person watching them from behind a tree. It could have been anyone. There were guests roaming the property. The figure was obscured by too much foliage, but when Sasha and the prince stood up, the figure disappeared.

It was very late. The estate was quiet, all the guests retired for the night. Unable to sleep, I went to Sasha's room. The door was open but she wasn't there. I went downstairs. A weak light burned in the vestibule near the front door but there was no light outside. I stepped out onto the porch, where it was pitch black, and felt my way to one of the chairs facing out onto the dark grounds. Beyond the high-pitched chorus of cricket song and the distant voices of frogs from near the stream, I heard my sister's soft voice over in the direction of the veranda. I recognized Prince Miranov's voice quietly responding, though I could not understand what either was saying. A breeze carried his resinous scent of amber in my direction.

As their conversation continued, Sasha's whisper sounded upset. The volume of the prince's voice rose. He seemed to be defending his friend Oleg for lying about being a cartographer. "You must understand! He is ashamed, I think, because he is not educated."

Sasha's half-whispers, often interrupted by the prince, were quick and hot, indicating impatience. My heart was beating hard. I had never seen evidence that Sasha spoke her mind to him until this moment. From what I could make out as they talked over each other, the subject changed and the focus became the fact that the prince's family had title but no money.

I could hear everything more clearly now. The prince insisted that this situation was not uncommon, that it was the merchant class that was growing richer, that his friend, Oleg Radzitsky had money because he knew how to make money.

"And I see that Volkhov presents an uncommonly good opportunity for him!" Sasha exclaimed. "And for you!"

"But why are you upset?" the prince demanded with fervor. "You said you had no ties to this estate. You said that you have no home!"

I stood up and a floorboard creaked.

The conversation stopped completely.

Struggling to get control of my breathing I became aware of a sound so subtle, that I had to strain my ears to make it out. It was closer than the crickets and the frogs, the quiet shaking suppressed sound of a presence, but it wasn't coming from the veranda. A funny cold sensation began at the base of my skull and sent shivers through my body. I went back to the vestibule, listened more and followed the sound into a dark front room. There was a bitter smell, vaguely familiar, though I could not place how. The presence was here but indistinguishable from all the areas of shadow.

Then, on the veranda, my sister or the prince lit a lamp and a rectangle of light came through the window at the far side of the room, the window the prince and Sasha were sitting outside of. The light illuminated a cross section of a man's chest, while his face above and his body below the waist remained cut off in blackness.

But the numerous rows of brass buttons on the archaic tunic caught light with each short atrophied breath. His presence was wrong here. How often had he trespassed into the house like this where he was not permitted? For a moment I felt afraid, pierced by what I can only describe as a primeval terror of his largeness. Did he often come into the house? Was he deliberately listening to their conversation? Had he ever climbed the stairs and stood outside my mother's room or my sister's?

The terror I'd felt passed as I listened to his struggle to quiet his afflicted breathing. His weakness was palpable. "I see you, Uncle Boris," I said.

Abandoning the effort to suppress his wheezing, he limped from his corner, the floor creaking under him. I moved away from the door and he escaped the room slowly, like a massive, injured animal.

I looked out to the porch. Sasha and the prince had gotten up with their lamp and were standing there, watching Uncle Boris stumble away in the direction of his annex house.

Chapter 22

I had dressed and was on my way from my room to go down to a formal dinner party being held on the terrace, when I saw my father sitting in a chair outside my mother's room, holding a crystal vase filled with roses and wildflowers. He was also dressed for the formal dinner. He raised his eyes when he saw me, looking puzzled and expectant.

"I knocked, Vera. She knows I'm out here."

"Did she tell you to wait?"

"No."

"Did you open the door?"

"No. I wouldn't presume to do that."

The flowers emitted a powerful, malodorous fragrance, making me slightly dizzy.

I went to my mother's door and knocked. "Mama," I said, then opened the door.

She was alone, sitting in her usual spot on the red couch, her head twisting around to look at me. I stepped inside.

"Close the door, Vera," she said in a muted voice.

I obeyed and came in, standing between her and the fire. "Papa would like to see you."

She looked through me with a resigned trance-like calm. "No," she uttered, barely audibly.

"Why not? He has flowers for you."

"I won't see him now."

"When? When should he come?"

She shook her head. "Tell him I can't see him. Tell him to go."

"But why?"

She lifted her hands and covered her eyes. "Stop, Vera. I can't see him."

The heavy dark perfume of the roses and the occasional sharp, almost bitter breath of the wildflowers managed to penetrate the door and enter the room like an emissary of my father's, come to plead his case.

My mother blinked her eyes and looked over her shoulder a moment, slightly panicked, as if someone had come into the room.

I felt unsteady on my feet. "Tell me why! Did Papa do something that upset you?"

She thought about this and said, "When I told him how sorry I was for breaking the music box he tried to come closer to me."

"But he stopped when you told him to. He misses you, Mama."

"He needs to understand that I can't . . . I can't."

I started to go, then stopped when, through the door, I heard the approach of Gabinskaya's distinctive footsteps coming from down the hall.

I turned to my mother again. "Is it because he's a man?" I asked.

She didn't respond.

"Is that all it is? Is that his crime?"

She closed her eyes.

"And what is my crime, Mama? Why have you stopped loving me?"

"I have not stopped . . ." she protested.

"I've been ill. You have to have known that. You never came to see me."

She reached for my hands. "Forgive me, Vera. Forgive me."

"Mama," I said, and knelt down before her. "What is wrong? Tell me."

She shook her head with resignation.

When Gabinskaya entered the room I stood up, moved past her, and exited.

My father looked at me as I came out. When I shook my head he sat forward and clutched at his hair in silence.

He left the vase of flowers on the small table near the chair he'd been sitting in. I held his hand and we went downstairs to join the dinner party.

With the prince at Volkhov, Sasha had become elusive. The two of them were, as a pair, mostly antisocial, but they appeared at the dinner on the terrace, followed by Oleg Radzitsky in his mustard yellow jacket. Prince Miranov introduced Radzitsky to anyone attending who had not met him before, as a former cartographer, now a businessman and a surveyor of land.

Beneath Sasha's stoic expression I sensed annoyance.

Uncle Pavel asked Prince Miranov to tell the story of the Ice Palace again for the newly arrived guests. I was sitting across from Sasha, and as the prince began by telling everyone that he was a collector of tales of the grotesque, she hung her head, looking down and to the side, avoiding my eyes. She seemed in pain, as if she were barely enduring the story, and perhaps even the prince himself.

Her eyes once shot up at mine, and before she quickly averted them I felt she was imploring me, but what was it she was imploring? I still felt she wanted to share something with me. She struck me as someone in prison, someone afraid, but I had to remind myself that she was a willing prisoner. Her breathing was deep and the emotion he inspired in her made her skin pale. This was a strange kind of passion that, instead of igniting a flame, drained her of fire.

Several conversations were going on at once, so I only half heard snatches of what was being said at the head of the table. At some point, the talk turned to the peach orchard.

The voices of Radzitsky and the prince overlapped.

"Too much herbaceous ground cover . . ."

"Diseased and damaged branches . . ."

"A lot of labor needed to bring that orchard back."

"It may be too late to recover . . ."

"The ideal area of land to build dachas on . . ."

I could not clearly hear the responses this was eliciting from my uncle and aunt, though their voices were there in the mix of everything. Soon my aunt managed to change the subject by asking Radzitsky about his past as a cartographer.

The prince interjected to say that Radzitsky had worked on mapping Siberia.

"Only for a short time," Radzitsky said. "But I will tell you this: we cannot trust that any map of Siberia is precise. The landmass is too large. I have heard some say that it is impossible to measure and much larger than any map shows it to be. A cartographer I know who worked on it for many years lost all his teeth and his hair turned gray. He eventually went mad."

My father had been listening quietly to everything. He was about to squeeze lemon over a serving of oysters when a tiny blue crab walked sideways off the iced platter, leaving a damp trail on the linen table cloth. My father looked at me with wide, amused eyes and lightly swept the crab onto a saucer with the side of his hand. It tweaked his index finger with its larger claw and would not let go. "The little Cossack!" my father said loudly, laughing and holding his finger in the air.

Having drawn the attention of everyone at the table, he stood up, smiling and holding up the crab on his finger for all to see. "The little Cossack!" he repeated, puffed up and smiling widely.

"Taking on such an enormous enemy!" Victor Victorovich said.

My father picked up a glass of water, lowered his finger into it, and shook gently until the crab disengaged and floated to the bottom. Everyone was still looking at him and laughing as he called Osip over, handing him two rubles. "Take this formidable little fellow to the river and set him free."

"Such a crab lives in saltwater, Sergei," my aunt said through her laughter.

"It probably traveled here by oyster truck all the way from the Baltic Sea," Anya Leonideyvna added.

"What else can be done with it?" my father asked. "It will be happier in the river than at our dinner party."

Holding the glass of water with the little crab bobbing in it, Osip left the terrace wearing the determined expression of someone setting off on a grand mission. Everyone laughed uproariously.

My father, still standing, poured a glass of vodka, drained it, then banged it down on the linen, looking energetic enough to break into a dance. "And now," he said, "a little water snake will come out of my carnation!"

There was less enthusiastic laughter and people turned their attention back to their meals or their interrupted conversations. My father hesitated then sat down. He kept looking around, as if hoping to catch an eye. I could feel his hunger for attention, his disappointment that the moment was gone. I smiled at him and he sighed and smiled back, but his mood gradually declined. As soup was served, my father had the uneaten oysters taken away and talked to me of innocuous things, a chance meeting with an old acquaintance, a recent craving for kasha and baked mushrooms.

In the midst of what my father was saying, I heard the conversation about the orchard beginning again at the far side of the table, and again, because of crosstalk and other conversations at the table I could not hear everything that was said. The talk went on for a while as people ate their soup.

At a certain point my father seemed to be listening to it also. Both Prince Miranov and Radzitsky were speaking persuasively to my aunt. I heard her say, "It is very hard to maintain. A tremendous devotion is required."

Radzitsky seemed to be agreeing with her, saying it must have been very difficult to be in charge of by herself. He mentioned again that it is ideal land and an ideal location, the best on the estate for building dachas.

There was also talk about the park just beyond the avenue of birch trees, the woods closest to the house. This area, Radzitsky said, would fetch the most money. "One of the most attractive areas of the estate."

A slight commotion ensued as soup dishes were taken away.

"Where is Anton Pavlovich, Vera?" my father asked as if he had just noticed his absence. "He isn't already gone to Moscow, is he?"

"I don't think so, Papa."

His brow wrinkled with concern. He lowered his voice and in a half whisper asked, "What happened?"

I ached to talk to him about Anton and thought I might be able to say a little, but was interrupted as the main course was served around the table, and after that, my father seemed to have forgotten again about Anton.

I kept thinking about the orchard and the park just beyond the avenue of birch trees, and had little appetite.

My father had only eaten a few spoonfuls of his soup and had waved away the main course.

"Papasha!" I pleaded softly, touching his sleeve.

A dampness glinted in his eye and he wiped it with his dinner napkin. "Lately, I wake up in the morning thinking I am a little boy. What a shock it is, Vera. What a shock it is to realize I am not."

Later that night when everyone had dispersed, I found my aunt in her office, bent over her ledgers, her glasses smudged.

"Aunt," I said and stood facing her. "Please don't let the prince and Radzitsky persuade you to sell anything but acreage in the back of the estate."

"The orchard is too hard to manage. I am the one that has maintained everything here. Your father can no longer help financially. He lost more through his investments than he had told me about. And I have made some bad decisions, the parties, as you know."

"I know why you did that, Aunt. You told me."

"I feel foolish for having placed such hopes in Father Ivan."

"I am so disappointed in him, too, Aunt. But you still have Volkhov. It's your home and it's mine."

"I don't want to take care of Volkhov anymore. My mother left it to me because she never would have burdened your father or Pavel with it, and she knew they probably couldn't run things, anyhow. I feel used." She looked at her ledger, then turned back to me again. "Who has loved me here, Vera?"

"I have loved you! I love you!"

I took her hands and squeezed them. "If you just sell allotments from the back acreage you'll have money and we'll be able to stay. And you can pay men to work in the orchard."

"Even with the men working I would be in charge. The orchard is a great weight on my shoulders. It always has been. No, I want to leave, go somewhere else."

"But I will help you, Aunt!"

She shook her head.

"You can turn it over to me. I will learn what I have to."

"I will not turn it over to you, Vera. You have no experience and everything is a mess. I would not do that to you."

"But this is my home, Aunt! I can't lose Volkhov!"

"You are young. Don't let your life become what mine has become. You'll get no help from anyone." Her eyes filled with tears. "I want the money. I want to leave."

"No, Aunt!"

"My heart is broken, Vera."

I threw my arms around her.

"You can come with me, Vera."

"Please, Aunt. Reconsider."

"And so can Pavel and your father. I will have enough."

"But my father will probably go back to Kiev."

"Your father won't be going back to Kiev."

"Why not?" I asked cautiously.

"He has nothing there anymore."

I broke the embrace. "He didn't tell me."

"How could he tell you, Vera? He can barely admit it to himself. He, too, is now dependent on me."

"I think when the moment comes, you won't be able to sign Volkhov away! I just don't believe you will do that!"

I could see that my hands were shaking, but I could not feel my body.

She stood up and led me to the settee where we sat with our arms around each other.

"You won't do it, dear Aunt Marya."

She rested her head on my neck and I stroked her hair.

"I am so ashamed," she whispered.

Early the next morning I wrote again to Anton, asking him to please come.

I asked Osip to ask Anton to read the note in front of him and give him an answer. But when he returned, Osip told me Anton said he would read it when he was alone.

And the day passed.

Chapter 23

The next day, in search of a sympathetic ear, I looked for Proskovia and found her asleep just to the side of the carriage road, a spot too exposed and possibly dangerous, the two dogs whimpering, circling the area. I would need Nickander to help me move her to safety and I was about to set out for the summerhouse, where he had, as of late, been repairing a broken window, when I saw him in front of the stairs to the veranda with a small group of inebriated guests. Victor Victorovich, probably because Anya Leonideyvna, who functioned as his moral compass, was not present, was insisting Nickander carry him up the stairs. Awkwardness ensued as Nickander struggled to lift him. It was not that he was too heavy, but being so wide around the middle made him difficult to grasp onto. Nickander managed to hoist him onto his shoulder like a wide piece of furniture, then carefully balance him there as he climbed up each stair, while the guests below cheered and clapped with laughter. Once Victor was delivered to the top of the stairs, the actress, Tolskaya, cried out from below that she was next. She was, as I had always seen her, decked out in orange and bright green, and with her long nose, reminded me of an Amazonian bird.

"I am feeling lazy and do not want to be bothered with the stairs," she said as the others laughed and applauded.

I ran toward them. "I am sorry to break up this absurd game," I said loudly, but I require Nickander for something important."

"Have a sense of humor, Vera!" Tolskaya said. "It is all in good fun."

"I doubt that it's fun for Nickander."

"He is like a bull. What can it hurt him?"

"Come, Nickander," I said and scowled at the lot of them.

"Young people do not enjoy life these days," she said and made a dismissive gesture with her hand.

Nickander picked Proskovia up carefully, while I retrieved her tapestry bag. He and the dogs followed me as I headed toward the remote wing where she had a room that she rarely slept in.

Proskovia awakened just as Nickander was laying her down on the bed, and with bulging eyes, clawed at him in horror.

He retreated quickly backwards from her into the shadow of her open closet, bumping his head on the doorframe as he did.

The dogs barked anxiously outside the window.

I rushed to her, explaining what had happened.

"I told your aunt that if I was found asleep, I should not be moved!"

"I am so sorry, but you were in a dangerous place, right near the carriage road."

She sat on the edge of the bed gathering her wits. "Besides," she said, looking around the room with alarm, "I am afraid in this room."

"Why, Proskovia?"

"There is the ghost of a child in the wall. I have heard a little voice talking and humming. I can tolerate ghosts but the ghost of a child is too sad!"

A straw hat with a dark attached veil sat at an angle over a lampshade. Proskovia looked at it as the veil moved, stirred by a breeze rushing through the open window.

"You are hearing Vova, a young chambermaid," Nickander said in a brokenhearted voice, his large moon-shaped face seeming to float there in the shadows of the closet. "She is not a ghost. She is lonely."

"Why is she lonely?"

"The others leave her the terrible jobs, like emptying chamber pots," Nickander replied, deeply and unhappily moved by what he was sharing

"Come out of there, dear young man," Proskovia said. "Please."

Nickander stepped forth from within the closet, bowing this time carefully so as not to hit his head again on the doorframe.

"Why aren't the others fair to her, the poor girl?" Proskovia asked.

"Because they say she is odd. Because she talks to herself," I said. "And because she does not tell them where she comes from."

"Why should anyone have to tell anyone where they come from? That is sensitive information." Proskovia rose to her feet and said it was urgent that she speak with this poor creature.

The three of us walked through the halls looking for Vova, Nickander on high alert, listening without breathing. We turned the corner when he stopped in his tracks and said, "The fumes of the furniture oil are strong! But no doors are open. She always leaves the door open when she cleans. She must have just departed."

"Like ether," Proskovia whispered, turning and facing Nickander, eyebrows high, the fingertips of one hand touching her heart. "Is she real, the dear girl?"

"Yes," he said and they exchanged expressions of profound sympathy.

Eventually, the mission ended when Vova could not be located.

"What does she look like, Nickander, so I will know her when I see her?"

"She is like a gazelle, Madam Proskovia. Only shyer and more graceful."

"Do not call me madam, dear boy. Call me Proskovia. I am as you are, just someone living each day as it comes to me."

That same afternoon, from my perch at a third floor window, I saw Proskovia walking with Nickander, who looked on the verge of tears as he spoke, as if he was sharing something from his soul.

Looking rapt as she listened, Proskovia pressed a hand to her heart.

Hours later I went out and sat on the veranda. Proskovia walked past near the carriage road with a tall slender young woman who was wearing a rumpled white dress, too large for her, her face obscured by the dark veiled hat I had seen in Proskovia's room.

Proskovia saw me and waved, and the young woman, who must have been Vova, nervously pulled on the veil to keep it still, the breeze threatening to lift it.

Hours after that, still feeling weak and unsteady on my feet, I ventured to walk a little deeper onto the property. I saw them again through the trees. Finches sang and chattered, darting back and forth in the branches above them.

Proskovia was lying on her side in the grass, mouth open, eyes visible but vacant, her expression a study in supplication. Vova sat near her, singing quietly, her face still hidden by the veil on the big hat.

Very gingerly, she removed a leaf stuck to the shoulder of Proskovia's dress.

I was about to slip away when I noticed Nickander standing between two trees looking at them sadly. He seemed embarrassed when he saw me approaching him and nervously fled, saying that Osip was waiting for him near the summerhouse where the window they had just replaced had been mysteriously broken.

Chapter 24

I am sorry, dear Desdemona, that I have not come to Volkhov. I trust that you are feeling better. You do not need to apologize for turning away from me the night of the fireworks. It was this that helped me realize how deeply you still love Petya Fyodorovich. I had convinced myself that your feelings for him had cooled, that you were more free of him than you are.

We were, those last days I visited, living together in a kind of romantic delusion. But the shock we both experienced that night broke the dream and reminded me that I am not free either.

Yesterday I received a letter from my sister, Masha. What I have waiting for me in Moscow is worse than I thought . . . Nineteen years old and I am the papa, saddled with the care of my family. And Masha, who is only seventeen but is the sibling with the most sense, tells me in her letter that she will be a kind of aid to me. She will help me as much as she can. I will never marry, Vera. But I don't know a woman who would want the job anyway. Dealing with all of us.

Though I had imagined it once or twice, marrying Anton was not in the forefront of my thoughts, but reading those words caused a hollow sensation to fill my stomach.

I am a permanent fixture in a big ruthless family. I have four brothers, and only one, Misha, the youngest, is capable of behaving with any manners. But that may change. He may also become impossible. How my mother and sister put up with all of us, I will never know.

And I am afraid I am very loyal to this ruthless family.

I hope you are recovering, my very dear friend.

Anton

It was almost dark; the trees looked more black than green. Except for the occasional breeze, the air was still. Crickets were chirping in the cool dark foliage and frogs were singing near the river. I had still not gotten my strength back after the loss of so much blood, and Anton's letter had unsettled me. Swallows flew towards me, brushing so close I felt them passing through me.

The world was on the brink of changing, becoming unrecognizable, but for now it was as it always had been, the trees standing tall, conferring peacefully with each other in the night air.

A light was burning upstairs in Dr. Mitrofan's house.

I knocked meekly and when there was no answer, went in. No one was downstairs. I went up to Anton's room. The door was ajar, held open by an iron doorstop.

He sat bent forward with his back to me at a desk near the half-open window, writing furtively in the lamplight, while the hem of the curtain gently stirred. He took a breath and looked at the open window as if considering something. When he applied his pen again with urgency, a spark of excitement moved through me. I watched him for a while, wondering if he would sense me there, but he was completely absorbed by what he was imagining and I could not bring myself to interrupt him. He said he would never marry. He was already married to his family. I could hear him breathing, his pen moving faster, his head bending closer to the lamp. He felt inaccessible. Mysterious.

I left the doorway and quietly descended the stairs.

It was darker as I made my way back to Volkhov, the ground black and far away beneath me. Each step I took I feared I might drop into a ravine.

I lay in my bed with the windows open.

The night outside felt so alive, so awake. I could smell the sweet honey-like fragrance of the night blooming flowers, the phlox and the tiny yellow primroses. I missed Anton.

Beyond the noise of crickets I could hear the occasional human voice or bark of a dog. I told myself to try and sleep but then I heard something else: the sound of a man coughing. A shock of adrenaline shot through me. Would Anton have come here this late at night?

I put on a robe over my nightgown and went downstairs. The main doors were wide open as they often were on summer nights. Moths flew in circles around the dimming light of the gas lamp on the porch, or clung to the screens.

I stood on the veranda, feeling the floorboards under my bare feet, listening for the sound of Anton's cough. Out here the cricket song was louder, a vibrant, high-pitched chorus.

A nightingale sang in a nearby tree, and smaller birds, pert little shadow figures, glided or flew quickly past, making commotions in the black leaves.

A group of voices wafted from a distance, people in what sounded like thoughtful conversation on one of the pathways. Someone laughed. Through the branches I saw a vague illumination from the lamp someone was carrying.

I stood on one of the wooden stairs that led down and heard the cough again, but the timbre was not Anton's. The pitch of the voice was lower. The cough became persistent like someone with a bad cold, but it gradually got closer and louder. It came from a figure moving haltingly a few yards away, but in an area of darkness so I couldn't make it out. It stopped moving and the coughing became convulsive, the man struggling to breathe.

I was about to run down when other figures appeared and surrounded the man. I heard my aunt's voice say my uncle's name: *Boris*. Others said his name, too, as they led him in the direction of his annex house.

Nickander ran by carrying a lamp, clearly on his way to get Dr. Mitrofan.

For hours I kept watch out the window. When I saw Dr. Mitrofan carrying a lamp, coming from the direction of the annex house, I went down and met him and asked after my uncle's health.

"Why are you up at this hour, Vera?" he asked in a scolding tone.

"Tell me about Uncle Boris," I said.

"He worries that he'll die this time. I asked him to rest his voice but he doesn't listen to me. He's been talking to me about the past."

"Did he say anything about my mother?"

"Only that he wants to see her. I have tried at other times when he's suffered hemorrhages to persuade her to see him, but she has made it very clear that she never will."

"No, she is very stubborn."

After a pause he told me that Anton had planned to come and see me a few days back, but he received a letter from his sister, Masha, that upset him.

"He wrote to me. I know he received a letter."

"Did he tell you that his brother Kolya was spitting blood?"

"No."

"Even coughing up blood he continues to smoke and drink. His moods swing violently from euphoria to depression. He has started sleeping on the street."

"No, he didn't tell me that."

"Anton is anxious and is going to leave in a few days, much sooner than he had originally planned."

"Oh no!" I said.

"He's devastated about his brother's health, but I think this has put the fear of God into him about his own health. He doesn't say this, but I've come to know him well enough that I see it." Dr. Mitrofan sighed and gave himself to momentary reflection. "He is disappointed that he never saw the white deer. It bothers him."

"I am also disappointed that he didn't see it."

As the doctor started to go, I told him that I would go with him back to his house, that I needed to see Anton.

"Go upstairs and sleep, Vera. I hope Anton is not awake now but getting a healthy sleep. Come later."

Anxious for the hours to pass, I tossed and turned in bed.

I heard quiet footsteps in the hallway. I sat up, listening hard, certain, for some reason, that it was Anton waiting for me outside my room. The door to the hallway was ajar. I got up, my heart hammering. "Anton!" I said, and opened the door a little more. The air was filled with the smell of the ancient woods at the far north of the estate, an intense redolence of petrichor, as if rain were about to fall in the hallway.

And I knew the white deer had come into the house. I went to the stairs and looked down. A white glow, a mist, was formed in the middle of the dark staircase. The deer, I thought, but she was more mist than form. If only she would materialize. But then I saw a figure of some kind on the landing below. A figure in a chair on the landing where a chair would never be. I took a few steps down the stairs and could see that it was Anton, sitting with his legs crossed, holding an infant in his arms. A rush of panic went through me. He could not nurse that baby. He could not take care of her.

I woke suddenly. At first I did not recall the dream in its entirety, only the sense that the white deer had come into the house. The smell of the perpetually damp ground in the ancient woods was still strong. I opened my door and searched. There was no light on the staircase and the smell gradually faded. As I began to accept that it had been a dream, I remembered Anton holding Katya and a burst of grief spread through my body.

Chapter 25

What had been a gray dawn gave way to a bright morning, cumulus clouds at steady sail across a blue sky.

Lika told me that Anton was reading behind the house.

I found him lying back in the sunlight on one of two wicker chaises that faced a field of flowering rye, bordered by red poppies. He was cracking a sunflower seed between his teeth, a paper bag and a few scattered shells on the small table next to him. I thought it would be one of his medical textbooks he'd be holding, but it was a slender black volume, which he closed immediately upon seeing me and set down on the small table next to the paper bag. As he started getting up, I told him not to.

I sat on the edge of the empty chaise and faced him. "I dreamt that a white mist stood on the staircase in my house. I knew it was the white deer. She was on the verge of materializing, but she didn't. It was one of those dreams that felt so real, like it was not a dream at all. It still feels real. I had such a strong feeling that she had come into the house to find me."

He looked at me with surprise and openness. "I would love to have such a dream," he said.

"The doctor said you are not here much longer."

"I leave the day after tomorrow."

"So soon?" I asked.

He nodded.

I picked up the slender volume. It was *Eugene Onegin*.

"I'm taking a little break from the medical textbooks," he explained.

I opened the little volume, stopping randomly on one page, pointing my finger to a spot, and reading to myself:

Tatyana, lonely heroine

Roamed the still forest like a ranger.

I closed the book and put it back on the table.

"I'm glad you've come, Desdemona Denisova."

The affection in his voice caused my eyes to dampen. I smiled at him. We were so instantly at home in the company of the other.

"You asked me once where I would hide if I was the deer. There is an area of ancient woods at the far north end of the property."

"Why did you not think of it before?"

"I am so accustomed to avoiding those woods. I've always been afraid of them, and it's a long walk to them. I am still afraid of those woods. But the reason they are in my mind, Anton, is because when the deer came into the house I could smell those woods. They have a certain fragrance like petrichor, even on the driest of days. And like wet, dark earth freshly dug. I think it was a message, that we need to go to those woods to look for her."

A flock of geese, honking overhead, threw sudden shadows near us. I watched them cross over the flowering field until they disappeared into the distance.

"You were in the dream, too, Anton, holding little Katya."

He looked at me with deep feeling in his eyes.

"My little stepdaughter," he said softly.

"Proskovia told me that a child is the anchor that holds a mother to the earth. I am no longer held in place. It's as if I am floating."

I put my hands over my face and bowed my head.

Anton touched my shoulder and softly sang a few measures of "*Bayu bayushki bayu . . .*"

He leaned in and kissed my forehead.

"When I was little, Sasha told me that the Baba Yaga lived in those ancient woods in her house on chickens' feet. She said she saw the old witch once moving through the branches in her mortar and pestle, spit dripping from her pointy chin."

"I always wondered whose forest the Baba Yaga lived in." He looked at me with a shine on his eye. "Of course it would be a forest at Volkhov!"

"It is so dark in those woods, Anton, that nightingales sing even in daytime."

"I will chance a meeting with the old witch herself for a glimpse of the white deer."

In the brightness of the day I could see slender spokes of orange in the brown of his eyes.

"It will be an excursion, it's the farthest reaches of the property. I have a very strong feeling that the white deer will be there."

"Let's plan on going there tomorrow," he said. "On my last full day here."

We heard a ruckus from a road in the distance, which cut through the flowering field. A troika raced along at full gallop, dust and chaff flying up from the wheels, the driver standing at the reins. "The man thinks he's a gladiator," Anton said, and smiled at the unexpected spectacle of it.

He offered me the bag of sunflower seeds. I took a few and passed it back to him.

We looked out at the field, poppies bobbing slightly and swaying in the breeze.

I picked a few wild daisies as we walked north together along the main cobblestoned road that ran between Volkhov and Dr. Mitrofan's property. We were going the opposite direction from Volkhov. It was always a quiet road but we saw no carts or carriages at all on this sunny day. We reached a wide intersecting dirt road, scored by centuries of wheels and sled runners, memories of deep mud parched now in the sun.

"This is the road to Eliade-Luria, a road that runs thousands of miles into Siberia."

"Your father mentioned this road the night of the fireworks."

"I was nine years old. You may be skeptical of what I tell you, but I will share it with you if you want to hear it."

He said he did, so I told him how my father took me out in the sled that winter to enjoy the first snowfall of the season. It had mostly stopped falling when we reached this road, the occasional flake floating by, drifting and circling.

We'd had to stop while a sled that was pulling a cart was passing. It got stuck for a little while and we had to wait. At first it was the horses that drew my attention, so gray and plodding, one of them with dappled hips, shaking snow from its mane. They were so much larger than the lithe brown mare pulling our sled, shifting her quarters as she waited, nodding her head and jangling the bells on her bridle.

I'd never seen a vehicle like it. A tarp covered everything but it had detached in one area and snow had fallen in. I had no idea what I was seeing at first. The figure in that exposed area of the cart, half lying, half sitting, looked like a life-size doll, wearing a pair of solid white shoulder pads and a tall white crooked peak of a hat on his head. The sun appeared from behind a cloud in that moment and the hat glistened. He looked like some kind of fairy tale soldier or one of the slender consorts of Nicholas of Winter.

I stood to get a better look and saw him move. This was a man, not a doll. He wore a bracelet of some sort, and as I studied that bracelet, something in my stomach collapsed. It was connected to a heavy chain, which was secured to the bars of the cart, partially hidden under snow. Through a narrow opening in the tarp I could see movement, what looked like several other figures lying down covered in gray blankets. My father tried to explain to me that the men were prisoners being taken to Siberia.

I asked about the man in the hat and my father laughed softly and told me that it was not a hat, that it was snow.

I'd stared. The man with the hat of snow had no coat on. It must have been the angle of the opening above him that had caused the snow to settle inches high on only his shoulders and head, the way snow leaves a thick blanket on top of a wall or a pediment.

I'd asked my father questions, why the man was sitting in a place that wasn't covered by the tarp, and he said that perhaps the man was being punished for something he should not have done. I asked why he didn't wipe off the snow, and the peculiar silence that comes with snowfall amplified my words. The man clearly heard me ask the question and slowly opened his eyes, blue and clear, and they looked directly into mine, sending a shock through me, the world turning for a moment upside down.

After the cart drove away, I started to cry, and my father asked me why I was upset, but I didn't know how to say that the man's spirit had shot out across the air between us and fled into me, that I could feel him there, taking refuge in my being.

My father struggled to distract me by singing. *Like a bird on the wing . . . I shall fly to old Mother Moscow . . .*

"I carried this man's spirit around for him for months, Anton. Then one afternoon, I heard something like a clap of air. And I could no longer feel him. And I was sure that he had died."

Anton gazed at me in silence, but he did not look skeptical.

My tutor, my aunt, and old Aniuta had taught me that Siberia, the place my sister had been born, was an open-air prison, a place of suffering; a land of chaos and lawlessness; an endless territory where people got lost. I was told people rarely returned, and many times were never heard from again.

"I will never forget how desperate the man was not to go where they were taking him."

For those months when I felt the man's spirit residing in me, I was terrified all the time that he was suffering. I was preoccupied with him, feeling confused and even ill over him, and also protective of what had passed between us. I couldn't bring myself to talk about him. And I couldn't say anything either about Siberia because Sasha had been born there, so instead I talked incessantly about my dread of this road to Eliade-Luria, as if the road itself were responsible for those carted away on it. "Dear little sister," Sasha said once in annoyance. "You have nothing to be afraid of. It's only peasants and servants that end up in chains."

"I have since found out that Sasha was wrong about that. But I believed her at the time. Maybe she thought these words would reassure me, but they did not. I thought of Petya and imagined him in chains. I became preoccupied with the fact that I lived in incredible comfort while Petya lived in a house that looked similar to the stable. I did not know how to balance the unevenness of things."

Anton stood in the sunlight looking down at the ground, the breezes tousling his hair. After a silence, he smiled.

"You are more like your mother than she knows or even you know, Vera. You believe in the old woman in the fire and the Vorsa running through the trees. You saw your grandmother, who has been dead for many years, in her purple dress near a stand of birch trees. And in your way of seeing the world there is much about the transmigration of souls, people's spirits inhabiting samovars or mirrors, or shooting out over snowy roads to take refuge in the heart of an empathetic little girl."

A chill rushed up over my back and arms.

"You don't recognize it, but you are full of a Siberian way of seeing."

I laughed softly, and my eyes filled. I wanted to somehow communicate Anton's insight to my mother. I wanted her to know I saw the world the way she did.

"Vera," he said. "I want you to understand why I am determined to go to Siberia one day. I feel compassion for that poor man with the snow on his shoulders as you so deeply did. And I want to know the same things that you do. What it means to be so helpless in the face of unmovable indifference. What it means to have your humanity so reduced that the snow mistakes you for a wall."

I tried to swallow back tears.

"What else could you as a child of nine have done for that man? Helpless in all ways but that one, to believe you were protecting his spirit, preserving something for him.

"Going there, seeing what is largely hidden from us, or we keep hidden from ourselves, and writing about it. Exposing it. That would be my version of carrying the man's spirit with me, trying to protect it. You and I are of the same convictions, dear Desdemona. It is suffering that confounds and preoccupies both of us."

We heard a faint clamor of music in the distance as we continued north along the road. A small band of gypsies appeared, moving in our direction. When we all met in the road, they bowed to us. A duo of musicians, a man with an accordion and a man whose guitar was missing one string, played a dissonant tune with great feeling. As Anton and I cheered, I threw a daisy at each of them. A woman jangled a tambourine, announcing a juggler, a birdlike figure with a large serious forehead and crooked nose. He juggled four balls but one flew off and got lost in the overgrowth. To replace it, he took an egg from a basket and juggled it along with the three balls, continuing to juggle when the egg cracked on his forehead, dripping down his face, a little of it in one eye. This caused Anton to applaud and whistle.

"It is summer!" the juggler cried out in a high-pitched, singsong voice, blinking egg from his eye. "The time to go a little mad!"

He then juggled plates, one of which crashed against a rock at the side of the road. But the man was unwilling to be discouraged, and relentlessly, unselfconsciously, kept juggling.

"More! More!" Anton cried in a state of rapture. "Wonderful!"

I had no coins but Anton dug into his pockets and gave them all the coins he had.

The entire time, walking back to Dr. Mitrofan's, we hardly caught our breath for all the laughing. "You must understand," Anton said with the gypsy's high-pitched, sing song inflection. "It is summer! The time to go a little mad."

He leaned over impulsively and kissed my shoulder.

Chapter 26

We had walked back in the direction of Dr. Mitrofan's house and Anton was going to walk me back to Volkhov, but Lika called out to us, insisting sternly that we come in and eat. She gave us large bowls of sour cabbage soup and warm black bread.

We had finished and were drinking tea when Anton told me that he had met my Uncle Boris.

"Two days after the fireworks, I went with the doctor on his rounds. We went to Volkhov to check on his health."

"Did you get to ask him about Siberia?"

"Yes. Your uncle is such a large man, and probably the most brooding presence I've ever been near. I told him about my aspirations to visit a labor camp and told him I believe that all Russians should visit Siberia, as Turks go to Mecca. He said it was unusual, but he did not try and dissuade me."

He told Anton to travel on the Post Road, where he could find the occasional roadhouse, and where there were places the driver could change horses or he could meet with a new tarantass. He told him to be careful of the escaped prisoners in the forest along that road. The escaped men struggling to make their way west were known as General Cuckoo's Army because the trees there were loud with the song of cuckoos.

He said that he had lived awhile among the Nakut people and described an area in Russia's far east, in the basin of the middle Lena River, along the Alden and Vilyuy Rivers, where it was mostly taiga and tundra in the northern area. It was partly mountainous, the climate dry, the winter long and severe.

He told Anton that he became a great hunter and always caught more fish than any other man. He was strong and respected and being much taller than the Nakut and with blond hair, they thought of him as a spirit man. He said that the wild deer and the musk deer used to come to him as if they sought him out so that he could kill them. Anton was struck by the authority with which Uncle Boris delivered his words, and the resonant bass of his voice, even as he struggled to catch his breath. He told Anton he learned to speak Nakut enough to communicate with the men. One of them told him that it is an honor for the deer to be killed by a great hunter, that the wind spoke to them in his favor.

"He asked me, Vera, if I believe in nature spirits. I explained that I was skeptical about such things."

I thought of the white deer but did not mention it.

"He told me I was a practical young man, but that everything changes when you live very close to nature. He had believed in God, but living among the Nakut he began instead to believe in spirits, because you are always negotiating with them in one way or another."

"And what did he say about my mother, Anton?"

"He was comfortable talking about his own prowess as a hunter but when I asked about your mother he was quiet." Uncle Boris talked more about hunting and when he was silent for a little while, Anton asked again about my mother. Again Boris was quiet, looking down at the floorboards. Then, speaking very slowly, he said a fur trader happened into the camp one day, the first person they had seen in two years who was not a Nakut. My mother pleaded with him to take her back to any of the villages around Lake Baikal. He agreed.

"Your uncle accompanied them. His plan had always been to return to the Nakut, but he said he delivered your mother to a community of Old Believers, some of whom they recognized from the gathering at the lake. He then set out back north but could not find where the Nakut had moved camp."

He'd had rubles that he brought with him and kept them with his papers. One night while staying in a roadhouse the rubles and his papers were stolen. After that, he got waylaid into a different life. He wrote to my mother at the place where he'd left her and someone wrote back to him that she was no longer there but had married one of the elders in the community and moved to an enclave on a mountain over Lake Baikal.

He never said what the life he was living those years entailed but he was eventually arrested, taken to be an escaped convict. He had no papers, nothing to prove otherwise. For three long years he was forced to do hard labor in the Kara Gold Mines, before his story was finally verified and believed. He was then given papers to travel with, but he had contracted tuberculosis in the filthy and often freezing conditions of the camp.

It had been six years since he'd seen my mother and he had gone to find the house where she lived but her husband had died and she had left with her small child for western Russia.

Boris then worked his way across Siberia, often having to stop and wait out bouts of illness or the merciless Siberian winters. He lost years.

"He told me that people will think I am mad to go to Siberia, but that life is not here in the soft, genteel world. The worst years of his life were at the Kara Gold Mines. The two best years were among the Nakut.

"He said to me that when he is feeling healthy he hates the complacent life he lives now. And he posed a question to me. He asked, 'Is this life? After what I once lived among the Nakut? I cannot believe that it is.' He said it is a refuge only, not a life, that a vital man does not spend his energy in mundane routine. But he said he was tired and ill and good now for nothing else.

"It was illness that drove him west and the need to see his sister. I asked why it was your mother would not see him, and he looked affronted by the question. I had clearly crossed a line."

But after a minute, Anton told me, my uncle sighed and his chest caved in. He looked down and seemed sad. When he finally spoke he said that his sister probably could not bear memories of the time with the Nakut. He remembers the time happily, but is sure she does not. She was grief-stricken for her mother the entire time, and she could not get warm, even in the summers. The cold haunted her like a ghost. She'd asked him repeatedly to find a way to take her back to civilization. He said he would but did not. He lied and told her he was trying but he was happy in the life with the Nakut. When he said this to Anton, his eyes grew damp.

When Anton walked me to the road, I said, "My poor mother. I wish he had said more about her."

"There was one thing, Vera. He may have just made a mistake, but when your uncle was talking about leaving your mother with the Old Believers, he said he was relieved to find that they were kind and willing to take *them* in." Anton repeated the word *them*.

"Maybe he stayed with them awhile, also."

"No," Anton said. "He left with the fur trader almost immediately."

"Willing to *take them in*," I repeated.

"Maybe it was a mistake," Anton said, looking at me carefully.

"Unless he meant Sasha," I said. "That Sasha was already born."

Anton nodded his head as if this was something he'd already thought of, but had not wanted to say.

"But that makes no sense," I said.

"It was clearly a mistake."

Chapter 27

Sasha had left the small slender volume with the deep purple jacket on my bed. I sat down and opened it. It was a collection of poems: *The Flowers of Evil* by Baudelaire, inscribed on the first page: *for the Sphinx Herself, Alexandra Iunosheva, from a Knight Templar.*

I skimmed through and saw underlined phrases on different pages, small stars in the margins next to them.

Fate, charmed and doglike, trails your petticoat . . .

What matter if you come from heaven or hell?

On another page: *Oh beauty! Monster huge, alarming, pure!*

On yet another page: *From Satan or from God, Seraph or fiend . . .*

I could not help but think he had underlined phrases because they reminded him somehow of her. If that was true, he had called her a monster.

The folded blue sheet of paper was stuck between pages in the book, the letter I was sure she had considered letting me read. In a strange, back-slanted penmanship, the prince had written:

My Sphinx, You would fit in with the women in the Symbolist gardens of Paris. You understand in your deepest being the Symbolist revolt against nature, because nature has betrayed you. Your hand is absurd, a mistake.

My throat and chest tightened. I could not separate the handwriting, compressed and elongated, from his prurient interest in my sister's small deformity.

You are something impossible, a chimera, conceived during a violent and unnatural union.

My breathing grew constrained as I reread the last phrase of that sentence.

Conceived during a violent and unnatural union.

Was he trying to match Baudelaire in metaphorical language?

You are the fruit of an unnatural conception. Your hand, one of nature's rare orchids, exquisite in its ugliness, is the very expression of rape.

The fibrous paper, not quite blue but more the color of smoke, trembled in my hand. Was he, in his florid and indirect way, talking about something real? The document issued a vague horror, which drained the air around me, rendering it unbreathable. I kept coming back to the word *rape*.

Sasha had wanted me to read this.

I folded the page and replaced it in the book. I carried the book to her room, hoping I'd find her there. But she wasn't. I left it on her bed.

I went to my mother's door. I heard her cough inside but I hesitated to knock. I was not certain what I would say or how I could talk about what I'd just read. I walked to the staircase but before descending, stood a moment thinking. Piano music played, rising from the depths of the house so its melody hummed quietly in the walls. I touched the banister and felt it shiver. I thought of my mother's cough behind her closed door. Gabinskaya would be alone at the piano.

I went slowly down the two flights of stairs, listening, drawn toward the music's tenderness, feeling the vibration of each note. I stood outside the open door of the empty ballroom.

When I entered, Gabinskaya's fingers paused. For as long as I had known her I had never attempted to speak with her. Even when I was small, she had always avoided my eyes, kept her head high in my presence and walked officiously past me. I was uncertain how she'd react to my approach.

She looked at me and a fleeting twitch of her eyelid told me that my presence disarmed her. Her eyes were pale green and small, her nose a long, perfect aquiline, beneath which her thin lips contracted, then relaxed.

She began again to play, at first quietly and in a slower tempo. Her eyes closed halfway as she allowed the music to infuse her. I kept my distance at first, remaining at the far end of the grand piano. Soon she returned to the previous volume and tempo of her playing. She had accepted my presence.

It was music I had never heard before, a slow, ceremonious rhythm, which seemed to quiet the heart, to offer solace. Encouraged by the music, I approached slowly along the length of the black, polished instrument.

When the last note resounded, holding the air, her hands went still, hovering over the keys.

I waited for the vibration in the room to become too faint to feel, and I ventured to ask, "What is that piece of music, Madame Gabinskaya?"

"Franz Lizst," she said, her voice a soft contralto. "*The Consolations*."

"Madame," I said in a hushed voice.

Her eyes lifted to meet mine.

I asked if she remembered a letter that came from Siberia twelve years before.

"Yes," she half whispered.

"Why did you burn it?"

When she didn't answer, I asked, "Was it from Uncle Boris?"

She waited then nodded. "Yes." She looked down again at the keys.

"What did it say?"

"He said he was on his way. He didn't know how long it would take. He wanted to see her . . . your mother . . . and his child before he died."

"His child?"

She looked at me sidelong and asked almost sadly, "Do you not know, Vera, who he could have meant?"

I felt cold. A shadow, terrible yet numinous, brought its dark light into the room.

Sasha had shared with Prince Miranov what she had not been able to tell me. The secret at the heart of her life.

Gabinskaya carefully closed the fallboard over the keys but remained sitting before the instrument. She spoke slowly as if still swept up in the rhythm of the adagio, as if the sound of it had not already settled and disappeared into the walls. "Your uncle learned the language of the native people. They thought your mother was his wife, not his sister, and he let them believe that." She breathed apprehensively and went on. "And so he lived with your mother as if she *was* his wife." Again she paused and seemed to struggle with her breathing, color having risen over her smooth face to the roots of her hair. "Your mother continues to blame herself for having needed him, for the complete dependence she had on him."

When she paused again I said, "I was told they lived with the Nakut people for two years."

"Yes."

I thought of the word *rape* but did not say it.

"Mostly," Gabinskaya began again, "your mother doesn't forgive herself for thinking she loved him as . . ." she paused, and though she spoke carefully, her pale green eyes were lit with angry tears. "Not at first," Gabinskaya emphasized, "but eventually she began to believe she loved him as a husband. I have had to remind her so often she was desperate with grief at the loss of her mother. And the terrible deaths of her father and her oldest half-brother, Dmitri. But especially the loss of her mother. She was isolated. While your uncle thrived among the primitives."

"She had only him," I said, my voice small and breathy.

Our eyes met and for the first time I felt as if Gabinskaya saw me. Her angry expression became a grimace of sadness.

A long quiet held the room.

"I know that a fur trader appeared . . . at some point . . . and my mother pleaded with him and he brought them back to one of the villages around Lake Baikal."

"Yes. The elder, Ilya Iunoshev married her to protect her and to give Sasha a father."

I struggled to take in everything that had been revealed, but I kept coming back to what she had said about my mother loving Uncle Boris as a husband. I was conscious of trying to be careful with wording things the right way.

"Did my mother keep loving Uncle Boris in . . . that way?" It was not how I wanted the question to sound.

Gabinskaya seemed momentarily stunned. "No, no," she said. "No. Everything became clear to her when she was with Iunoshev."

I nodded but Gabinskaya focused on me, looking vaguely horrified. And my question rang on the air like a heavy bell, a vibration felt deep in the sinews.

I quickly changed the subject. "I know that when Iunoshev died, my mother left Siberia and took Sasha to Petersburg."

"Yes, she fled Siberia, a terrible, dangerous journey, because she was afraid Boris would find her. That in itself proves that your mother never wanted to see Boris again."

"Yes," I nodded, but the way she had worded this suggested to me that she was not really sure what my mother felt.

Gabinskaya went on to say that once my mother was in St. Petersburg, and after that in Volkhov, as long as Boris remained in Siberia, the past remained there with him. But that letter that arrived twelve years ago, the letter in the yellow envelope, said he was coming.

"Do you see? Do you understand that your mother never wanted him here?" It struck me that Gabinskaya was still responding to my question asking about whether or not my mother went on loving Uncle Boris in that unnatural way. "I have told your mother that he should be driven from the property but . . . he is ill, she says. And he is her half brother, by blood. No one else is left of her family." It was this last sentence that seemed to calm her a little, and justify to her why my mother wanted him to stay and be cared for.

We heard a footstep outside the room. "Who's there?" Gabinskaya called out. I rushed into the hall in time to see the hems of Sasha's dress as she went quickly up the stairs. I went back in and told Gabinskaya.

"Your sister," she began, "didn't know until she read the letter days before it was burned. Since then she has been living with the knowledge of who she is."

From the front patio, I saw Sasha standing near the stable with Prince Miranov, whose carriage was prepared for departure. She spoke angrily to him and her tone seemed to agitate the horse tethered to the waiting carriage. It stepped back and forth, shifting its haunches, causing the vehicle to jolt.

Prince Miranov grasped Sasha's shoulder, but she wriggled free of his hold and walked with determination away into the park.

He called out to her, demanding that she come back. When she didn't he yelled after her, "A family does not allow its orchard to go to seed without inviting its own demise!"

I started quickly in his direction. "What do you mean by that?" I demanded. He made a dismissive gesture with his hand, jumped into his carriage, and it drove away.

I looked for Sasha, calling out her name, but if she was nearby, she didn't answer, and I eventually tired of yelling. I kept thinking of the prince's words. In spite of how much I hated him, I heard truth in what he'd said.

At the first light of dawn I went into my mother's bedroom and found her and Sasha asleep in their white nightgowns. The curtains were closed, the candle just guttering in the green lamp. From the glass flue, a black wisp of smoke wriggled upwards and exhaled, dissolving on the air.

My mother lay under the blanket on her right side facing toward Sasha. I climbed carefully onto the bed beside her and settled gingerly under her blanket, my face close to the back of her neck. I breathed her in and cried quietly, suppressing the sound.

The past had come back to her. Some things always come back, I thought. Things come to an end, but they are never over.

She had told us when I was very small about leaving a cold and terrible place, to return to a certain vast Siberian Lake that was said to be one of the deepest on earth. I had not understood the significance of her memory until now. Iunoshev had been taking her to safety.

I half closed my eyes and had what I can only call a waking dream:

I was with my mother and sister. I could feel their presences but could not see them. I did not know how old any of us were, but I felt like a child. We were passengers in a carriage of some kind, which hugged a narrow pass along the wall of a mountain on one side. Only feet away from the wheels of the carriage on the other side, a deep drop into a wide forested gorge, a vast canyon of trees. The air was silver. Birds swerved and circled below us and then above, their piercing cries echoing. We were all filled with a trembling optimism, the world opening into something new. Lake Baikal was still miles away, but its proximity made us sharply alert. The sun appeared as we descended and patches of snow melted before our eyes.

At first light of morning the larks began pouring out their songs.

Chapter 28

Anton waved from the avenue of birch trees.

"I received a letter this morning, Vera!" he called out. When we reached each other he continued. "*The Dragonfly* is going to publish my story, 'A Letter from a Learned Neighbor.'"

"Anton, that's wonderful!"

"I sent it well over a month ago so I was beginning to despair of hearing anything, especially after accumulating so many rejections from other places."

He went on for a little while in excitement about how *The Dragonfly* was his favorite of the different periodicals he'd been sending his work to. And that at five rubles a line he was being paid 275 rubles.

"You are looking at a published author!"

"I knew it would happen, dear Anton!"

I had put together a basket of food, which Anton took from me and carried as we set off for the ancient woods.

I had wondered throughout the night if I would share with Anton any of what had been revealed to me the day before, but his good news and his exuberant mood decided me against it. I was relieved, in a sense, feeling a kind of muteness around it. Gabinskaya had used words to describe those years my mother had spent with the Nakut, but the words had not adhered. They had fallen away. What remained were slow cloud fronts of feeling, solemn and gray.

I had a vague but urgent notion that seeing the white deer would soothe something, would put the world right. I had all but promised Anton that we would see her, having presented my dream to him as her message beckoning us to the ancient woods.

Mostly I walked ahead a bit, but sometimes we walked side-by-side and I took Anton's hand, or he took mine. We stuck as much as possible to the shade, neither of us speaking in case the deer was nearby, though we shot each other the occasional smile. When we heard stirrings in the leaves, we'd slow our steps and exchange looks, but mostly it was just birds making little disturbances as they took wing from branches and treetops.

After a long trek, the ancient woods announced themselves by a marked difference in the trees: massive and ivy covered with gnarled trunks, old branches encrusted with lichen. And they grew close to each other, interlocking their roots as if to enclose the green, twilit interior.

"It is something out of an old fairytale," Anton said.

I remembered coming here, standing outside these woods when I was small, holding Sasha's hand as she tried to show me the thrill of being afraid, telling me that if I listened I could hear the Baba Yaga breathing and snoring in her sleep.

Years later, Petya had persuaded me to come here, and I had been afraid. I felt sparks now of the old childhood fear and hesitated. Seeming to recognize this, Anton took my hand, as Petya had done years before, and led me into the green dimness between two trees. Anton's hand was hot, not cool as Petya's had been when he had led me in, and less rough. The moment was otherwise so similar, and the shock of it moved me, joining Anton and Petya together again, blurring them.

The dim interior had not changed since I had come with Petya. It echoed with birdsong and still smelled like old rain. We had to tread carefully in the dark green shadows, the ground uneven with heavy gnarled roots. In other places, the earth under our feet became loam, thick as a mattress, and Anton leaned forward for balance, carrying the basket with one hand while keeping hold of my hand with the other. We weren't far in when we heard the voice of a nightingale echoing at a close distance. When the way became more precarious, Anton slowed down, focused on guiding me forward, and the two of us balanced together like one many-limbed being, utilizing the tension between us.

As we went deeper, the way became dense, darker and more forbidding. Soon there were more nightingales singing and there were moments when I did not know if it was a branch or the wing of a nightingale brushing past my face.

We reached a clearing, a spot Petya and I had once come to, the high network of interlocking branches forming a canopy overhead. We sat next to each other on a gnarled root and waited, raking the surrounding trees with our eyes.

The quiet was filled with soft noises, the movements of birds in flight, and other unseen life causing leaves to shift and chafe and twigs to snap.

Clusters of bright yellow mushrooms glowed like tiny lanterns at the foot of a tree. They would have seemed like a good omen if Petya had not told me long ago that such mushrooms were poisonous.

This was the last day Anton might see the deer.

He proved capable of absolute stillness and I tried to emulate him, his body something solid, his spirit still and focused. Watching his profile, I could tell that he was listening for a particular noise, the hesitant step of a slender leg or the pressure of a hoofed foot in the overgrowth. Now and again Anton's head would turn or he would sit forward, gazing in one area where he seemed to have heard something and my heart would rise with hope. In each instance when nothing appeared, I restrained an urge to reach over and touch his hair where it grazed his neck in the back, near his collar.

We kept to that heightened stillness for an hour, or it could have been two hours. Time became impossible to read. I was growing tired of yearning for her to come, tired of numerous disappointments when there would be sounds that turned out only to be a bird swooping to a lower branch or a squirrel scampering up a tree. Eventually, a note of impatience came into Anton's breathing.

I pointed to a little light filtering through the trees. "We should go that way."

When we left the woods we found ourselves back in daylight, moving past lilac bushes and through a delicate cloud of frenzied insects. I led him beyond the pea-tree hedges to where the tributary narrowed and fell over a wet ledge of rock, and tall sunflowers with thick, tight stems grew on the banks, and beyond that to a small hill with a wide vista before it.

I spread the blanket I had brought onto the ground and set the picnic out before us: apples, soft green cheese with pistachios, black bread. I'd brought two small blue china plates and a cheese knife.

We tore pieces from the bread and spread cheese with the small knife.

"Dr. Mitrofan told me that the talisman you have, with the white deer on it, is Siberian."

"Yes, the charm comes from a northern oblast on the Arctic Circle, where a family friend, Lev Katkov, spent three years in a work camp. He'd been sent there for a very small crime, a small theft, and was released eventually and allowed to find his way back over the Ural Mountains. We were children when he came to visit. I was fourteen, I believe, and my sister, Masha, was twelve. She loved the little image of the deer in the green woods, so he gave it to her."

"And Masha gave it to you?"

He nodded. I had wondered if he'd tell the full story that Dr. Mitrofan had told me about how ill Anton had been, that he had been on the verge of death, and that he likely believed, though he would never admit it, that the gift of the white deer talisman from Masha healed him. But he didn't tell it. There was so much around illness that he would not talk about or that he tried to underplay.

He commented on how much he liked the cheese, how good it tasted with the apple.

We ate, watching a slow parade of cumulus drifting past.

"Don't go to Moscow yet, Anton," I said.

He raised his eyebrows.

"You can bring your books here and we can sit in different spots in the quiet and I will not bother you. For as long as Volkhov remains."

He looked at the broken clouds. "I have to go back to Taganrog to get my ticket of absence and my permit to study at Moscow University. And there are many furnishings and keepsakes my family expects me to bring to Moscow. I will have to hire a cart."

"I don't want you to go."

"They are waiting for me."

I gave him a pleading look. "What will I do when you go, Anton?"

"You will help out more often at the Zemstvo School and you will visit the little girls and boys with rickets in the hospital."

I looked out over the landscape, areas of meadow and woods, wild grass and leaves edged in sunlight.

"Proskovia told me that a child holds a mother to the earth. I began to see myself as little Katya's mother. I started to know who I was." My words came with effort and too much breath. "No matter what happened in the outside world, being Katya's mother would give focus to my life. I would have gotten through the family's disapproval. Everyone, maybe even Uncle Pavel, would have gotten over their disappointment in me and loved her. She and I would have shared an indescribable closeness. I already loved her, Anton. I know you know that."

He nodded.

"I cannot publish humorous sketches or study medicine, and I cannot draw like Petya. But I, too, want to do something with my life, Anton. My mother has often told Sasha and me that because we are women, we have to wait for something to happen to us. My cousin, Nadya, in Kiev, wants to introduce me into society but I have no interest in that."

He cocked his head sideways and focused on me. "Dear Desdemona Denisova, you are an actress. Do you know how many histrionic natures there probably are in the world that will never have the opportunity to step on a stage? And it is so easily within your reach."

"My grandmother has cursed acting for me."

"You are not your grandmother, Vera!" he said almost sternly. "She has given you a distorted idea about actresses."

I thought about this and then said, "The theater has broken my father's heart."

Anton smiled at me as if he understood what I was doing, throwing out my reasons why I should not be an actress so that he could knock them down.

"And you are not your father. You are, in many ways, more resilient. You are someone else entirely. You may not be able to see that, but I can. And," he gave me a sidelong smile, "I think maybe you can see it. You just want to hear me say it."

He looked at me so intently I felt transparent and had to lower my eyes. I let my gaze settle on the half-eaten apple in my lap.

"I don't want you to leave," I said. "What's happened to our plan to stop time? I can't do it without you."

"Did you listen to what I just said to you? Did you hear it?"

"Yes," I replied, "I heard what you said."

He turned suddenly away and coughed into his handkerchief. I watched him hunched forward, struggling to stifle the cough.

When he put his handkerchief away, we sat a little longer, looking at the clouds with a certain solemnity. We got up and both began gathering the picnic things. I went around a stand of trees to the stream to rinse off our small plates. Kneeling at the water's edge, I spread a cloth napkin over a rock and dipped each of the two plates in the cold moving current, washing them as best as I could with my fingers. I set each aside on the cloth napkin. As I was washing the small silver knife a chill spread over my neck and shoulders, and my heart seemed to rise into my throat. I lifted my eyes. The white deer stood less than two yards away on the other side of the stream.

She was big, much taller than I imagined she would be, her eyes liquid and dark. She seemed unafraid as she focused on me. And then, from out of the leaves right behind her, came a fawn, beige with pale speckles on its back and sides and pale beige tufts in its ears. Carrying itself awkwardly on tall, spindly legs, it stopped and stared at me, swaying slightly, its ears pointing up like its mother's. It seemed to accept me and began to nurse. I remained there on my knees, the white deer gazing at me with what felt like an easy familiarity. I thought of little Katya and experienced a state of vertigo, the world pulsating, becoming all echo and uncertainty.

In the same moment that the doe's ears swiveled in the direction of a sound coming from the other side of the trees, the fawn stopped nursing. I blinked and the two of them vanished, branches moving and rustling with their passage.

Anton appeared, circling from around the trees.

He understood, from the flustered way I turned to look at him, what had happened.

"You saw her," he said.

For all the hours that remained of the day, we walked the acreage, sometimes circling around back to the place where I'd seen her. All the while as we searched, I was reliving the moments she'd stood before me and felt myself filled with light, something I held back from sharing with Anton until he would see her himself. We stopped on the tops of hills and other places that offered wides vistas.

Eventually, Anton said with resignation that he needed to leave.

When we reached the end of the avenue of birch trees we stopped near the shortcut back to Dr. Mitrofan's. He reached into his pocket and took out the talisman, held it on his palm, and looked at it in silence. I thought he was going to give it to me, and I was ready to refuse it, to tell him he should keep it, but he seemed to think better of offering it and put it back in his pocket.

"Quite a few people have seen the white deer on your property and you saw her when I was nearby. I didn't see her, though I have probably been searching for her more than anyone else."

"I wish you had, Anton, with all my heart."

"Maybe this will sound silly to you, Vera, but I told myself that if I saw the white deer I would think of it as a message from Nature or from God, if he exists, condoning the journey I want to one day make into Siberia."

"Dr. Mitrofan told me that the white deer is the vanquisher of illness."

He colored slightly. After a pause, he nodded. "I told you that the white deer is a good omen for exchanging one life for another, and that is true, but it *is* known in a certain northern area of Siberia as the vanquisher of illness. Seeing a white deer is a promise of strong health in the future."

"Maybe this means you shouldn't go to Siberia, Anton."

He shook his head. "It's silly that I've placed so much hope in seeing the deer. This doesn't change my mind about going. I want to travel through Siberia. I want to face its difficulties."

Anton talked about Gleb Katkov, the man who brought the charm back to the western part of the continent, saying that he'd had a unique experience in Siberia, one rarely heard of. If he had not been sent there, into that particular prison near the Arctic Circle, a place where for more than half the year there was only one hour of daylight in a twenty-four-hour period, he would never have been educated. In that particular camp, they had access to books and another prisoner taught him to read.

"Imagine your first books being Dostoyevsky, Uspensky, Turgenev. He searched to understand the forces of life, studying arithmetic and geometry. He focused on the meaning of existence. He laughed as he read, Vera, because he could feel light coming into the darkness he had always lived in. And he said the skies were alive, the northern lights performing fantastic undulations.

"In the freezing darkness, he might have fallen, like most poor souls, into complete despair. Instead he discovered inner light. I know how rare that is, but his story shows us how unpredictable life is and how potentially resilient a human being can be."

"If you go, will you at least let me keep your spirit in safekeeping for you?" I said this, laughing a little but holding back tears.

"Thank you, Desdemona Denisova," he smiled. "But I need to take my spirit with me."

"Alright, but if you ever need me to, I will take excellent care of it."

"I would not ask you to part with your spirit, dear Desdemona," he smiled.

"But you can, Anton. I will give it to you."

"You must keep it. You will need it when you go on the stage."

"Am I really an actress, Anton?"

"I know you are."

"How do you know?"

"Are you fishing for compliments, Vera?"

"No. For reassurances."

"You read what I said about your performance in my letter to my brothers."

"Maybe that was an isolated incident, something that happened by chance and will never happen again."

He gave me a wry smile. "Are you finished yet saying things like that so I can tell you how wrong they are?"

I felt myself blush. "I confess, that is what I was doing. You know me well."

"You will resuscitate the roles your grandmother desecrated." He lifted my hand and kissed it, then held it between both of his hands.

"Ask your father for recommendations about the best companies in Kiev to audition for. Go before the first axe hits the first tree."

We put our arms around each other. I closed my eyes and breathed him in, feeling that steady hum, that vibration that lived in his bones and his blood.

It was Anton who broke the embrace. He started on his way, but turned and said, "The stage awaits you, my dear Desdemona."

While I watched him go, quail called out to each other across the bright nocturnal orchard, and I knew I would never disassociate that plaintive sound from those summer days and nights with Anton.

Part 4

"Dawn. Soon the sun will be up. It is already May, the cherry trees are in bloom, but it is chilly in the orchard . . ."
—Chekhov

July 11, 1904

St. Petersburg

During a break in rehearsal today I was making a note in my script when one of the actors announced that Anton Chekhov had died.

My pen froze. I stopped breathing.

"He died in Germany," the actor said. "At a spa in Badenweiler."

I listened in silence as people exchanged exclamations of sorrow or disbelief. Most had met Anton over the years. All admired him as a great playwright and acclaimed author.

One of the actors who had been in the initial run of Anton's most recent play, *The Cherry Orchard,* earlier this year, told a story about Anton sitting in a back row at the Moscow Art Theatre during a rehearsal, wearing a heavy coat, two scarves, and a fur hat.

"He was unhappy with Stanislavsky's directorial choices and kept sighing and groaning. Three times I saw him slap his hand against his forehead. He hated that Stanislavsky was treating the play like a tragedy. He insisted it was a comedy."

He'd been so ill, the actor explained, that he shook when he walked and needed a cane. "The poor man was only forty-three but he looked seventy." Fits of coughing caused tears to run in steady streams down his face and get lost in his beard.

I could not feel my body.

People began to talk about *The Cherry Orchard*, which I had not seen. The actor who had been in it said it was about a family of improvident landowners, charming and good-hearted, just deaf to reason, who lose their orchard and their estate out of fecklessness.

I felt a stab in my gut at the description.

In the last letter Anton had written to me he'd told me that *The Cherry Orchard* had the longest germination of any of his plays. As he wrote it he kept remembering that summer at Volkhov when we were nineteen.

One of the actresses said that she'd found it interesting that several important characters, some living and some dead, never appear on stage. "In that way it is a play about ghosts."

I felt a chill rush over me.

The actor who had been in the production said that the couples who seem at the beginning of the play destined to marry, never do.

An older actress had a copy of yesterday's *Petersburg Gazette*. In it she found a short article about Anton's body being returned from Germany. It had come back in a refrigerated train car with the word *Oysters* painted on the side. Many people were outraged that such a great Russian writer should be treated with such indignity.

But I kept thinking that Anton would have found it funny. "It sounds like something from one of his stories," I said. A few people smiled and seemed to agree, but most stayed silent as if I was being disrespectful.

"I think he would have laughed," I said.

People shared more memories and eventually went silent.

Someone lit a candle.

The older actress cried.

Somehow I managed my way through the rest of the rehearsal. I followed new blocking I'd just been given, met each of my cues, remembered all my lines, and spoke them clearly. All the while I was aware of a shadow in my peripheral vision. I imagined it was Anton sitting in a middle row in the empty theatre, watching me.

That night I sat alone in a dark room.

I lit a lamp and for the next hours I read and reread the letters he had sent me over the years.

7 November 1879
Moscow

Greetings from Moscow, dear Desdemona!

I have just completed my first months as a medical student and I'm still trying to get settled in this crowded, noisy, ramshackle room with my family.

I love the church bells of Moscow! They ring every day but especially on Sundays. I walk for hours listening, or I open a window in the university library, even when it's freezing, just to hear them!

I wanted to let you know that my sister, Masha, recalls the story of the girl and the grasshopper. The tiny weeping girl was not escaping the grasshopper at all, but in search of him. He hopped away and seemed to have disappeared. She rode on the back of the blackbird looking for him! That was all Masha could supply. She does not remember the rest of the story but she is sure of that much.

My eyes are weakening from all the reading I'm doing and I have decided to purchase a pince-nez, though I will have to pawn my shoes in order to do so. A stipend due me is late in coming through.

If I am going to strain my eyes I would rather do it writing a long letter to you, but if I am going to be a doctor, I better study.

Write me at this address:
AP Chekhov
c/o Vnukova
Grachovka, Moscow
I kiss your palms.
Please take good care of yourself, tiny girl.

Your Anton
(a negligent grasshopper who hopped away)

21 April 1880
Moscow

Vera!

How grateful I am to your aunt for forwarding my letter to you! And how thrilled I am to have received your reply. It is the first letter I've ever received not written on terra firma, but written from a deck chair as you sailed north along the Volga, watching the passing shores! Congratulations for having found a place with the Replov Theatre Company. You did not tell me enough about the Replov and left me to find out for myself that it brings productions to the far ends of Western Russia, from the gulf of Finland to Yekaterinburg, at the threshold of Siberia.

In your letter, you said you left Volkhov out of desperation. Perhaps desperation is a gift if it helps us to break through into a new life. How gratified I am to think of you working on stage, where you belong. And how interesting that two of your fellow actresses talk to you endlessly of spiritualism, homeopathy, and hypnotism! But Vera, in spite of what you said in your letter, I am **not** *looking down dismissively at such things. And I confess that you are right when you said that I am secretly interested in all of it. I would not confess that to anyone but you, but you see so clearly through me. The two actresses have found a fertile field in you for such ideas, although they will probably learn more from you than they can teach you.*

I am so deeply sorry about Volkhov, about the orchard being cut down and the trees carried away without ceremony. I am glad you did not stay there to witness more destruction of your childhood home.

I am heartened, however, to hear that Vova left with Proskovia for Gabinskaya's estate, to live freely and with leisure (who would not want such a life?), caring for two borzois and three dachshunds. I can imagine Vova wearing the big hat with the veil, leaving with Proskovia in a carriage, while the other maids run after them cursing Vova for bolting and leaving them with all the chamber pots to empty. And poor Nickander. What will become of our dear pious, heartsick Atlas of Volkhov?

You say that the ground is now gone from under your feet and you must surrender to a life of impermanence, that there is no safe, steady harbor without Volkhov. I know you are grief-stricken, but please remember that we are all living in a state of impermanence.

There is a little bit of news in my life since my previous letter. You can congratulate me on publishing more of my less terrible stories in two issues of a journal called The Alarm Clock. The editor there has expressed interest in another of my stories as well, one that is equally as bad. Each story, I will just say, is a testament to my lack of refinement and my crude immaturity, qualities that are popular these days.

I must go now, back to studying the intricacies of the nervous system, what small bit there is known about it. Even the most learned doctor little understands its mysteries. As with so much else about the human body.

I know the Replov visits remote places, but might you ever come to Moscow?

Your ever devoted,
Anton

9 September 1881
Moscow

My dear Vera,

Medical school gets more and more stomach churning. I am, when I am not studying or in classes, writing the usual irritating little stories to make people laugh. They are bad and I am ashamed of what I stoop to in the name of a few rubles. Perhaps I write so many of these little sketches as practice, hoping to get better and better so that one day I might write something important and revelatory about Siberia.

But there is one story I am less ashamed to show you: Late Blooming Flowers, recently accepted and published in installments in Talk of the World. I show it to you hesitantly, including a handwritten copy with this letter.

I had high hopes for my play, Platanov, which I have been working on somewhat secretly, but it was rejected by the Maly Theatre and now I am thinking of burning it.

Tell me about your life as an actress. Tell me your observations and any amusing little anecdotes or yarns, keeping in mind that I might use something you share with me as fodder for a story.

Forgive the brevity of this letter. It is noisy here among my family and I can barely hear myself think.

I am still your faithful servant,
Antosha Chekhonte,
the Man without a Spleen

21 February 1882
Moscow

Vera Sergeyevna,

Please accept my deepest condolences at the loss of your Uncle Boris. It was kind of Father Ivan and Dr. Mitrofan to arrange for him to stay in the sanitorium after everyone fled Volkhov. I heard that his last six months were especially difficult. Up until the end, Dr. Mitrofan told me, he was asking for your mother. Only one person visited him regularly, someone who barely knew him at Volkhov: the pious Atlas of Volkhov, who has found work with the blacksmith in Korablin.

Do your mother and Sasha still live with Madame Gabinskaya? Like you, I thought Sasha would marry one of her many paramours and find her way in the world. But who am I to begrudge family members from keeping to each other?

How difficult it must be for you being so far away from your dear father. How he must miss you!

I recently tried to publish a book of humorous stories, but humor is considered subversive in this new climate of repression. Since the assassination of Alexander the Second, censorship has become impossible to navigate. The censor finds the most innocent things threatening. Everything is assumed to be a metaphor, ridiculing the current political situation. And so my book of silly stories, illustrated by Kolya, remains unpublished.

But I will stop complaining and share with you something of which I am proud. I am fully supporting my family now with scholarship money and the earnings from selling my stories, however crude and second rate they are! My writing is paying the bills!

And I am writing a play now in which I am doing dreadful violence to stage conventions.

I miss talking to you, dear friend. I miss your unique way of feeling the world. I once called it primitive, but that feels wrong. Primitive is a word that evokes mud and earth, and your way of seeing is filled with air and light. You, my dear Desdemona, are a mystic! But if you tell me you have felt my spirit near you watching you, I will guarantee that you have not. I never let my spirit go off on its own.

I miss you and often think of how we watched clouds together one evening under the shade of that very old willow that is probably, tragically, no longer there.

I am sending you my deepest regards, Desdemona. I bow before you.

Always your Anton

A letter written but never sent:

19 March 1883
Ishim

Anton,

Your letter, postmarked February 21, 1882, came to me a year late! It was forwarded from place to place and finally reached me in Yekaterinburg. You said you were including a story, Late Blooming Flowers. Did you change your mind at the last minute or did you send it in a separate envelope? The letter has arrived, but not the story. When we are in a more civilized corner of Russia, I will search for a copy of Talk of the World, where you said it was published.

It would have been a perfect time to read your story. We are snowed in in a small village in the Ural Mountains. This interruption of the tour has been a wonderful reprieve. Ordinarily in the places where we stop, I share a room with two or three other actresses or members of the crew. But the rooms here are very small and I have my own. Privacy is such a luxury. The snow keeps falling so our stay keeps prolonging.

I have been sleeping so much in the past few days. And I have been dreaming and remembering my dreams.

When I was small, lying in my bed, I would hear the movement of skirts made heavy by embellishment, the clicking of tiny beads. It was my mother come to check that I was covered. I was sure that my mother was here earlier in the dark when I sensed a female figure in the room.

"I just came to light your stove." It was a woman who had been burning fragrant coal earlier in the tearoom. There were no beads on her skirt. Snow was storming outside the window. She lit the stove and left me with a fresh candle and took the other, which had almost guttered.

I slept again and had a dream: My mother was outside the small window, shivering in the snow. I brought her in and she sat before the stove but wasn't able to get warm. I woke up with an awful sense of helplessness. But when I slept again, the dream continued and I was determined to make her warm, giving her teaspoons of hot tea, wrapping her in a blanket. And this time, she seemed to be getting relief from the cold.

And I dream about Volkhov and wake wondering what has become of it. I am so far away from what might be left of it. And I am so far away from my mother and my sister and my poor father, and from you. Impossibly far away from you. The last word I had, Sasha is still living at Gabinskaya's, though she continues to insist that it is temporary.

It is dark and I write this by the light of the candle flame. The snow is blowing in soft gusts outside.

Can we not, Anton, leave the demands of our lives behind a while and meet somewhere where we can be alone? For weeks, or even months? Please answer this. Please let us try.

How I miss you, my dear friend.
Always yours.

I made several attempts to send this letter from Ishim, but the heavy snows had disrupted the mail, and I was told, the third time I tried, that I was better off sending it from somewhere else. I held on to it, keeping it in one of my trunks. I had the opportunity to send it when we were traveling again and stopped in another village, but I could not find it in my trunk and thought I had left it behind. A year would pass before I would find it between the pages of a small volume of poetry one of the actors had given me.

17 July 1884
Zvenigorod

My dearest Vera,

I am in Zvenigorod where I have volunteered to treat patients at a zemstvo hospital. The cholera epidemic has hit here hard.

It is now three months since I saw the Replov's excellent production of The Trojan Women with you as Cassandra (another great role you have taken back from the abuses of your grandmother). I hope I praised you enough when I saw you, but if not let me tell you again how moved I was. Some nights on the verge of sleep I see you standing alone in the near darkness of the stage, illuminated by a single limelight, focused on the dark air high above the audience as you chant your prayer to Apollo.

I only wish I could have spent more time with you afterward. One glass of champagne was not enough, but as you know, the play ran late and I had examinations very early in the morning.

I am happy to report that I have finished medical school! It is difficult to believe that I, a lowly son of a serf, who spent childhood selling herrings and pickles, might now be called by the respectable title of Doctor Chekhov!

Some good news I cannot help but share. I have published a collection of stories about the theatre called Tales of Melpomene. And my crime novel, The Shooting Party, is being serialized in Daily News.

Another opportunity to see each other will surely come soon, and we will spend much more time together. Urge the Replov to bring their next production back to Moscow or send me the schedule for the coming year and I will try to come to you.

With affection from your most sincere admirer.

PS In another month you may write me at a new Moscow address:

AP Chekhov
Golovin Lane
Stretenka Street

29 March 1886
Moscow

The most extraordinary thing has happened, my dear Desdemona. The great writer, Dmitry Grigorovich, has sent me a letter, which has struck me like a bolt of lightning. I almost burst into tears, I was so overcome with emotion.

He tells me I have talent, a talent that demands respect, though up until now, he sees that I have not respected it. And he is so right. I have written and published scores and scores of stories, writing them quickly without editing them, with barely a second look before sending them off to one of the periodicals that have published and keep publishing my half-baked efforts.

I have sensed that I have some talent, Vera, but I have treated it as worthless. No one until now has given me a word of encouragement. My father, who loves to read, turns up his nose at anything I have written. I have been viewed, even by those who publish my stories, as a literary non-entity and I have, until now, accepted that view.

I have, I confess, approached my writing in a frivolous, irresponsible and meaningless way. I have been writing my stories the way reporters churn out pieces about fires: mechanically, half asleep, caring as little for the reader as for myself.

Dmitry Grigorovich's letter came to me like a jolt might come from a magistrate with an order to leave the city immediately. I felt urgently that I had to extricate myself from the position in which I have mired myself. I must stop writing against short deadlines and stay longer and go deeper with each story.

I remember you struggling with the scene from Twelfth Night before you performed it with your sister. You said that you kept entering the scene through the wrong door. I see that I have been entering my writing through the wrong door every time.

We are only twenty-six, my dearest Desdemona, but time is rushing by and I want to write something of substance.

Grigorovich has encouraged me to use my own name rather than Antosha Chekhonte or The Man Without a Spleen. He says I must take myself seriously as a writer. So from this moment on, I will write as Anton Chekhov. The kindness he has shown to me has so inspired me, my dear. I do not feel like the same man. His letter has left a deep imprint on my soul.

At this moment, the bells are ringing for Matins. Everyone here is asleep.

You and I will try again soon to see each other. You are almost always in the hinterlands of Russia so please let me know when you are near Moscow again or even Petersburg. I sometimes travel there but if I'm not there when you are I will, barring epidemic or flood, happily take a train to come and see you. Let us try, my dearest Desdemona.

I miss you and kiss you three times from afar.

From your close friend, Anton, the person in whom you inspire deep respect and emotion.

The following is a draft I kept of a letter I wrote and rewrote several times, struggling for the right tone. This one was the closest to the one I finally sent.

12 April 1889
Archangelsk

My Dear Anton,

I am so deeply sorry to have learned about the death of your brother, Kolya. So sorry, my dear friend. I learned this sad news at a party in Petersburg after a performance. I heard your name spoken, a man talking about your power over women and another man replied, by saying that in medical school, you received your highest marks in gynecology. And they all laughed.

If women are in fact drawn to you, why do these men make it into something coarse, or make it ridiculous by laughing at it?

But back to the conversation, which became disturbing. A bulbous-faced man, casually fingering shreds of tobacco as he stuffed them into a pipe, asked if you were really serious about your suicidal venture.

The word suicidal dealt a blow to my stomach.

Questions were asked, and the answer came that you were preparing to leave for Sakhalin, the Siberian penal colony, to study the prison conditions.

People were stunned.

"Imagine that!" someone said. "Why would he travel to that barren devil's island?"

The man, who I would learn through eavesdropping was your publisher, said that you had given him an outline of the route you planned to take and that it would be a three-month journey at least, perhaps four, just to get to the godforsaken place. He said you have to cross Siberia in the backs of rickety coaches, probably eating the most vile food. All along the way you would be in danger of the vandals and escaped prisoners who are not above murdering to steal a wallet. And if you survive all of this, you then have to cross the Okhotsk Sea.

Someone asked if there was a woman you were trying to flee from. "As I said," your publisher replied, "women are drawn to him. In Moscow they are known as Antonovkas, like the Russian apples." There was more laughter.

Another man said that he had heard that some of those Antonovkas were doing research about Sakhalin for you in the libraries of Moscow. More laughter before the conversation turned serious. "Many writers," someone said, "have gone to Siberia involuntarily." You are the only one this man has ever heard of going there of your free will.

And then I heard something that truly upset me. That you are quite ill, suffering from pulmonary and intestinal tuberculosis. And that this is the reason you should not go. But that you will not admit to being ill. "Imagine!" someone said. "And he is a doctor!"

They all agreed, Anton, that you are in denial of how sick you are. And that is when someone mentioned that your brother, Kolya, died recently from the same white plague they say you have, and that perhaps you are trying to prove to yourself that your own health is fine. Another man, who apparently is a doctor, said that such a journey, if you survived it, would shorten your life.

And so I am writing to you now to tell you how deeply sorry I am at the loss of your brother, and to object to your going, to urge you to please not undertake such a journey.

I know this is an argument we had years back at Volkhov, but I let it go because it was just an idea then, an idea I hoped would never become a reality. But now here it is, and if you weren't ill, though you probably still tell everyone you are not, I might just leave it. But please, Anton, my dear friend, do not go and leave the rest of us worried and sleepless over your safety and your health.

My aunt wrote me from Smolensk, where she lives with my father and Uncle Pavel. My father, she tells me, is not doing well. He is forgetful and thinks my mother is somewhere in the house. He looks for her in different rooms or he watches for her out the window. Aunt Marya says it breaks her heart. I plan to go there as soon as I can.

If you respond before May 1st, you can reach me at this address:

V. Denisova
c/o Demochko
Kuzminky, Kiev

Again, dear Anton, my heartfelt sympathies for your loss of a most beloved brother.

Your true friend,
Vera

I don't know if Anton ever received this. The next letter I got from him came from Siberia.

June 1890
Amur River, Siberia

My wonderful actress,

How happy I am right now. The Amur River is beautiful and I am finished forever with riding in tarantasses. If you have never heard of a tarantass, it is a terrible contraption, a springless, horse-drawn conveyance. Why the invention of springs has not yet reached Siberia is a mystery to me! The roads are rocky and uneven and one suffers the shock of every bump. After many hours, one gets out of a tarantass, bent, wobbly and ten years older than when one went in. No one should become so painfully familiar with their own skeleton!

The steamer is so smooth in comparison and my cabin is clean. I am eating the freshest sturgeon I've ever had. Since Listvenichnaya I have experienced no signs of bronchitis. My lungs are as clear as an infant's.

My family is due a long letter but I had to write you first. The strangest thing happened. In a tiny remote village past Nerchinsk, populated by many Chinese, I came across a pile of books in a fishing tackle shop, of all places. There among Bibles, holy books, and a volume of the sayings of Confucius, written in Chinese, I found a slender volume of Othello! As I read it, sitting on a rock near the river, of course I cast you as Desdemona.

Back in Moscow last year I met a man who told me that in Venice there is a house known as Desdemona's house. The water slaps right against the door. He said that Venice is the most romantic place on earth. Falerno wine and the gondoliers singing at night as they row! You must find your way there one day, Desdemona Sergeyevna Denisova. If you do not, it would be a tragedy of the worst proportions.

The trip across Lake Baikal was wondrous, unforgettable. The only bad thing was that I was in third class, the deck being fully taken up by the merchants' wagon horses, and they were stamping around during the whole voyage like raving lunatics. These horses added a certain flavor to my voyage: I felt as if I was on some sort of pirate ship.

I will not bore you by telling you too much about the lieutenants from an infantry regiment that I traveled with for a while. One of them sang constantly, bits from operas, but with as much ear for music as a smoked herring. Another one could have talked the hind legs off of a donkey and insisted on shoving his oar into every conversation.

At Klyuyevo, the watchman agreed to take our luggage to the station; he set off in his cart and we followed behind on foot beside the lake to the most magnificent and picturesque scenery. The track led through the forest: woods to the right of the mountainside, woods to the left dropping down to the lake. What ravines, what crags! The colors around Baikal are warm and gentle. Selinga is utterly beautiful, and in Trans-Baikal you can be galloping through the Caucasus in the afternoon, and by nightfall you are on the Don steppe, and next morning you wake from a doze and find yourself in Poltava, and it's like that for six hundred miles. We covered one hundred and thirty miles a day, and that's the most you can do in summer. We were completely dazed. During the day the heat was terrible, too, and then it got very cold at night.

I have almost crossed Siberia completely. Even as I experience its greatest beauties, I know I will never come back again. It is not something a westerner does more than once in a lifetime, if it can be helped.

My felicitations to you, my dear Desdemona.

I bow before you. I kiss your foot.

Forever your Anton

For years I didn't hear from Anton, though I wrote him two long letters and sent them to his home in Melihovo, where I knew he was living with his sister and his mother. He had become famous, his stories winning high praise and awards. He had suffered several very public humiliations with his plays but had persisted and they were being successfully produced by The Moscow Art Theatre.

His humanitarian work was well known. He organized famine and cholera relief, built rural schools, planted trees and began a campaign to build a sanitorium for sufferers of Tuberculosis. He contributed thousands of books to libraries, and worked to reform the inhumane Russian penal system. He had become famous for the solicitude with which he treated his patients, offering medical services free to peasants.

A decade after I'd last heard from Anton, I received a large envelope containing two letters, one postmarked two years before (1902) and returned to him, and a new one (1904). On the envelope of the old letter he'd written: *Please read this one first.*

18 March 1902
Yalta

Vera Sergeyevna,

Each time I send a letter to you I feel I am throwing a stone into a lake.

The last letter I received from you contained your very kind words about The Seagull and I wrote back. But since then, nothing.

I don't know that you would have heard, but I got married. After having told you with such arrogant certainty that I would never marry! I have not been well, and this has changed me. I am sometimes driven to using a cane. But I will not bore you with those details, my sweet friend. Because of my health I live much of the time in Yalta, in the south. My wife, the actress Olga Knipper, lives in Moscow.

Is it true that you are no longer traveling but settled in Petersburg and working with a new company? I've also heard that you married an actor from the troupe you used to travel with. Are you happy? He must be good to you. If not, tell him your dear friend, Anton, uses a cane and will come after him with it.

Here is something extraordinary that I want to share with you: Recently I was in a neighboring Crimean town and went into a shop known as The Red Corner to buy an icon for my aging mother. The shop was accessed through a lone door located at the back of the Holy Church of the Transfiguration, adjacent to the rectory. Three walls were taken up by gilded iconostasis, lit by hanging lamps and numerous candles flickering in red glass votives. The cold air smelled of frankincense.

Many travel icons were displayed on the long table beneath the hanging images and I picked one up, The Holy Mother with Three Hands. There was something familiar about the image, perhaps the blowing veil, or the way the figure loomed ever so slightly to the right.

And then I saw another icon next to it, a female figure even more familiar. I picked it up and held it before me and the room trembled around the eyes of this icon. I waited for the face to resolve itself into one less familiar, but it would not. It was your face, so clearly your unforgettable expression from the drawing you allowed me to look at that summer. It was as if doing the drawing had prepared the artist to paint this icon. I asked and was told that these icons were in fact painted by Piotr Fyodorovich Zarov. Our Petya.

He has covered your nudity, clothed you chastely in robes, but your face is still a study in nakedness, an expression of unguarded yearning.

The original drawing had been all shadows, but in this painted one, standing before a background of gold leaf, your skin looks lit, as if from within. Studying it closely, I can see hundreds, maybe thousands of tiny pinpoints of different colors. Your Petya has become an incomparable artist.

On the back there is an inscription: Saint Eudoxia: She Who Does Good Deeds.

The proprietor in the shop told me this is a popular icon. I imagine hundreds, maybe thousands of candles burning all over Russia before this image of your face. (I know you will not lose an iota of humility over this idea. How odd life is!)

I purchased it, of course, and continue to contemplate it. I will hold onto it until I hear from you. Then I will send it to you at any address you say, though it will pain me to part with it.

Ever your friend,
Anton

12 February 1904
Yalta

Dearest Vera,

I have a new play, The Cherry Orchard. Act One takes place in spring. There are trees on stage covered with white blossoms.

This play has the longest germination of any of my plays. Writing it, I kept remembering that summer at Volkhov when we were nineteen. We talked about stopping time and perhaps we did, because remembering that summer, time feels transfixed around those woodland walks in search of the white deer. In a way, I have never stopped searching for the white deer.

I wrote the youngest character, Anya, with you in mind, thinking you might take the role, having to constantly remind myself that you would be as old as I am now! You are eternally the girl in the green light of that long ago summer!

I should be gratified that The Moscow Art Theatre has been producing my plays, and I am, but it is complicated. Stanislavsky and Vladimir Nemorovich-Danchenko claim to love my new play but do not understand it! Vladimir has gone as far as to tell me that I am the one that does not understand my own play. He calls it an exquisite tragedy. It is a comedy!

Please write me! But do it soon. I am leaving in a few weeks for a spa in the Black Forest in Germany with my wife, a place where they specialize in helping people with advanced tuberculosis.

Long before you rescued Petya Fyodorovich from a life of servitude (one of your good deeds), you "rescued" the spirit of the man with the snow on his shoulders and head, on his way to the penal colony. Back at Volkhov that green summer of our youth, you tried to discourage my dream of Siberia, but I was too stubborn. Still, you tried, Saint Eudoxia, to rescue me.

Do I regret going? No. Never. Did it shorten my life? Yes, certainly. For many years I would not admit this, but I am tired of pretending, to myself and to those I care about.

Perhaps you'd consider letting me take the icon with me to the Black Forest? It is, after all, a travel icon. If I do not hear from you, I will definitely take it with me and if, when I return, you have written that you want it, I will send it right away.

You used to tell me that you felt Petya Fyodorovich's presence in your room even when he was as far away as Sevastopol. Lately when I look at the icon I feel your presence here in my rooms. Are you here with me, dear Desdemona? As I lie back and close my eyes, are you in a chair in the corner looking at me? Lately, the world does feel filled with that mystical Siberian way of seeing. Things feel less solid, more fluid. I do not want to attribute these perceptions to illness. Do spirits really take refuge and reside temporarily in the chests of others? I laugh when I remember the things you used to say, yet they are so compelling to me.

As I'm preparing to leave for Germany, something you said once that summer keeps coming to me. The actress, or in this case, the actor (me), knows the arc of the story in every cell of his body, and yet, he must not know it. In this way, a strong performance is a paradox, because everything must be filled with the tension of uncertainty. He must believe that something else could happen, that the play could end differently, that the doors of fate remain open.

Do not forget your warmly devoted
Anton

(In the envelope along with this letter was a small, hard object enclosed in a fragment of muslin. I unwrapped it to find the talisman of the white deer.)

Acknowledgements

For feedback on recent and much earlier drafts of this novel I am forever grateful to Therese Handley, Stefania Amfitheatrof, Laurie Kutchins, Sheila Kohler, Edward Hamlin, Margot Livesey, Sarah Fleming, Nancy Graham and Lilia Levin.

Grateful acknowledgment is due to Joseph Olshan for his belief in this book, and to Isaac Peterson, Jessica Hammerman, Murray Weiss and Louise Crawford, each with an important role in shepherding this book into the world.

I am grateful for Donald Rayfield's exhaustive biography, *Anton Chekhov, a Life*, as well as his studies of Chekhov's work, including: *The Cherry Orchard: Catastrophe or Comedy; Understanding Chekhov: A Critical Study of Chekhov's Prose and Drama;* and *Chekhov: The Evolution of his Art*, as well as his introduction to *The Chekhov Omnibus, Selected Stories*, and his various essays and chapters in other critical works on Chekhov, including *The Cambridge Companion to Chekhov*.

Other works that have brought me closer to Chekhov are: Janet Malcolm's, slender, passionate *Reading*

Chekhov: a Critical Journey, charting her literary pilgrimage into Chekhov's Russia; Rosamund Bartlett's *Chekhov: Scenes from a Life*, V.S. Pritchett's *Chekhov: A Spirit Set Free; Seeing Chekhov: Life and Art* by Michael C. Finke; *Reminiscences of Chekhov* by Maxim Gorky; *Anton Chekhov's Life and Thought, Selected Letters and Commentary*, edited and annotated by Simon Karlinksy; *The Chekhov Theatre* by Laurence Senelick; *Speak Memory* by Vladimir Nabokov; *Natasha's Dance, a Cultural History of Russia* by Orlando Figes; *Former People, the Final Days of the Russian Aristocracy* by Douglas Smith; *My Life in Art* by Constantin Stanislavsky; *My Life in the Russian Theatre* by Vladimir Nemorovich-Danchenko; and most important of all, the treasure trove of publications of Chekhov's plays, short stories, novellas, and letters in their many translations.

And thank you, of course, to Neil and Miranda. My loves.

About the Author

Neil Scott Johnson

Regina McBride is the author of six novels, one memoir, and one book of poetry. Her novel *Stranger from Across the Sea* was also published by Green City Books. Her novels have been translated into five languages. Her novel *The Nature of Water and Air* was a Booksense pick (Independent Book Stores selection), a Barnes and Noble Discover Great New Writers book, and a Borders Original Voices choice. It was optioned for a film. A recipient of fellowships from the National Endowment for the Arts and the New York Foundation for the Arts, she lives in New York City where she taught fiction writing at Hunter College for thirty years, and continues to teach privately.

www.ingramcontent.com/pod-product-compliance
Lightning Source LLC
LaVergne TN
LVHW101156140926
848013LV00029B/255
9781963101232

Praise for *Born of Malice*

"*Born of Malice* is a dark delight from beginning to end: a plunge into a visceral world of spellwork and power struggles portrayed in gorgeous prose. I was instantly captivated by the characters and the extraordinarily original magic system."
— **Emmi Itäranta**, award-winning author of *Memory of Water*

"*Born of Malice* hooks you from the start—a fiery tale of ambition and vengeance set in a city where magic is illegal and music can unmake the universe. The story is told through the eyes of two demigods, chaos and nightmares made manifest, and a scholar-musician striving to make magic accessible to all. Expect gorgeous prose and horror aplenty, but know that it's the fascinating lore and tormented characters that will reel you in: insecure gods and ill-fated loves, centuries-old feuds and fragmented texts hinting at magical secrets... Drawing from African traditions to create a world so vivid you can smell the carnage and taste the entropy, this is Xan van Rooyen at their bold, bloody best."
— **Cheryl S. Ntumy**, author of *Black Friday: Short Stories from Africa*

"In chiseled, confident prose, the expansive world containing the city of Savat blooms to life in Xan van Rooyen's *Born of Malice*. Characters with the depth of the Nether that birthed them rage across the pages in this vivid tale that asks whether our motivations ultimately matter when our actions destroy even the little we might hold dear—and questions whether those motivations are as noble as we contend. An autistic academic, neglected god-child with chronic pain, traumatized siblings, and a city broiling with a history of colonization, religious suppression, and magical malpractice across class lines—what could go wrong? I was riveted. Book two now, please!"

—**Naseem Jamnia**, IAFA Crawford-, Locus-, and World Fantasy-nominated author of *The Bruising of Qilwa*

"Xan's lush prose is always a delight to immerse the imagination, equally matched by their cunning, layered characters whose motivations keep you guessing what they're really up to in the shadows. Assume nothing and trust no one. With characters you can both admire and loathe, this is a richly imagined world and a silky-smooth narrative, barbed with ancient familial angst for good measure."

—**Stephen Embleton**, 2024 Nommo Award winner for Best Speculative Fiction Novella for *Undulation*

"The musical magic echoing through this blood-tinged story is captivating, and the unique world Xan van Rooyen has built feels real and complex with its multiple languages and cultures. An epic family drama with (demi)gods, revolution, and amazingly creepy transformations of the body."

—**Sara Norja**, author of *Kummajaisten kesä* (*The Summer of Strangelings*)